"You may not remember me, cowboy, but I remember you.

"You were something of a legend. You know—rodeoing, in trouble with the law, giving your rich father fits, breaking the girls' hearts.

"It's embarrassing to admit, but I had one helluva crush on you, Jenner McKee, and it stayed with me a long, long time. I thought I was well over it, but then, a few years ago, I saw you again....

"You bought me a drink and, even though I was old enough to know better, one thing led to another. To make a long story short, we spent the night together, and in the morning you were gone. No note. No loose ends. No promises to be broken. End of story. Except..."

"Except?" Jenner's lips barely moved, but his nostrils flared with fury.

Beth took a deep breath. "Except I got pregnant."

Dear Reader,

Welcome to Silhouette **Special Edition**...welcome to romance.

Some of your favorite authors are prepared to create a veritable feast of romance for you as we enter the sometimes-hectic holiday season.

Our THAT SPECIAL WOMAN! title for November is *Mail Order Cowboy* by Patricia Coughlin. Feisty and determined Allie Halston finds she has a weakness for a certain cowboy as she strives to tame her own parcel of the open West.

We stay in the West for A RANCHING FAMILY, a new series from Victoria Pade. The Heller siblings—Linc, Beth and Jackson—have a reputation for lassoing the unlikeliest of hearts. This month, meet Linc Heller in *Cowboy's Kin*. Continuing in November is Lisa Jackson's LOVE LETTERS. In *B Is For Baby*, we discover sometimes all it takes is a letter of love to rebuild the past.

Also in store this month are *When Morning Comes* by Christine Flynn, *Let's Make It Legal* by Trisha Alexander, and *The Greatest Gift of All* by Penny Richards. Penny has long been part of the Silhouette family as Bay Matthews, and now writes under her own name.

I hope you enjoy this book, and all of the stories to come. Happy Thanksgiving Day—all of us at Silhouette would like to wish you a happy holiday season!

Sincerely,

Tara Gavin
Senior Editor

Please address questions and book requests to:
Silhouette Reader Service
U.S.: 3010 Walden Ave., P.O. Box 1325, Buffalo, NY 14269
Canadian: P.O. Box 609, Fort Erie, Ont. L2A 5X3

LISA JACKSON

B IS FOR BABY

Silhouette®

SPECIAL ▽ **EDITION**®

Published by Silhouette Books

America's Publisher of Contemporary Romance

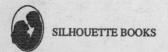

SILHOUETTE BOOKS

ISBN 0-373-09920-7

B IS FOR BABY

Books by Lisa Jackson

LISA JACKSON

has been writing Silhouette romances for over ten years. With over thirty titles to her credit, she divides her time between writing on the computer, researching her next novel, juggling her teenaged sons' busy schedules and playing tennis. Many of the fictitious small towns in her books resemble Molalla, Oregon, a small logging community, where she and her sister, Silhouette author Natalie Bishop, grew up.

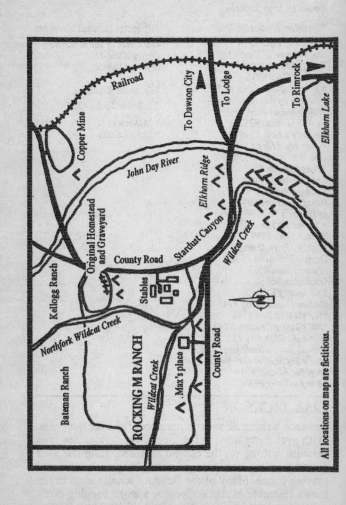

All locations on map are fictitious.

Prologue

Dear Miss Crandall,

I know you probably didn't expect this letter and I must admit that I never thought I'd be writing to you, but I feel as if I have no choice because my grandson's future—his very life—may depend upon it.

Before you disregard me as an old, overly melodramatic woman, please read the enclosed article and know that Jenner McKee, my late son's boy, needs your help. Six weeks ago he was injured while trying to save my granddaughter and the livestock from a horrible fire at the Rocking M Ranch. He was pinned beneath a ceiling rafter that had fallen, his leg was crushed, and now the doctors aren't sure if he'll ever walk on his own again. I assure you I'm not stretching the truth. By all accounts, Jenner should be dead, as his father is, God rest his soul. I fear that if he finds no reason to look toward his future, his will to live may shrivel up altogether.

But there is hope. You see, I know your secret. Before his

death, my son, Jonah, confided in me that you bore Jenner a son, but that you kept the secret of your pregnancy to yourself, never letting Jenner know that he was to be a father.

I believe with all my heart that if Jenner knew he had a boy of his own, he would find the will to live that he seems to have lost. I beg you, please, come home to Rimrock. Tell Jenner the truth. Let him see his son with his own eyes.

I'm afraid that if you don't comply, I will simply have to take matters into my own hands, and I vow to you, as God is my witness, I will see to it that my grandson is told that he's a father.

Please return. I'm afraid meeting his boy is Jenner's only chance.

Sincerely,
Mavis McKee

FIRE DESTROYS MCKEE STABLES

An explosion and three-alarm fire ripped though the stables of the Rocking M Ranch owned by McKee Enterprises. Several firemen were injured in the blaze along with Dani Stewart, 28, Hillary McKee, 5, and Jenner McKee, 33. Stewart and the McKee girl were treated for smoke inhalation and released from the hospital. Jenner McKee is in critical condition at Dawson City Hospital, where he is being treated for smoke inhalation, second degree burns and injuries to his spine and one leg.

Due to McKee's efforts, no horses were killed in the blaze, which destroyed the stables, a building housing machinery, as well as a pump house and part of a barn.

The cause of the blaze is under investigation, but Fire Chief Fred Swaggart hasn't ruled out arson....

Chapter One

Sometimes you just plain run out of luck. Especially with a man like Jenner McKee.

Angrily, Beth Crandall stuffed the rest of her mail into the pocket of her jacket and kicked at a stone in the parking lot, sending it skittering across the wet asphalt to land near the row of dripping rhododendrons that was the barrier between one sixplex and the next.

As if she hadn't tried to tell Jenner he had a son! A vision of Jenner, rugged and leather tough, flitted through her mind. Roguishly handsome, tall and lean, he'd used her as he'd used a dozen women before her, and she'd been foolish enough trust him.

She couldn't imagine him injured . . . crippled. He'd been so vital, so alive, so strong.

She stared down at the embossed letterhead and wished she'd never seen the letter from Mavis McKee, never ripped open the envelope, never scanned the words that were bound to control her destiny.

For nearly three years she'd convinced herself that she'd never have to deal with anyone named McKee again, but she'd been wrong. So very wrong. "Fool," Beth muttered as she climbed the steps to her second-story apartment in Oregon City.

The building was situated on a bluff overlooking Willamette Falls where the river tumbled over rocks and spillways to move steadily northward. On either bank were industrial buildings—factories and mills of different sorts with tall smokestacks that billowed steam into the gray sky. Highway 99 sliced along the shoreline, running parallel to the river and the railroad tracks that followed the Willamette's path.

Yes, she was far away from the sleepy little town of Rimrock, Oregon where she'd grown up and spent a lot of her adolescent years adoring a lonesome cowboy rodeo star, the rebellious second son of the richest man in the county.

Jenner McKee. Her heart squeezed at the thought of him. Beth had told herself she'd gotten over her schoolgirl crush long ago, that in the past three years she'd matured and given up the silly dreams she'd built around a man who probably didn't even remember her name.

And now he could find out about Cody.

Her insides turned as cold as ice. Numbly she walked to the edge of the cliff and looked over the railing to the sluggish gray waters of the Willamette. How had Mavis found her? Probably through Jonah McKee. Beth suspected that while he was alive, Jonah had kept track of her and her son.

Whether she liked it or not, she had no choice but to return, to come clean and admit to Jenner they had a son.

Otherwise, should she try to run, to hide Cody, she might lose her little boy forever. If Jenner decided he wanted custody, he could afford the most expensive lawyers in the state, he could buy witnesses and line the pockets of crooked judges, and Beth could lose her only son.

Her throat turned as dry as dust at the prospect.

How would it look to the judge?

In her mind's eye, Beth conjured up her worst nightmare. She stood alone on one side of the courtroom; Jenner and his team of lawyers swarmed together on the other. Gone were his faded, worn Levi's. Instead, he wore an expensive three-piece suit with a white shirt and solid-colored tie. His days' growth of beard had been neatly trimmed away and he was solemn and serious, no longer the rough-and-tumble rodeo rider who had never spent more than two weeks in any one spot. He'd inherited part of the vast McKee fortune and owned property, a huge house, acres of ranch land, timber and mineral rights, as well. Along with ranch hands, he had a maid and nanny on his payroll.

The judge's voice was stern. "Ms. Crandall, you're the daughter of Harriet Forrester, correct?"

"Yes."

"Let's see . . . Crandall . . . that makes you her daughter from her second husband. . . ."

"Her first husband," Beth corrected.

"Winward was her maiden name?"

"Yes."

"Humph." The grim-faced judge leafed through a thick sheaf of documents and scowled, clucking his tongue sanctimoniously. "Harriet Winward Crandall Lambert Jones Forrester. My God, she's gone through enough husbands, hasn't she?"

In Beth's mind's eye, the judge smiled down at her, exposing yellowed teeth.

"I don't see what my mother has to do with this hearing," she countered, once again feeling the pain, the embarrassment she'd lived with all those years in elementary and high school. She'd heard the whispers, endured the taunts, knew that most of her classmates thought her mother was nothing more than a cheap hussy, a whore who went through husbands as quickly as some people went through toilet paper. At least that's what Dale Bateman had said to her when they were in the fifth grade.

"It's simple. You're the daughter of a . . . well, a very colorful woman. Why, she's practically legendary here in Rimrock, the way she's slept with just about every single man in town, and Mr. McKee, here, is the son of one of the most revered men in three counties." He leaned even closer, his judicial robes settling around his broad shoulders as he folded his hands and smiled. "Now, isn't it true you didn't tell Mr. McKee he had fathered a son?"

"Yes, judge," she imagined herself saying in a strangled voice.

"And is it also true that you took money from Mr. McKee's father—kind of a bribe to stay away from Jenner McKee?"

"Well, it wasn't really a bribe—"

"But it helped you pay off your education debts, allowed you to make ends meet while you had the baby and started looking for a nursing job, didn't it?"

"Yes, but—"

"Hold on a minute." In her painful vision, she could see him adjusting his reading glasses to peruse thick stacks of depositions. "While you work during the day, Mr. McKee's son is being cared for by an elderly woman who you only met once you moved into your apartment in the city."

"Mrs. Taylor is far from elderly! She's very active and has more energy than I do on some days. Besides, she loves Cody."

The judge sighed loudly. "And did you, or did you not, keep your son hidden from his natural father?"

"Yes, but—"

The courtroom was suddenly as silent as the tomb. Only the paddle fans whirring softly overhead made any sound. Shaking his head, the judge picked up his gavel. "I hereby grant custody to Jenner McKee! Ms. Crandall will have visitation rights, of course—" The imaginary gavel pounded down with a bang. Beth jumped, her heart drumming in fear, and her fingers tightened around the rain-slicked railing of the overlook.

Losing Cody was her worst nightmare. One she'd had over and over again. In the past couple of years, she'd convinced herself that it was only that—a worrisome dream. She'd never been to a custody hearing, and certainly they were much more fair than the horrible one she'd envisioned. And yet . . . She shivered inside.

Don't let Jenner get away with it! He never wanted Cody and he didn't want you! Fight him, Beth! Don't give up!

Hunching her shoulders against the rain, she headed back to her apartment. There was no reason to panic. Just because she'd received a letter from Jenner's grandmother was no reason to believe that he'd changed. He might not care that he had a son.

Except now he's injured—unable to walk on his own. That would change a man; make him realize what was important in life.

She stopped dead in her tracks as she reached the stairs to her second-floor apartment. What would Jenner do without the use of his legs? How would he function? She tried to imagine him behind a desk, pushing papers for McKee Enterprises, and she failed. He'd never be happy confined to a wheelchair, never be able to accept the fact that he couldn't ride a wild rodeo bronco, or rope a calf, or best a man in a barroom brawl . . . or make love.

Beth's throat caught and she took in a short, swift breath. She'd given up thinking about her one night with Jenner long ago, tried to forget how it felt to have him hold her, kiss her, touch her anxious nipples with his callused thumbs. Theirs had been a night of lovemaking, a single, special night that Jenner probably didn't even remember, one that she had treasured for months.

But that was all in the past now. Before she had her new life here in the Willamette Valley. With Cody. At the thought of her son, she raced up the stairs, her heels ringing on the metal steps. Suddenly she had to see his smiling face, hold his small body close to hers, convince herself that he wasn't going to be taken away from her.

She unlocked the bolt and threw open the door.

"Cody!" she called, sensing the apartment was empty. Panic swept through her. Maybe Mavis had already made good on her threat. "Cody!" She ran to her son's small bedroom, but the crib was empty. "Lela?" *Get a grip, Beth. They're just out. They'll be back in a minute.*

Fingers trembling, she slid out of her jacket and flung it onto the corner of her bed. Forcing herself to remain calm, she splashed water on her face in the bathroom, then kicked off her high heels and changed from her skirt, blouse and jacket into a soft pair of jeans and her favorite sweater.

Today had been her last day at the clinic. She'd been granted severance pay, of course, but not much because the clinic, run by government funds, was closing. The entire staff had been discharged, and there had been tears and laughter and worried goodbyes this afternoon.

Beth was certain she'd get another job; she'd applied at three hospitals, but she just didn't know when she'd be hired. Her life was falling apart at the seams, and now here was this letter with the horrid news that Jenner was hurt, maybe permanently.

It looked like his luck had run out, as well.

Beth felt a jab of guilt. Ever since opening the damned letter, she'd worried about Cody and herself and hardly given a thought to Jenner and his plight. Despite the way he'd treated her, he didn't deserve the injuries he'd received while trying to save the others.

Jenner McKee. Noble. Who would have thought?

She heard the door open and she raced into the living room, where Lela Taylor was busy unbuttoning Cody's jacket. Beth's heartbeat slowed a little and she forced a smile as Cody's blue eyes focused on hers and his face broke into a happy smile.

"Mommy!" he yelled, holding up his arms despite the fact that Lela was trying to.shuck off his jacket. "Mommy! Mommy!"

Eagerly Beth plucked him out of Lela's arms. "Where've you been, big boy?" she asked. Planting a kiss on his soft cheek, she smelled the traces of baby shampoo in his hair.

"Oh, we took a big walk today, didn't we?" Lela chuckled. "We went over to the park and what did we see there, hmm?"

"Dog. Big dog!" Cody said, his eyes, so like his father's, shining brightly. "And puppies."

The two women exchanged glances.

"They were giving them away for free," Lela said a little sheepishly.

"Lela, you didn't!"

"Well..."

"I want!" Cody said excitedly.

"I couldn't resist."

"But we can't have a puppy here. Not in the apartment."

Lela lifted her hands in silent surrender. "Oh, I know, honey, and I respect that. But there's no reason Al and I can't keep the dog until you get a bigger place."

"Oh, no..." Beth felt as if her world was collapsing.

"If you don't want the dog, Al and I will just add him to our litter. One more won't hurt anything."

"As long as Cody understands," Beth said, but she was beginning to feel manipulated by a two-year-old imp and the woman who adored him.

"He can come over and see Barney any time he wants."

"Barney? You already named him?"

"Not me." Lela winked at Cody. "Your son did." Reaching into her pocket for her keys, she added, "Oh, I locked the stroller downstairs in the bicycle closet." She checked her watch. "Better be running along. Al will be home in half an hour and he doesn't take kindly to waiting for dinner. Turns into a bear if he has to watch the news before he eats."

"You should make him cook his own," Beth said, thinking of the giant of a man who had been married to Lela for over forty years. A quiet man who rarely voiced his opinions, Al Taylor was the most unlikely person she knew of becoming a "bear."

"I do. Every Friday night. We usually go out for pizza."

As Lela reached for the door, Beth hugged her son and decided she had to start making arrangements to return to Rimrock. "You know, since I don't have to go into work next week, I think Cody and I might be taking a few days off to visit my mother."

"Next week?"

"Who knows when I'll get some free time again?"

Lela's gray eyebrows rose over the tops of her tortoiseshell glasses. She had never pried, but she knew that Beth had left Rimrock for reasons involving Cody. Though Harriet Forrester had visited her daughter in Oregon City a few times, Beth had never gone back home in the few years that Lela had been Beth's neighbor and friend.

"Not bad news, I hope."

Only the worst! "No, I, uh, just think it's time." Beth hated not confiding in the friendly older woman, but she had reasons to keep her secrets to herself. She'd never divulged the name of Cody's father to anyone other than her mother.

Until a few minutes ago, she'd thought her secret was safe; the only people who knew that Jenner McKee had fathered a son were Beth, her mother, Harriet, and Jenner's bastard of a father, Jonah P. McKee. Beth had heard that Jonah had died, of course. Her mother had informed her of the news, and now there was speculation that he might have been murdered. Mistakenly Beth had assumed he'd taken the secret of Cody's birth to the grave with him, but apparently he'd confided to Mavis that she had a grandson.

A grandson who no one was supposed to know about.

Lela promised to pick up the mail and water the plants, then left Beth clinging to her son. How many other people knew about Cody? Who else knew that Jenner McKee was a father? She'd hoped that once Jonah was dead, she'd be free of the McKees forever, but the damned letter had only proved that there would always be an invisible cord, as strong as steel, binding her to the richest family in Rimrock.

Beth felt the urge to run, to flee to some distant spot where no one would ever find her. But that was impossible. With the McKee wealth, influence and connections, she would never truly be safe. No, she had no choice. She had to go back to Rimrock, face Jenner, and tell him he had a two-year-old son.

"Just leave me the hell alone!" Jenner roared, his voice thundering through the halls of the old ranch house.

"Why should we?" Casey, his younger sister, snapped back. "So you can pour yourself into a bottle?"

Growling obscenities that would make a sailor blush, Jenner gave the damned wheelchair a kick and watched the useless contraption roll across the wood floor to land with a thud against the couch. "Good riddance." Grabbing his crutches, he stumbled to his feet. His left leg dragged, refusing to move on its own. "What I do is my business," Jenner said as he swayed, his weight shifting precariously. Gritting his teeth, he managed to balance on the crutches. He, who had once had the ability to stay astride a thousand pounds of ripsnorting, mean horseflesh, reduced to this. Hell. The doctors had predicted he might never walk again and he'd proved them wrong. He could walk, damn it, but he had to use the stupid crutches. And he limped. Badly.

He tried to turn his back on his muleheaded little sister, but she was having none of his stubborn streak. She stormed up to him, her hazel eyes sparking with fury, her chin thrust forward. A little thing, she had a temper that matched his own. A McKee trait. "Mom, Max, and Grandma and me—we're only trying to help," she said, poking him in the chest. "Why do you think Max is working like crazy getting that apartment fixed up for you? And Mom, with what she's going through since Dad died, it's a wonder she can put up with your mood swings. Then there's Grandma. She's as fit to be tied as I've ever seen her. The least you can do is smile once in a while."

"Did I ask for any of your help? Huh? Did I beg you to try to cheer me up, bring me food on trays, offer to push me around in *that?*" he sneered, raising up one crutch and pointing at the wheelchair. "Hell, no!" The crutch landed on the floor again, rubber tip sliding slightly on the polished wood. "I didn't ask you or Mom or Mavis for anything."

"You're an ingrate, that's what you are!"

"And that's the way I like it!" Jenner hobbled across the room to the window where he could stare out at the blackened remains of the stable. His skin crawled when he thought about the damned fire where he should have died. Even in the growing dusk, he saw the charred rubble and ash that had once been shelter for the McKee horses. Two other buildings—the machine shed and a pump house—had also been engulfed in the hideous flames that had devoured the stables. His head suddenly pounded with the shrill sound of neighs of terrified horses, the thunder of steel-shod hooves kicking in panic, the wail of his own screams....

Damn it all. He turned quickly, nearly fell over, and moved toward the bar, his father's bar, where a bottle of opened whiskey beckoned.

"Oh, great. Just what you need."

"What I *don't* need is a lecture." Propped upright with the crutches, Jenner poured himself a short glass from a bottle his father had barely tapped before he died.

"I just want you to pull yourself together!"

"Like you have? Hell, you don't even know why you're still in Rimrock. You're always spoutin' off about leaving but you never quite make it to the door, do ya?"

Jenner caught Casey's gaze in the mirror mounted above the brass sink and liquor cabinet. Concern engraved her skin with little lines around the corners of her mouth, and he suddenly felt like a heel. But he didn't want her worries. Nor her pity. He just wanted everyone to go away and leave him alone. Managing a hard smile, devoid of even the tiniest hint of humor, he lifted his glass. "Cheers."

"Jenner—"

"I don't need a mother, all right? I've already got one. And you don't have to nag like a wife—*that* I'll never need." He tossed back his drink and poured a second. Dark clouds gathered in his sister's usually clear eyes. "Keeping count?" he mocked.

"You're impossible."

"Damned straight!" He downed half of the second drink, savoring the smoky flavor that hit the back of his throat and burned a welcome path down to his stomach. His blood began to warm and his muscles relax. He caught a glimpse of himself in the mirror, unshaven, hair too long, except in the places it was growing in again in fuzzy patches where it had been singed by the flames. There was a scar near his right ear. His skin had been seared by an ember, but he'd been lucky. Or so the doctors had tried to convince him. With a snort, he eyed the whiskey bottle again.

"Have you ever wondered what you're going to do with the rest of your life?" Casey asked.

No doubt about it, she as a pest. "Have *you?*" he countered.

"Every day."

"And you get nowhere. Face it, Casey, you're spinning your wheels."

Even the insult didn't fend her off. She bristled a little and said, "I'm taking care of you. And Mom. Besides, we're not discussing me. You're the one who has to think about the future—to come up with some kind of game plan for the rest of your life."

Turning slowly to face her, he felt his fingers tense around the glass. "If you want to know the truth, Casey, I don't really give a damn."

She clenched her teeth. "You know, I believe you. I was going to offer to stay with you since Mom and Grandma have gone into town to meet Rex Stone, but—"

"What, my company's no good?" he mocked. "Gee, Casey, you make the popcorn and I'll turn on the TV. If we're lucky, we might not miss the final round of 'Jeopardy' and after that we could have us a rousing game of checkers." He drained his glass. "Well, no, that sounds a little too strenuous. I think I'll just have another drink instead."

"Do what you want. I'm tired of baby-sitting!"

He laughed then cringed a little at the hollow sound it made ricocheting through the hallways of the house where he'd grown up.

Muttering something under her breath about hard-headed, good-for-nothing men, Casey stalked out of the room.

Jenner snagged the bottle, settled into his father's favorite oxblood leather chair, and relaxed a little. He clutched his empty glass. Though the whiskey beckoned, he ignored the temptation. Instead, he laid his head against the back of the seat and closed his eyes. Why did she have to bring up the rest of his life?

The damned thing was he couldn't even think about tomorrow.

* * *

Beth's old Chevy Nova wheezed a little as she pulled into the driveway of the little bungalow she'd called home for most of her life. The house hadn't changed much and was still painted white with green shutters complemented by a black shingled roof. The lawn needed mowing, but the flower beds, her mother's pride and joy, were a virtual rainbow of pansies and petunias that flanked the sidewalk and peeked from low-growing shrubs next to the house.

"Come on, Cody," she said, sneaking a glance at her son as she cut the engine. "Let's stretch our legs."

"Stretch legs!" Cody said, his blue eyes shining as he held out his chubby little arms to her. A rambunctious toddler, he smiled easily, ran full tilt most of the day, and repeated everything that was said to him.

Slinging her purse over her shoulder, Beth climbed out of the car. Cody impatiently started work on the buckles to his car seat. "Out! Out!"

"Hold on a minute, peanut."

"Not peanut."

"Okay, okay." She unstrapped Cody from his car seat and hugged him close. "So where are we?"

He turned sparkling eyes up at her. "Where are we?"

"Grandma's house." Balancing him on her hip, Beth walked up the cement path to the front porch. The screen door opened before she could reach for the doorbell, and Harriet Forrester, beaming at her only grandchild, stepped onto the front porch.

"I was wonderin' when you'd show up," she said as she pried Cody out of Beth's arms. "How are you, big fella?" Nuzzling her grandson, Harriet sighed happily. "Oh my, how Grandma's missed you."

Just forty-nine, Harriet looked a decade younger. Her brown hair was devoid of gray and cut into a pageboy that feathered softly around her chin. Her eyes were still clear and green with only a trace of webbing near the corners.

She'd always been a beautiful woman, a woman men noticed. Not shy of the altar, Harriet had been married more times than Beth could imagine. Her current husband of the past six years was Zeke Forrester, who had three ex-wives himself and was a foreman at the sawmill.

"My Lord, he's grown," Harriet said, clucking her tongue and pressing a kiss into Cody's downy blond curls. "Why, you're just getting to be Grandma's big boy, aren't you?" With a smile at her daughter, she said, "Come on inside. I've got coffee brewing, or if you'd prefer a soda, there's a six-pack in the fridge. I've got beer, too, and oh, why don't we open a bottle of wine? It's been so long since you've been here! We've got to celebrate, don't we, pumpkin?" She pressed another kiss to Cody's forehead and breezed into the kitchen, where Cody wiggled until Harriet set him on his slightly unsteady feet.

"I don't think I should have anything to drink," Beth said, reminding herself of her mission. Her palms turned sweaty at the thought of finally facing Jenner with the truth.

"Just a glass..." Harriet opened a drawer and searched for a corkscrew. A bottle of chilled rosé was sweating on the counter near the sink.

Beth hesitated, then decided she'd better get the worst over with. She didn't want to chance losing her nerve.

"No, Mom, really. I've got to drive out to the ranch and visit Jenner McKee."

Immediately her mother's sunny disposition faded. "Oh, God. You're going to tell him," she said stonily as she gripped the open drawer for support. The age lines that hadn't been apparent before seemed to suddenly appear at the mention of Jenner's name.

"I have to."

"Do you?" Harriet cast a glance at Cody, who was already exploring the open pantry. She began to chew on her lower lip and shook her head as if she was having a silent argument with herself. "They'll want Cody, you know. And whatever the McKees want, they get. It's kind of the law of the land, or code of the West, or whatever you want to call it." Cody reached for a can of peaches. "Oh, dear, I've got mousetraps in there." Harriet scurried after her grandson and hauled him out of the pantry.

"I think it's only right that Jenner should learn the truth from me rather than his grandmother. It's something I have to do, my duty. Besides, I think it's time to close that chapter of my life."

"You're not closing a chapter, you're opening a can of worms and mark my words, those McKees will want Cody."

"They can't have him," Beth said.

"It's not that simple."

Cody was already wriggling to get back to the floor.

"What's Jenner going to do—try to buy him from me?" Beth laughed, but even to her own ears the sound was hollow and lifeless. She'd thought about it a million times— what Jenner would do if he ever found out he had a son, a baby boy. Each time the thought had crept into her mind, she felt a chill as cold as death course through her blood. She was in no position to fight the McKees, but she shouldn't have to. Cody was hers, and though Jenner had inadvertently fathered the boy, he had no claim to him. Of course the courts would see it differently, especially if the courts were run by judges whose election coffers had been filled with McKee money.

"You don't know what Jenner might do," Harriet said, kicking the door to the pantry shut and reaching into the cookie jar. "He's a McKee, isn't he? And even if he didn't get along with Jonah, Jenner's as ruthless and self-righteous as the rest of the clan. Look how the family won't give up on the fact that they think Jonah was murdered. *Murdered!* In a town the size of Rimrock. That's the craziest notion I've ever heard." She handed Cody a peanut butter cookie.

"Jonah made his share of enemies," Beth said.

"Haven't we all?"

Beth held her tongue. Her mother's face was suddenly crossed with an expression of extreme sadness and pain. Beth didn't have to be reminded of the rumors that had surrounded the older woman. For as long as Beth could remember, she'd heard the harsh whispers, noticed the raised eyebrows, witnessed the good, churchgoing women of Rimrock turn their backs on Harriet Winward Crandall Lambert Jones Forrester. Tongues had wagged about Rimrock's most flamboyant divorcée. Between marriages to her four husbands, Harriet had dated many of the locals, though, as far as Beth knew, she'd drawn the line at married men. Harriet's view of marriage was that it was binding and monogamous as long as both parties were happy, but at the first sign of rough going, it was over. Harriet was a free spirit who didn't believe in relationships that were too difficult. When either party was dissatisfied, it was time to call it quits and move on.

Beth, on the other hand, had a romantic, fairy-tale belief that marriage should last a lifetime; that despite the ups and downs, a couple should cling to each other, give to each other, help each other through any crisis. Even though, considering her ill-fated relationship with Jenner, she'd been proved wrong already.

"What does Stan think of all this?" Harriet asked.

Beth sighed. She hadn't confided in Stan, the man she'd been dating and thought she might marry one day. "I haven't told him. I thought I should tell Jenner first."

Harriet clucked her tongue and poured them each a glass of wine. "You may not know it, honey, but you need this." Harriet handed her daughter a long-stemmed glass, then sipped from her own.

"How's he doing?" Beth asked, taking a swallow of wine.

"Jenner?" Harriet shrugged and settled into a worn kitchen chair. "Ornery as ever, I've heard. He's not paralyzed like they first thought, but one of his legs isn't working right. Mandy Crawford—she knows Kiki, the McKees' cook—says Jenner's as mean as a nest of yellow jackets in October. Always angry. Kiki has to walk on eggshells around him."

"But he is walking?"

"I haven't seen him myself, but that's what I hear."

Relieved to hear that he wasn't going to be confined to a wheelchair, Beth took another sip of wine, then set the glass on the counter. She couldn't put off the inevitable. "I hope you don't mind watching Cody while I go break the news," she said.

One of Harriet's arched brows lifted a fraction. "Aren't you going to take him with you?"

"Not yet. I think I should do this one step at a time."

Harriet smiled at her grandson who was covered in cookie crumbs. "Well, that's just fine with me. How about you, pumpkin? How would you like to stay with Grandma and fix supper for Grandpa Zeke?" She took a long swallow from her glass. "Of course, we won't start for awhile. He doesn't get home from the swing shift till later."

Cody's eyes clouded a little, but Harriet didn't seem to notice. "Now if Jenner gives you any trouble, you just leave him to stew in his own juices. And don't let him intimidate you just because he's got McKee attached to his first name. We may not have as much clout in this valley as the McKees do, but we're family just the same. I'm here for you, and you know that Zeke will be, too."

"Thanks, Mom," Beth said, "but I'll be fine." She let the remark about Zeke slide. So far, her mother's marriage seemed to be holding together, but Beth didn't kid herself. Zeke didn't give two cents what happened to his wife's daughter. He had enough children and grandchildren of his own to worry about. Beth and Zeke weren't close and never would be. After her own father had left, Beth knew better than to expect anything more than cordiality from any one of her mother's husbands.

This included Zeke Forrester, a silent man who had barely glanced up from his newspaper on the night Beth had left town after making the announcement that she was pregnant and was moving away from Rimrock forever.

Harriet finished her glass of wine. "He thinks of you as his, honey."

Beth didn't believe it, but she held her tongue. Let her mother spin her little fantasies. When Harriet was in love, she adored her spouse. When the love faded, Harriet didn't believe in holding on to old baggage and she divorced the man promptly. No hard feelings. No bad-mouthing. No alimony. And no children. Except for Beth, Harriet had always made a clean break. Beth had often wondered if her conception had been a mistake, but she supposed it didn't matter. Throughout all the pain of growing up, she'd never doubted her mother's love. "I'll see you later then."

"Okay, but before you go, I want to give you a little advice." She lifted the bottle and filled up her glass again. "I know that Jenner hurt you and I don't want it to happen again."

"He didn't mean to—"

"Don't go protecting him, okay? Look, Beth, I've known a lot of men in my life and not one of them—well, aside from Zeke maybe—is worth a broken heart. If you think you've got to tell Jenner about Cody, so be it. I won't interfere, but don't let yourself get all brokenhearted again."

"I wasn't ever—"

"Shh. Just remember. Jenner McKee's no saint."

With her mother's words still nagging at her, Beth drove to the McKee ranch. A blanket of darkness had settled over the valley, and the Blue Mountains, rising like sentinels in the distance, seemed to blend into the sky. She'd forgotten how black the nights were here, outside of the lights of the city. With only a quarter moon and a few stars winking behind a thin veil of clouds, the night seemed vast and endless.

Her stomach was in knots, her hands sweating at the thought of seeing Jenner again. Did he know? Had his grandmother warned him that she would be returning? Would he remember her? It wasn't as if they'd had a long affair.

Oh, Lord, how had it come to this?

The beams of her headlights splashed upon the row of trees lining the drive of the Rocking M Ranch. Her heart began to drum wildly as she turned off the highway.

What would she say? What could she?

Her stomach cramped with fear, the numbing fear that Jenner might demand custody of his son. Well, it wouldn't happen. She wouldn't let it happen. She'd never, *never* give up her child.

The ranch house was nearly dark, light shining from only one window as she parked near the garage and sent up a quick little prayer for strength.

Crossing her fingers, she climbed out of the old Chevy and stopped dead in her tracks when she noticed the charred ruins of the stables—ashes blowing in the wind, blackened beams and pipes, a pile of useless, burned rubble.

She imagined the horror that Jenner had lived through and felt a stab of guilt for her own selfish interests. How would it feel to survive a raging inferno wild enough to consume a huge building? In her fervor to keep her son, she'd thought of little else, not even the sheer terror and pain that Jenner must have experienced. Hadn't that been why his grandmother had written her in the first place?

A breeze, cool with the breath of autumn, whipped her hair and brought the smell of ash and burned wood to her nostrils. She hiked the collar of her jacket up around her neck as she walked on wooden legs across the asphalt lot to the path leading to the front door. There was no time for turning back or second-guessing herself. As she stepped onto the porch, a low growl rolled through the air. The hair on the back of her neck rose as she spied a dog lying under a decrepit rocker, his eyes glowing with the reflection of the security lights. "It's okay," she heard herself saying. "Good boy."

The animal's tail gave a short thump. Determination mingled with fear as she pushed the doorbell and waited, hearing the chimes peal softly.

But then there was nothing. Not even the sound of a footstep on the floor.

Again she rang the bell and waited, the seconds ticking by slowly in contrast to her rapid heartbeat.

Not a sound.

"Come on, come on," she muttered, pounding loudly on the doorframe. This time the dog let out a sharp bark.

"It's open!" a male voice roared and she suddenly could barely breathe.

She would recognize that voice even if she hadn't seen Jenner McKee in fifty years. It was a voice that still haunted her dreams and belonged to a man she'd never forget. Cody's father.

The screen door creaked as she opened it and her hands were clammy. She wiped them on her jacket and walked slowly through the darkened hall and toward a sliver of light shining through a partially opened door.

"God help me," she whispered as she stepped into a den and found Jenner, propped up in an old recliner, a glass in his hand. He looked just as she remembered him, ranch tough and cynical, his eyes slitting a little. Faded work shirt, worn jeans, scuffed cowboy boots, unshaven jaw—the image of the cowboy still intact. "Hello, Jenner," she said, forcing a smile so brittle she thought it might crack.

His gaze raked up and down her body and he rolled his empty glass in his hand before his eyes found hers again. With a look of undisguised disgust he asked, "Who the hell are you?"

Chapter Two

Beth didn't move a muscle. "You don't remember me." It wasn't a question, just a simple statement of fact that shattered all her silly dreams. What had been so special to her had meant nothing to him. Nothing!

"Should I?" he said, glowering at her. She noticed crutches propped against the end of the couch, a wheelchair tucked into a corner near the bookcase and a half-filled bottle of some kind of whiskey on the table.

She managed a thin smile. "It would make things easier."

"Things? What things?"

"I'll get to them, but for now I think you should know that I'm Beth Crandall." Was there just the flicker of memory in his blue eyes? "Until I finished college, I lived here most of my life with my mother."

"And I knew you?"

"Not really." She remembered silently adoring him from afar. A real cowboy who won awards riding in rodeos all over the country. A man who had shunned his inherited wealth and given his father nothing but grief. A rebel. She'd been only sixteen when she'd first seen him in a local rodeo and since that time she'd fantasized about what it would be like to be the woman who might tame his wild spirit.

What a fool.

"You and I saw each other briefly about three years ago."

His eyebrows knit. "I've seen a lot of women briefly," he said, suddenly wary. The lines near the corners of his mouth deepened. "So why're you here?"

Oh, God, he's not making this any easier. Her throat felt hot and tight. "Actually, we spent a night together."

"Just one?"

"Yes."

"Too bad." He snorted, but didn't comment further, and Beth realized he didn't remember their lovemaking at all. For nearly three years, she'd dreamed of it, remembered the passion, the soul-jarring explosion of desire, the afterglow that was just long enough for rest before he kissed her again, his arms wrapped possessively around her.... Blushing foolishly, she realized that her fingers had curled into tight fists. Slowly she straightened each one as she walked all the way into the den until she was standing in front of him.

"This isn't easy for me," she admitted, staring down at him sprawled haphazardly in the recliner. Even unshaven and wearing clothes that hadn't seen a washer for quite a while, he was sexier than any man had the right to be.

"So get on with it. Oh, hell, I forgot all about my manners," he said with undisguised sarcasm. "How about a drink?" He reached for the bottle.

Yes! "No. I think one of us should be clearheaded."

"Your choice." He raised his glass and gave her a wicked smile that once would have melted her heart. "It ain't gonna be me."

She saw it then—the anger in his sharp gaze. Fury, dark and deep, colored his eyes to a reclusive shade of midnight.

In her peripheral vision she noticed the wheelchair. Though she knew that thousands of disabled people lived productive, normal lives, she couldn't imagine Jenner unable to walk or ride or make love.... He was just too tough, too independent, too damned stubborn.

Her heart gave a little lurch and she tried to ignore it, but as she watched him pour a thin stream of liquor into his glass, she remembered the cowboy she hadn't been able to tame. He'd been as reckless and free as the northern winds sweeping down from the mountains. Tall and lanky, he'd walked with a swagger, offered women a grin guaranteed to break their hearts, and loved no one but himself. Cowboy tough, with muscles honed from years in the saddle—not just on the rodeo circuit, but on the ranch where he'd grown up as the rebellious second son of the richest man in the county—Jenner McKee would never be able to accept living his life bound to a wheelchair. He was just too damned proud.

He took a long swallow of his drink, then reached for his crutches. He eyed her again without quite so much hostility. "So what is it you're doing here? I assume you came to see me, since everyone else is gone and you haven't asked about them." With a grunt he pulled himself up right. "So, is this just a friendly little chat, or did you come to get a good look at me to see if I'm in one piece, or do you really have something to talk about?"

She screwed up her courage as he, using the crutches for support leaned on the padded braces that tucked under his arms. "I think I'd better talk to you when you're sober."

"Now's as good a time as any."

True, he didn't seem drunk, but she didn't know how long he'd been sitting alone in the dark with only a bottle for company. He took a hobbling step and was suddenly so close to her that she caught a whiff of the scent that had been his that one night long ago—soap, leather and male all tangled in a smell so distinctly Jenner it couldn't be disguised by the liquor. Her insides turned to water.

"I think I should remember you."

"That would help," she said, her voice husky. He was so close. Too close. But at least one of his legs worked and his back seemed to support him. He almost seemed as virile as before.

"Beth . . . that was it, right?"

She was dying inside. This was the father of her child and he had trouble remembering her name. "Yes."

"What'd you come here for?" His smile was devastating, but his voice bitter. "Don't tell me. You're lonely, remembered that we'd been together and wondered if I could still get it up."

Her fantasy shattered, and shock must have registered on her face.

"No?" Swaying a little, he reached for his drink. "Then maybe you've come here to read to me from the Bible, just to let me know about the joy in life and the fact that God has a plan for everyone even a heathen like me and the reason he decided to have a beam fall down and crush my back was to make me look into my real self, find my soul. If that's why you're here, sister, forget it. I've already talked to Reverend Jacobson and I don't think he'll be back." He snorted with some kind of grim satisfaction, and when she didn't respond, he lifted a finger as if a sudden light had flicked on in his mind. "Or, if it's not a personal reason, or a calling from the Almighty Himself, maybe you want me to do a little work for you. Got some steers you want branded? Or maybe a wild colt that needs breakin' or—"

"Stop it!" she screamed, suddenly angry. She couldn't believe how hard and cruel and jaded he'd become. Where was the laughter she remembered, the look of irreverence she'd found so endearing, the knowing smile? "Look, Jenner, I don't want you to work for me, I don't care what religion you profess to not believe in, and I certainly didn't come all the way over here to ask you to sleep with me!''

"Then I guess we don't have anything to talk about."

"Just your son!"

The words seemed to echo from the beams and walls of the old ranch house. Jenner reacted as if he'd been slapped, stepping back quickly, nearly falling over, then recovering to stare at her long and hard, not saying a word. His face turned stark as granite, the set of his mouth unforgiving, as if she'd crossed some invisible moral line.

Seconds ticked by, measured by the rapid thudding of her heart.

"My son?" he finally hissed, though no trace of emotion registered on his face.

"Yes."

"And yours, I assume."

"Of course."

"Of course." Slowly he reached for his drink. "So you're claiming that you and I slept together, what, a few years ago—?"

"Nearly three, when you were in Dawson City for the rodeo. You won the—"

"I remember *that,* but I sure as hell don't remember you." His nostrils flared slightly. "But you're trying to tell me that you and I met somewhere, ended up in bed, and the result of this *one night* of passion is your—wait a minute, *our*—son. Am I following so far?"

"That's right," Beth said firmly, though she saw the doubt in his eyes, the skepticism carved in the hard line of his jaw. "His name's Cody."

"But you didn't bother telling me until now because . . . why?" She could almost see the wheels turning in his mind. "Oh, no, don't tell me. Let me guess. I was just a dirt-poor rodeo jock, right? But now that my rich daddy's passed on, you think I might be worth a small fortune and because of this accident I wouldn't be able to scare up a sperm sample, so if the blood types are close enough, you could pawn your kid off on me. Is that what this is all about? A shakedown?''

She was flabbergasted. "A *shakedown?* You think I'm here for your *money?* Are you serious?''

"Are you?''

"About your money? Oh, God, no!''

"Then what—why show up here?''

"Because it was time!" she snapped, her temper escalating with all his outlandish insults. "If you want to know the truth—''

"That would help.''

" —I didn't want to come here in the first place, but I felt it was my duty." She thought about showing him his grandmother's letter, but decided that that was between him and the older woman. The letter might cloud the issue. All she needed to do was explain about Cody—nothing else.

"So now you're duty is done.''

That was all he could say? After learning that he had a child? Well, that's what she wanted, wasn't it? She didn't really expect him to smile, throw his arms around her and tell her that she'd changed his life, did she? She should be pleased that he wasn't interested in Cody, that she wouldn't have to give up her son on weekends or vacations. "Okay, so now that I've said my piece, there's really no reason for me to stay.''

"You're going to give up?" he mocked. "Just like that— turn tail and run? Hell, if you're in this for the money, you'd better get a little more backbone, be ready to stick up for your lies—''

"It's not a lie!" she hissed, stepping so close to him that she had to angle her face up to glare at him. "It's the God's honest truth. You have a son, Jenner McKee, a wonderful little two-year-old boy that I'd just as soon never met you. I don't want a red cent of your money and I don't need your sick attitude. I made a mistake when I slept with you, but I don't regret it, because I've got a child that I wouldn't give up for the world. So now that I've had my say and you've had yours, let's just call it even!'' Fury pulsed through her blood as she turned on her heel, started for the door, then felt fingers as strong as steel wrap over her forearm and jerk her around again.

She nearly slammed up against him and noticed his face had changed. No longer merely mocking, his features had turned harsh with disdain and disbelief. The slashes of cheekbone and rigid angle of jaw revealed a deeper emotion, a hatred so intense it burned in his eyes. "I don't know what you're game is, lady, but don't think for a minute that just because I can't walk on my own yet, or that I might never be able to, that I'll let any woman walk in and stomp all over me.''

"Wouldn't dream of it," she said icily.

"Good. 'Cause if I hear that you've been spreading your lies around town, believe me, I'll make your life a living hell. My family's been through enough grief and scandal in the past few months—they don't need any more.''

"Don't worry about it, Jenner," she said, attempting to yank her arm away. "As far as I'm concerned, we never met!''

His nostrils flared as he studied the lines of her face. "You'd better not be lying," he growled, his fingers still painfully gripping her arm. "'Cause you'll live to regret it.''

She wondered why she'd ever been so naive as to dream about falling in love with him. "You know, that's the trouble with you McKees. Every last one of you. Always making threats to get your way. You think that all your money gives you the right to run people off their land, force them to sell their businesses, give up whatever it is they think is valuable, and then tell them what to do in the bargain, but you're wrong, Jenner. All of you are dead wrong. You're no better than the rest of us!'' She wrenched her arm away and stormed out of the house.

The nerve of the man! To think that she'd fantasized about him!

Outside, the air was cool against her hot cheeks, and the dog let out a bark as she ran down the steps and across the asphalt to her car. Rage burned through her body as she climbed into her little Nova. Pumping the gas, she switched on the ignition and wondered at the tender little spot of disappointment and hurt beneath her blind fury. What had she expected? That he would tell her that he'd been searching for her, that he loved her, that he was thrilled to know that he'd fathered her son? Did she really think that he'd want to know about Cody, that he might even want a family? "Damn it, Beth, you are a fool!" she told herself as the car's engine coughed and died. "Come on, come on, not now!" Again she pumped the gas and twisted her key in the ignition. With a bang, the engine fired. She threw the car into reverse, pulled a U-turn, then slammed the gears into drive and sped out, her tires screeching a little. She snapped on the radio. Garth Brooks was wailing a country tune with some kind of love-gone-wrong lyrics and she changed the station to hear on old Rolling Stones tune about getting no satisfaction.

"You and me both, Mick," she grumbled, twisting the steering wheel and roaring away from the Rocking M Ranch and Jenner McKee. Now she could go forward with her life, close the chapter containing her silly dreams about a lonesome cowboy, and think about her future. There was Stan to consider. Stan who wanted to marry her, Stan who swore he loved her, Stan who accepted Cody, even though he had grown kids of his own.

Unlike Jenner.

Her throat tightened over a sob and she forced it back; she refused to give in to tears. She was too mature to cry over a lover who couldn't even recall her name. She sniffed loudly, turned up the volume, and told herself that she'd visit her mother for another day or so. Then she'd make hasty tracks back to the Willamette Valley and begin her life with Stan, a life she'd been putting off for reasons she'd never been able to name. On Monday she'd start looking in earnest for a new job.

She should be on cloud nine. Obviously Jenner would never be a stumbling block in her life—she'd have her son all to herself.

Why then did she feel so miserable?

Jenner watched the Nova's taillights disappear down the lane. He took another sip of his whiskey, but felt no pleasure from the drink.

Who was that woman? She was pretty enough, he supposed, and only a few inches shorter than his own six feet. Long red-brown curls had cascaded down her back, and her eyes, a shade somewhere between green and gray had blazed with defiance, almost as if she had been challenging him not to believe her. Determination had been chiseled into the set of her jaw and her cheeks had been flushed.

A woman to reckon with. A beautiful woman. A smart woman.

But the mother of his child? No way!

He hobbled over to the bar and splashed the remainder of his aged Kentucky whiskey down the sink. He wasn't drunk, just felt a little fuzzy around the edges and wished that he'd been stone-cold sober when he'd faced her. Then maybe he could make some sense of her visit.

He caught a glimpse of himself in the mirror and snorted. What would she want with him? An unshaven, broken-down cowboy with a bad attitude and a taste for expensive whiskey. What was she really asking for?

Money. Women always wanted money.

Then why hadn't she started making demands right then and there? Maybe he should have offered to write her a check, forced her hand, made her show her true colors. Or maybe she wasn't sure she could pawn the kid off as his.

Maybe his remark about blood types had scared her. But surely if she'd had the nerve to show up here, she would've covered her bases. She seemed too bright not to have taken care that her story would hold up.

He wondered if he *had* slept with her. Probably. Though he wasn't proud of it, he'd slept with a lot of women, had a lot of one-night stands three or four years ago, in a vain attempt to erase Nora Bateman from his mind. Funny, he hadn't thought of Nora in months, and yet at one time he'd thought she was the love of his life. Well, he'd been a fool. There was no such thing. He knew that now. Nora was married to a stockbroker and living in Denver, spending the man's money faster than he could earn it.

Good riddance, Jenner thought. The pretty daughter of a neighboring rancher, Nora had shown her true colors before Jenner had been stupid enough to ask her to marry him. He was lucky to be rid of her.

So what about Beth? He tried to remember her. Could he really have spent a night alone with her, made love to her, then completely forgotten about her? Or was she just trying to get at him and the McKee fortune? It had happened before and would certainly happen again—as long as his family had money.

Wasn't that the reason there was so much speculation about his father's death and concern that he'd been murdered? A man as wealthy and ruthless as Jonah P. McKee was certain to make more than his share of enemies. At first, everyone had thought that Jonah had downed one too many at the Black Anvil Saloon and had lost control of his Jeep in the foothills, but now the sheriff's department along with a private investigator the family had retained were certain that Jonah had been intentionally killed—run off the road somehow so that his Jeep plunged over the guardrail rimming the highway on Elkhorn Ridge, then nose-dived into the bottom of Stardust Canyon.

Lately, more and more townspeople seemed to have come to the conclusion that Jonah had been murdered. Even Jenner's older brother, Max, believed it. Jenner didn't know what to think.

The fire at the stables where Jenner had been injured had been set by an unknown arsonist, and now the authorities believed that the two incidents—Jonah's death and the devastating fire at the ranch—were connected. Max had seen a suspicious figure near the stables just before the blaze had been set, but no one knew who the culprit was.

In Jenner's opinion, it was a helluva mess and complicated by his own circumstances. Whoever had set the fire had been the cause of his injuries, and if Jenner ever got five minutes alone with the guy, he'd strangle the bastard with his bare hands. He shoved the hair out of his eyes and hobbled back to his father's chair. He needed time to rest and think. Beth Crandall, whoever the hell she was, had dropped a bomb that was sure to explode if he didn't do something fast.

He closed his eyes and the image of Beth's face floated through his mind. It seemed as if he almost remembered her, as if a likeness of her teased the corners of his mind. Her name wasn't completely unfamiliar, and he felt, if he really concentrated, that he could recall a night of lovemaking in a hotel in Portland with a beautiful woman with green eyes and an easy smile.

But he'd always been careful. Never trusted a woman to keep herself from getting pregnant. Even when a woman had sworn to have taken care of birth control, he'd used condoms. He didn't want any disease nor did he want to inadvertently spawn a child.

Another hole in the woman's story.

He thought back to the woman in the Portland hotel. It had been soon after he'd won first place riding bareback in Dawson City and he'd ended up in the Willamette Valley, still celebrating his victory. She'd been pretty enough and her name had been Beth or Bess or something similar, but he didn't remember her as being so determined or so stubborn... or so damned alluring.

Maybe he'd been without a woman for too long. Ever since his affair with Nora Bateman had ended badly, he'd made it a point never to get too involved with a woman. He hadn't had any trouble keeping that vow.

As far as he could see, nothing had changed.

Jenner's grandmother and his mother returned less than an hour later. Though Mavis and Virginia had never been close while Jonah was alive, his death seemed to have given them a common purpose. Mavis had doted on her only son and accepted Virginia as her daughter-in-law, but Virginia had resented the older woman's intrusion into their lives. Now that he was gone, they found solace and comfort in each other, their shared grief bonding them when even the birth of Jonah's children had not.

Jenner heard them prattling on, talking loudly as they entered the back door and snapped on lights from one end of the house to the other. They found Jenner sprawled in his father's favorite chair. They didn't believe he had his own plans or that he'd made a vow to himself. Come hell or high water, he was going to leave the Rocking M and make a life for himself.

Mavis, her black cane more decorative than functional, walked quickly into the den. Though she was pushing ninety, she was still spry enough to get around without much help and she kept herself up. Her white hair was rinsed with blue to set off her eyes and she had it done faithfully every week at the Cut and Curl Beauty Shop on Elm Street. Though slightly stooped in the shoulders, she didn't look her age. No cataracts marred her shrewd vision, no arthritis dared flare up in her joints. Mavis McKee was still a strong woman, one to be reckoned with.

"I don't completely trust that man," Mavis was saying. "Too... oily. He doesn't tell you everything he knows."

"You don't have to trust him. Rex Stone is the best private investigator for miles around," her daughter-in-law disagreed. "Without him, the Sheriff's Department would have closed the investigation and Jonah's murderer would have walked free."

"He still may," Mavis insisted. "Hammond Polk is an idiot."

Virginia sighed loudly. "I know, but at least until the next election, he's the only sheriff we've got. That's why we have to be thankful for Mr. Stone."

"Not much better, if ya ask me." Mavis made a sound of disgust deep in her throat, but managed a smile for Jenner who had only listened to their discussion with half an ear.

"Still up?" Virginia asked her son and Jenner felt the urge to bolt again. His mother bounced from one end of the emotional scale to the other. Her smile was always bright and cheery for him, but at other times, when she thought he didn't see, her expression turned bleak and sometimes her bottom lip trembled as she struggled with her new role as widow. She slid a glance at the opened bottle of whiskey on the table, but held her tongue. "I thought the doctor said you should rest."

"All I can do," Jenner said sullenly. Hell, he hated dealing with this. He tried not to snap, but he resented having to be cared for and treated as if he were a child. "I've had enough rest to last me the rest of my life. Besides, I had company." He might as well tell them what had happened here before Beth decided to contact the family herself.

"Company?" his mother asked, and Mavis's gaze seemed to sharpen on him. "Who?"

"A woman. Said her name was Beth Crandall."

"Harriet Forrester's girl," his mother said, the corners of her mouth tightening with disapproval.

Tucking her cane beneath her legs, Mavis took a seat on the edge of the couch and tried to act disinterested, but

Jenner caught the glimmer of fascination behind her glasses. "What did she want?"

Jenner's smile was humorless. "She had some cockamamy story about her kid. Claims I'm the father."

"Father? Oh, Lord." Virginia's back stiffened slightly, the way it always did when she felt the need to defend herself or one of her brood. "But that's impossible...isn't it?"

"I think so."

"Don't you know?"

"Nothing's ever certain."

"But Harriet Forrester's daughter...did you ever...I mean..." A scarlet flush bloomed from her neck, coloring her cheeks. "How old is the child, anyway?"

"Two. His name is Cody."

"Well, there you go. You were involved with Nora Bateman three years ago." Relief threaded through her voice and she managed a smile, which Jenner didn't answer.

"That's about the time Nora and I parted ways." From the corner of his eye, Jenner saw a movement of his grandmother's head. As if she was nodding.

"Certainly you weren't so foolish as to get involved with her while you were seeing Nora."

"Not during, but maybe after." Jenner closed his eyes. "I don't remember her."

"Not at all?" Mavis asked.

Jenner shrugged his shoulders and wished he hadn't brought up the subject. The less his mother knew about his personal life, the better. As for his grandmother, she seemed more interested than he would have expected.

"She's as callous as her mother. Imagine, after all this time, coming here and demanding—"

"She didn't demand anything." Jenner cut Virginia off. His eyelids flew open.

"But she must want something. Money, I suppose."

"She said she didn't," Jenner said irritably. Why was he defending Beth Crandall? Didn't he have the same suspicions his mother was voicing?

Crossing the room, Virginia rubbed her arms as if experiencing a sudden chill, then turned on the gas and struck a match to light the chunks of oak resting on the grate in the fireplace.

"So you're telling me there's a chance she could be telling the truth."

"As I said, I don't know."

"What do you mean—?" The fire caught, blue jets sizzling upward as the gas-fed flames sought new fuel and licked hungrily at the mossy logs.

"I mean there was a time in my life when...when I didn't really pay much attention."

"That's vulgar!" Virginia said. "How could you?"

"I'm not saying it was right. It just happened, okay? I'd see a pretty woman, we'd start talking, have a few drinks, and next thing I knew...oh, hell, what does it matter now?" He didn't have to explain himself to his mother, for God's sake. The time of one-night stands, of loving 'em and leaving 'em had only been a short period in his life—the time after Nora. He'd been a fool. He didn't need his mother or his grandmother reminding him about it.

"Jenner—" Virginia began to reproach her son.

"I'm not in the mood for a sermon."

Mavis waved her hand in the air as if to dissipate the argument simmering between mother and son. "Right. What's done is done. Water under the bridge and all that. Maybe we all just need to calm down. I don't know about you, but I could use a cup of coffee and some of Kiki's berry pie if there's any left."

Virginia didn't like being dismissed, but she cast her son a look that indicated the argument wasn't over and headed off to the kitchen at the far end of the house. As the click of her heels on the hardwood floor faded, Mavis's smile disappeared. "I think you should know about Beth," she said in a whisper, "but there's no reason to upset your mother."

"I should know what about Beth?" Jenner said, feeling the hairs prickle at the back of his scalp, the way they always did when he smelled trouble.

"I'm the reason she's here." Mavis seemed almost proud of herself.

"I don't understand—"

"I wrote to her. Told her to come and visit you."

"You did *what?*" Jenner thundered, anger surging through his veins as he glared at his grandmother. "Damn it, Mavis, tell me this is some kind of sick joke." But he could read the single-minded glint of determination in her eyes as she met his furious gaze.

"No joke, Jenner."

His hands clenched the arms of his father's recliner, and for the first time in his life, he wanted to strangle the feisty little woman who he had heretofore adored. She'd actually written to some woman to come and visit him—some small-town girl he barely remembered. To do what—claim that her son was his? Was Mavis crazy?

"I don't get it. This girl…woman…she's nothing to me. Or you—" He stopped suddenly, understanding his grandmother's motivation. She had to think that the kid was his! But why? How had that Beth woman gotten to her? In the past hour or so since she'd left, he'd begun to wonder about her. She'd seemed so straightforward, so sure of herself. But to trick an old lady…

"What's she told you?"

"Nothing. As I said, I contacted her."

This wasn't making sense and yet Jenner was beginning to get that same feeling in his gut that he'd experienced more than once years ago when his old man had tried to pull his strings. "What did you say in the letter?" he growled.

She hesitated a second, then glanced down at the age spots on her hands as her fingers curled over the smooth handle of her black cane. "That she should come visit you."

"Why?"

"Because of the boy."

"Her son."

"*Your* son, Jenner."

"Mine? How do you know? Hell, Mavis, I don't even remember the woman and now she's got you believing that the kid's got McKee blood running through his veins. Don't you see this is all a setup? For the love of God, when will you learn to keep your nose in your own business?"

"Just as soon as you learn to walk again!" Mavis inched her chin up a notch, then picked up her cane and nudged the crutches lying by the chair. "Without those!"

Jenner ground his teeth together in frustration and stared at the flames hungrily licking the logs. As he gazed into the fire, he felt his skin crawl with the gut-wrenching fear that interrupted his sleep and had been with him ever since the stables had burned.

"That boy is yours!" Mavis insisted stubbornly.

"Unless I'm mistaken," he said slowly, "you weren't there when it happened, so how the hell do you know?" Furious with the woman, he climbed to his feet, grabbed the crutches that his grandmother so disdained and moved toward the window to stare out at the charred rubble of the stables. He still remembered the blinding heat, the smell of scorched horsehair, the squeals of the terrified animals. Miraculously none of the livestock had been killed, only a few horses singed by falling embers, but all in all, no lives, either human or animal, had been lost. A fireman had sustained minor burns and two others had suffered smoke inhalation, but only Jenner had been permanently damaged.

Bulldozers were scheduled to scrape up the remains now that the fire department and insurance adjusters were finished with their jobs. The fire chief was convinced the burning of the stables was arson; the insurance company was balking at paying because they suspected that one of the McKees had intentionally set the blaze to collect on the policy.

Jenner snorted in disgust. Fools. The whole lot of them. No one at the ranch would risk injury to millions of dollars worth of horseflesh for the price of the building. He suspected the insurance company was stalling.

His grandmother cleared her throat. "I wrote Beth a letter telling her how you were doing," she maintained calmly.

"How'd you even know about her?" Jenner itched to shake some sense into Mavis.

"Your father didn't keep any secrets from me."

"My father?"

"He told me about the boy."

"Jonah knew?" Again Jenner felt that prickle at the back of his scalp, the signal that things weren't as they seemed. "How?"

"He made it his business to know everything about his children. You may have forgotten Beth Crandall, but Jonah didn't, and when he found out she was pregnant—"

"*How,* Mavis?" Jenner demanded. "How could he know? Hell, isn't anything sacred?"

"Ralph Fletcher was one of his closest friends. They did business together."

"And Doc Fletcher didn't mind that he was breaking a confidence with his patient by gossiping with Jonah?"

"I don't think he saw it that way. Ralph was just being loyal to his friend."

"Bullsh—" Jenner grabbed a crutch, lifted it and pointed the rubber tip squarely at his grandmother's chest. "This is just crazy! That kid can't be mine! How does Ralph Fletcher or anyone else know who I was with?"

Mavis cleared her throat. "Your father knew—well, guessed really. He was in Portland on business that weekend and he saw you with Beth. He always stayed in the

Armitage Hotel. You should have thought of that before you registered.''

"The Armitage?" Vaguely, Jenner remembered. "That's quite a leap, isn't it?"

"He just put two and two together."

"He couldn't have seen me."

"But you can't remember, can you? So how do you know?"

Jenner dropped the crutch as he realized that he was trying to destroy his grandmother's dream. While his older brother, Max, had been Jonah's favorite, Mavis had always been partial to Jenner and his rebellious ways. And she wanted a McKee grandson. Max's daughter, Hillary, was fine, but Mavis wanted a boy to carry on her own son's name, especially since Skye couldn't have children. So she'd found herself one. Sick at the thought, Jenner shook his head. "I can't remember, but I'll tell you this. I'm careful, Mavis. Damned careful. I've never trusted a woman who told me she was taking care of birth control. I don't take those kinds of chances."

"Every time?" she asked.

Thunder seemed to roll in his head. "I don't think this is the kind of conversation I should be having with my grandmother."

"It is when we're talking about my great-grandson."

"There is no great-grandson!"

"Well, it's a good thing your father had more sense than you. He checked things out. The timing's right, the boy's blood type is right and Beth wasn't involved with anyone else. Cody's yours, Jenner, and it's time you were responsible for him."

Jenner snorted in disbelief and gnashed his back teeth together. His father, Jonah P. McKee, had been a first-class bastard.

"You had no right to contact her," he growled, angry at his grandmother, the world and God for letting him survive the fire. The damned fire.

"I had every right."

"I don't want to see her again." Jenner's voice brooked no argument, but the old lady wouldn't back down.

"You might not have a choice. If you want your son."

"He's not my—"

"At least look at him. My guess is that he'll look like a McKee. There's a family resemblance that goes on for generation after generation. If that's not good enough, have a blood test or one of those newfangled paternity tests where they match your genes...."

She really believed it. Always a stubborn woman, Mavis was getting downright ornery in her old age. But she wasn't foolish and she wasn't one to kid herself. If she believed the boy was really his... oh, hell. His insides cramped at the thought of it. A child? By a woman he couldn't remember? A woman who would just as soon shoot him as talk to him? His throat was suddenly sandpaper rough and Mavis was prattling on.

"You may have given up on yourself, Jenner, but I haven't. And the doctors might be satisfied that you're not paralyzed, that your legs, well, at least one of them, seems to be healing, but that's not good enough for me and it certainly shouldn't be good enough for you! Keep in mind you're a McKee, and we never give up." Two high spots of color darkened her cheeks, and she thrust her chin upward a fraction as if she expected him to understand that McKees were considered royalty in the small town of Rimrock, Oregon. In Jenner's estimation, her pretensions were worth about as much as a pile of manure.

He forced the words over his tongue. "So you've suspected for some time now that I have a son and you didn't say a word."

"Because of your father."

"What did he have to do with it?" Damn the old man. Even dead, Jonah was still pulling Jenner's strings.

She sighed wearily. "Jonah had such high hopes for you, Jenner, but you were always thwarting him, fighting him every step of the way. Sometimes he thought you rebelled just to get his goat."

"So he hid the fact that I had a son?" Jenner was incredulous. He'd known his father played dirty, but he never expected this. Without another word, Jenner hobbled across the room, snagged his keys from the mantel and headed toward the front door.

"What do you think you're doing?" Mavis demanded.

"Finding out the truth."

"But how—?"

Jenner nearly collided with his mother, who was carrying a tray laden with coffeepot and cups and thick pieces of berry pie oozing purple juice. She took one look at his face and the keys dangling from his fingers and her skin turned the color of chalk. "Jenner? What's going on?"

"Ask her," he said, cocking his head toward the den where his grandmother was watching him with a satisfied smile playing upon her thin lips.

"But you can't leave. You're not supposed to drive—"

"Don't wait up for me."

"Stop! You can't—"

"I might not be back."

"You can't just leave."

"Watch me." He shoved past Virginia and threw open the front door. A cool autumn breeze cut through his open shirt, but he hardly noticed. He plunged the crutches in front of him and moved as quickly as possible to his old pickup parked by the garage.

"Jenner!" His mother's voice trailed after him. "Jenner McKee, you come back here right now!"

"You can reach me at the apartment!" he yelled back.

"But you can't possibly climb the stairs.... You can't just take off... oh, my God."

Jenner tossed the damned crutches into the pickup bed and hoisted himself into the cab. Slamming the door, he ignored his mother and grandmother standing on the porch, pumped the throttle, switched on the ignition, and shoved the truck into reverse.

The old Dodge lurched before he managed to work the clutch as well as the gas and brakes with his right leg. The left leg was useless, but he wasn't going to let that stop him.

Not until he'd hunted down Beth Crandall and figured out just exactly what kind of game she was playing.

Chapter Three

"I take it things didn't go all that well."

"That's the understatement of the year." Beth threw her purse onto an old rocker and tried to quiet the anger that screamed through her brain. She'd been a fool to try to talk to Jenner McKee, and in her heart of hearts she'd known it. But she'd let Mavis's letter convince her that telling Jenner he had a son was the noble, right thing to do. Well, it was done and it was a far cry from anything noble or right.

"That bad?" Harriet, curled in a corner of the couch, dog-eared a page of the mystery novel she'd been reading and kicked off the afghan that had covered her feet. A thin black cigarette smoldered unattended in a glass ashtray on an end table.

"He didn't remember me and he didn't want to believe that he had a son."

"Oh. Well, you want to talk about it?"

"Not really. It's over and done with. Something I won't have to worry about ever again." She should have felt relieved, but the undercurrent of rage that had been with her ever since she'd left the Rocking M still lingered, simmering in her blood, ready to ignite.

"Maybe you'd like that glass of wine now." Harriet took a final drag from her cigarette and rolled onto her feet.

"I don't think so, Mom. How was Cody?"

"An absolute angel." Through the haze of exhaled smoke, Harriet jabbed out her cigarette. Her face brightened at the mention of her grandson. "We had a ball. Any man who doesn't want to claim that child for a son should have his head examined. Oh, by the way, Stan called. Said he'd be up until eleven if you wanted to call him back."

Beth felt a little niggle of guilt when she remembered the message she'd left for Stan on his answering machine. He'd been out of town and she hadn't wanted to call him at his hotel in Buffalo, so she'd just left a quick recording telling him that she'd gone to visit her mother for a few days and would call when she returned.

She should have been elated that he'd phoned her, but all the doubts that had been with her since she'd started dating him assailed her. She told herself that Jenner had upset her, that seeing him made Stan all the more attractive, but she couldn't convince herself.

In the kitchen, she dialed Stan's number from memory and felt a slight disappointment when the call began ringing through. What could she tell him? That she'd met with Cody's father? That now she was free from the past? That an unfinished chapter of her life had now been completed?

"Hello?" Stan's voice sounded distant.

"Hi."

"Beth!"

She cringed when she heard the joy in his voice and felt a pang of remorse that she didn't love him with the wild abandon that he deserved. At fifty-eight, Stan Cole was twice her age, had been married for fifteen years and divorced for eighteen. His children were grown and he had two grandchildren already with a third on the way. An insurance salesman, he would retire before he reached sixty-five. He loved to ski and camp and he was kind to Cody.

"What're you doing in Rimrock? I thought you hated it over there." Was it her imagination or was there a trace of irritation in his usually calm voice?

Hating herself, she hedged. "You know my job ended and I thought Cody and I should spend a little time with my mom before I started the old eight-to-five grind again."

"Oh . . . so when are you coming home?"

"I'm not sure. . . ."

"Monday?"

"Probably not," she said.

"Tuesday then. I'll meet you—"

"Stan, let me give you a call later. When my plans are set."

"Oh, well, of course. I just thought we could get together. I could take you out to dinner. Tuesday is two-for-one night at The Countryside—"

"I know, but I can't promise Tuesday or even Wednesday, for that matter. Mom and I have a lot of catching up to do." As she wound the telephone cord around her fingers, she tried not to hear the wheedling tone of his voice or the disappointment in his sigh.

"Well, all right. Do whatever it is you have to. I just miss you, you know. I've been out of town over a week. . . . Well, how is your mother?"

Why don't you ask about Cody?

Beth shot a glance at Harriet, who had taken her position in the corner of the couch again. She'd turned on the television, probably so that she wouldn't have to eavesdrop. "She's fine. Happy to see us."

"Good, good. I guess I'll just catch up on my work and when you get home we can go out."

"I'd like that."

"I'll put in a word with Lela, see if she can watch Cody."

"No. I'll talk to her when I get home," Beth said, leaning against the wall and staring out the window into the night. Street lamps washed the yards and sidewalks in a thin blue light and a neighborhood cat slunk through the shadows.

"Come home soon, honey."

"I will," she promised and hung up with an empty feeling in the pit of her stomach. He hadn't even inquired about Cody; only brought up the boy because he was anxious to find a sitter for him. The uneasy feeling that Stan would be happier if Cody didn't exist settled over her heart. Not that Stan was ever cruel or callous toward her son. But he just seemed to accept and tolerate Cody.

"Trouble?" her mother asked when she walked back into the living room.

"No. Things are fine." No need to worry Harriet any more than she already was. Fine lines crossed Harriet's usually smooth forehead.

"You're sure?"

"Everything's just a little unsettled right now—"

The roar of a truck's engine drowned the rest of what Beth was saying. Tires screeched as the vehicle swung wide at the corner and braked to a stop in front of the house.

"What the devil?" Harriet said, twisting on the couch to peer through the venetian blinds. "Oh, my God—"

A door slammed.

"Brace yourself, honey," Harriet said as she hastily closed the blinds. "It's Jenner McKee and he looks mad enough to spit nails."

Now what? Beth's stomach cramped as she heard the sound of Jenner's uneven footsteps on the front porch, and she steeled herself for another emotion-wrenching confrontation. The bell rang insistently as she opened the door and found Jenner leaning on the tops of his crutches, his eyes blazing with fury. "Son of a—" He caught her stare. "You and I have unfinished business."

"I don't think so." She stood her ground, not moving an inch, but he shoved his way through, maneuvering his crutches so that she was forced to step aside.

"Where is he?"

"Who?"

"The kid who's supposed to be my son!" he growled, glaring at her. Beneath the anger and rage, there were questions in his eyes as if he didn't quite believe everything he'd heard tonight.

"I thought you were convinced I was trying to fleece you."

"You might be."

"So why're you here?"

His face twisted with frustration. "Because you've managed to convince my grandmother that the boy's mine."

"I've never met your grandmother."

"But you wrote to her—"

"*She* wrote to me," Beth clarified. "In fact, she threatened me."

"You're trying to make me believe an eighty-seven-year-old woman scared you?" He snorted at the absurdity.

Beth's patience snapped. "You have no right to barge in here and start making accusations."

"You started this."

"No way. Your grandmother did." She crossed the room, snatched her purse from the seat of the rocker and dug through the contents until she came to Mavis's letter. Holding it out like a shield, she walked back to the door and handed him the envelope. "Read it. You might find it interesting." She flicked on the lights and crossed her arms over her chest as if protecting her heart.

Jenner tore the letter from the envelope, scanned the contents, and let out a long, low whistle. His face drained of color, but the line of his jaw was still rock hard and defiant. "Jesus," he whispered, and it sounded like a prayer.

"I didn't drive across the state to lie to you, Jenner. Why would I? Believe me, my life was much simpler without you."

A quiet cough caught her attention, and for the first time since Jenner had stormed into the house, Beth remembered her mother. Great. Just what she needed. "Listen," she said stiffly, "why don't you come in and meet my mother, Harriet Forrester."

Jenner lifted his head and his gaze touched Harriet's for just a second. "Excuse us," he said and drew Beth out onto the porch. "I don't think we need an audience."

"My mother knows the whole story."

"Well, then she's one step ahead of me, isn't she?" His lips barely moved but his nostrils flared with a single-minded fury. "I think you'd better tell me all of your little story, starting at the beginning."

"I tried to earlier."

"I know. I wasn't in the mood."

"And now you are?"

The fingers around her arm tightened just a fraction as if he wanted to shake the living daylights out of her. "Now I am," he said so slowly the words seemed pulled from his lips. "Start."

Beth yanked her arm away and rested her back against the door. She'd been humiliated and infuriated by this man already tonight, so she didn't have much to lose. *Except Cody!* Alarm bells sounded in her head, but she decided it was time to come clean. This was it—her one shot.

"You may not remember me, cowboy, but I remember you. From the time I was eleven or twelve you were already something of a legend in town. You know, in trouble with the law, giving your rich father fits, breaking all the girls' hearts. I remember when you rode your first rodeo, right over in Dawson City. I was there and I saw you win first prize riding a wild bull or some such nonsense.

"It's embarrassing to admit it, but I had one helluva crush on you, Jenner McKee, and it stayed with me for a long, long time. Of course, I thought I was long over it, but then, a few years ago, at the Independence Day celebration in the park, I saw you again. You were still the same cowboy I'd adored from afar, but now I wasn't a scrawny little kid anymore." Beth choked on the sudden gush of memories that teased at her mind—memories she'd tried for years to hide—even from herself. Rather than dwell on them now, she cleared her throat. "Anyway, the next time I saw you it was at the roundup in Dawson City, then we happened to run into each other in Portland the next week, bumped into each other in a restaurant downtown. I mentioned that I saw you win, you bought me a drink, and even though I was old enough to know better, one thing led to another. To make a long story short, we spent the night together and...in the morning you were gone. No note. No loose ends. No promises to be broken. End of story."

"Except that you claim you got pregnant."

"I did get pregnant."

His teeth gnashed together as he stared at her so intently she thought she might crumble right in front of his eyes. It seemed as if he thought he could tell if she was lying or not simply by studying her with a gaze meant to cut through steel. "Maybe I should see the boy."

Her heart nearly quit beating. She'd considered this moment a thousand times, and though she accepted that it was bound to happen someday, she didn't know if she had the constitution to witness father and son meeting. What should be a joyful experience was certain to be agony. Gathering up her courage, she said, "He's asleep."

"Doesn't matter. Not if he's my kid."

She notched her chin up a bit and met his gaze boldly. "First, I think we should get a couple of things straight. Yes, Cody is biologically your son, but he's my child not only by blood but because of my emotional commitment to him. In that respect, he only has one parent. You mean nothing to him and so I won't have you saying or doing anything that might upset or scare him."

Jenner considered this, his blue eyes narrowing in the darkness. "Fair enough," he finally agreed.

"And I'm not going to wake him up. If he happens to open his eyes, okay. But other than that, he sleeps."

Jenner's lips curved in grim amusement. "What're you afraid of, Beth?"

"Nothing."

"Think I might get all caught up in some latent fatherly feelings and try to swipe the kid from you?"

"I don't know what you'll do, Jenner," she said, reaching behind her and opening the door. "But if I thought you'd do anything to hurt Cody—and that includes 'swiping' him from me—I wouldn't have come to see you, and you might have spent the rest of your life not knowing your son." She shoved open the door with her back and he hobbled inside.

"Just show me the kid."

Back ramrod stiff, Beth led Jenner past the open archway to the living room and down a short hallway past the kitchen. She didn't bother glancing at her mother, though she was certain Harriet had overheard most of the conversation and was apt to come to her own conclusions.

The door to her old bedroom was ajar and Beth leaned against it, allowing light from the hall to slice into the room and spill over the playpen shoved up next to a small closet. Cody rustled around a little and snorted but didn't wake.

The strings on Beth's heart tugged as usual when she saw the curly blond down of his hair, his pink cheeks and the soft motion of his lips as he sighed. Gold-tipped eyelashes curved against his smooth skin and he slept with his legs tucked under him, his tiny rear end high in the air.

Sneaking a glance at Jenner, she wished she could read his mind. Without expression, he leaned forward and squinted at the boy under the faded blue blanket.

Jenner was determined to prove her a fake. One look at the kid and he was certain he'd know the boy didn't belong to him. But standing in the hallway, he'd begun to second-guess himself.

Could she be telling the truth? Could that little bit of a human be my son, for God's sake? For the first time since Beth had charged into his father's den at the ranch, Jenner began to doubt his own convictions. Not that there was any resemblance that he could determine—the fact that the kid was white and had pale hair didn't mean a thing—but there was something about the woman, her aura of determination and hostility, that bothered him.

Unwillingly he admitted that he admired her grit. He'd insulted her, tried to reject her, and she'd given as well as she got. But to think that this two-year-old... He glanced at her. While gazing at her son, her expression had softened. It was obvious she adored the child, so why would she put him at risk and claim he was Jenner's?

For money?

Because she still harbored some feelings for him?

For revenge?

She had to know that the McKee wealth could bring her— along with her child—to her knees. She risked being exposed as a fraud, an unwed mother trying to scam a rich man, a woman with no moral standards who didn't deserve the child she'd borne. The McKee team of lawyers were merciless and would tear her story and reputation to shreds if they were ever unleashed. She wasn't stupid; surely she must realize how tenuous her position was.

Disgusted at the turn of his thoughts, Jenner stepped aside as she quietly closed the door. He didn't move from the hallway. "You know, you never answered my question earlier."

"What question?"

"I asked you what you wanted from me."

Her gaze, which had been rock steady, slid away. "I came back because your grandmother thought you'd want to meet your son. Now that it's done—"

"It's not done. I haven't met him yet." He rubbed a hand impatiently around the back of his neck. "I want you to bring him to see me tomorrow."

"I don't know—"

He couldn't stop himself from reaching forward and gripping her arm. He felt the involuntary tightening of her muscles and saw a spark in her gray-green eyes. "You started this," he reminded her in a harsh whisper.

"Did I?" She tossed her hair away from her face. "It started three years ago, Jenner. And I wasn't alone."

"Well, it's time to finish it then, isn't it?"

"Finish it?"

Was it his imagination or did she tremble a little? "Bring the boy to my apartment."

"I thought you were living at the ranch."

"Not anymore. I've got an apartment in Doc Fletcher's old clinic on Pine and—"

"I know where it is," Beth said. "And I remember the doctor. He took out my tonsils right before I entered kindergarten and set my broken arm after I fell off my friend Mary's old horse when I was twelve. And, if I'm not mistaken, he's probably the one who informed your father that he was about to become a granddaddy."

Again the fire in her eyes, and Jenner wondered how it was possible that he'd made love to this woman and barely remembered her. "Just come around, okay?" he asked, his voice more gentle than it had been. "I should meet him."

"And then what?"

"I wish I knew," he admitted as the shape of his future seemed to change before his eyes. Not only was he a cripple, but he might have fathered a child...or had he? What if this woman, this seemingly sincere woman, was just a common con artist, a user who fed off men and their mistakes?

Or, God forbid, what if she was telling the truth?

Sagging against the front door, Beth waited until she heard the sound of Jenner's truck fade into the night. She'd seen the change come over him and realized that finally he might believe her.

And then what?

Shuddering at the thought that he might change his mind, might decide he wanted to be more than a blank space on a birth certificate, she slowly forced her legs to move back to the living room where her mother was shaking a long cigarette out of a nearly empty pack.

"He's not father material," Harriet said as she found her lighter on the table. "Not that many men are. From my experience, it seems that most of 'em would rather be little boys themselves than help raise a child right." She clicked her lighter to the end of her cigarette and inhaled deeply. "I guess I can understand how you were attracted to him. Like all the McKees, he's a handsome devil. But he's so damned irresponsible...." She glanced through the window and watched as a car crawled down the street. "Same with your father, you know. Probably the best-looking of all the men I ever dated and oh, what a charmer he was. I knew I'd marry him the first time I laid eyes on him, but I didn't expect that he would leave at the first hint of trouble. He sure wasn't father material, but I guess you know that."

Beth couldn't disagree. Growing up, she'd seen little of her father. He always made a half-hearted attempt to visit her around her birthday, though the demands of his job and new family often interrupted his plans. And Charlie Crandall had been content to let Harriet's string of husbands help raise his firstborn daughter.

A little pang of doubt entered her heart. Cody, too, would grow up not really knowing his father.

"You're better off marrying Stan," Harriet said, gazing thoughtfully at her daughter through the smoke curling from her cigarette. "He's stable and trustworthy, won't be running around on you chasing other women or elusive dreams. You should count yourself lucky."

"I wish I could be sure about that," Beth said, feeling that ever since coming face-to-face with Jenner again, her luck wasn't getting any better.

Cursing under his breath, Jenner slowly climbed the front steps to the apartment house where he'd once planned to live in a unit on the second floor. Since the fire and his accident, the owner of the house, Skye Donahue, had hastened to make some efforts to fix up the basement apartment for him. It had a ramp as well as a short flight of exterior concrete stairs. Skye was a doctor in the clinic next door; she'd bought out Ralph Fletcher when he'd retired. Skye was also engaged to Jenner's brother, Max.

Sweating by the time he'd negotiated the five steps, Jenner plowed through the open door to the foyer and rapped loudly on the door to Skye's apartment. "Come on, come on," he growled under his breath.

An upstairs door opened at the racket he was making, and Mrs. Newby, a short, elderly woman with apricot-tinged hair poking out from a nightcap, peeked through the opening. "Oh, Mr. McKee, it's you," she said, obviously relieved as she bustled into the upper hallway and leaned over the rail. "My goodness, I thought you were supposed to be recuperating."

"I am." Jenner was in no mood for small talk.

"You're a hero around here, you know. Saving Max's daughter and those horses and all."

Funny, he didn't feel like a hero. In fact, in light of the past few hours after meeting Beth and that kid of hers, he was beginning to feel like a first-class jerk.

"I'm looking for Skye."

Behind thick, rimless glasses, Mrs. Newby's eyebrows lifted. "And good luck finding her. Between the clinic and your brother, Dr. Donahue doesn't have much time for this place, let me tell you. Why, half the things I requested to be done to my apartment haven't even been started! Just last week I spoke to her about the carpet—"

The door on the opposite side of the landing opened and Tina Evans, Skye's other tenant, stepped onto the landing. Her smile stretched wide at the sight of him. "Well, look who's come home," she said.

Jenner gritted his teeth and forced a smile. "I'm trying to track down Skye so I can get into the basement."

"It's not finished yet."

"No? I bet it's close enough."

Tina's smile faltered a little. "She's probably with your brother, but I've got a key so that I can show prospective tenants the vacant apartments."

Mrs. Newby snorted. "I don't know why she'd want more occupants seein' as she can't take care of the ones she has."

Tina tried and failed to suppress a grin. "Give me a minute to get the keys and I'll meet you downstairs."

Tina disappeared into her apartment, and Mrs. Newby, still leaning over the rail, said, "Be careful you don't trip over the cat. It's always up to no good, slinking around, carrying fleas and shedding everywhere... never giving my allergies a rest, let me tell you! I've talked to Skye. But does she listen? Of course not—"

Jenner didn't hear the rest of her complaint. He headed out the front door and down the steps to the concrete path leading to the side entrance that once had led to Doc Fletcher's clinic. There was enough light from a security lamp so that he didn't stumble, and true to her word, Tina

used the interior staircase, cut through the basement, and
opened the door for him.

"See," she said, snapping on the overhead lights, "it's a
long way from being finished."

"It'll do," Jenner said as he crossed the threshold and
looked around. Fresh Sheetrock had been nailed to the
walls, taped together and mudded, but only half the apartment had been painted. The cabinets were up, but the doors
hadn't yet been hung and the tile floor was bare. Appliances were still packed in boxes, but he turned on the
kitchen sink and was relieved to find that the plumbing was
working.

"The painters are due to finish up this week and the carpet's coming next Wednesday. Skye didn't expect you to be
moving in so soon."

"Neither did I," he admitted as he crossed the room to a
closet where all of his worldly possessions—a bedroll, duf-
fel bag and a few odds and ends—had been stashed.

"If there's anything you need...?" she said, offering him
the keys, and Jenner flashed her a smile he didn't feel.

"I'll let you know."

She glanced at his crutches and bit the corner of her lip
before shrugging and waving goodbye. He listened as her
footsteps clomped up the interior stairs, then he shut the
door and threw the bolt.

"Home sweet home," he said to himself as he tossed
down the bedroll. The apartment didn't have the comforts
of the ranch, but at least here he was his own man. It had
been a long time since he'd felt this free.

Slowly easing himself onto the faded sleeping bag, he
thought of Beth and her son. A pain shot up his leg, reminding him that he was no longer a complete man, that he
might forever be chained to crutches or a wheelchair. He
could no longer support a family by riding the rodeo circuit
or training horses or hiring on as a hand at one of the
neighboring ranches.

But he wasn't foolish enough to think that he was poor.

Max would probably let him run the Rocking M. Jenner could handle the paperwork and supervise the work in the fields from a truck. Chester, the ranch foreman, could run interference with the rest of the hands.

Max had already given him three hundred acres that old Jonah hadn't included in his will. Wildcat Creek slashed through one corner and the old cabin built by a great-grandfather needed some work, but was sound. A little bit of elbow grease and it would do just fine. For one.

But could he really just give up the life he'd known?

He wondered what kind of a father he would be. He'd never be able to play baseball, shoot baskets or teach the kid how to rope a calf. Swimming would be tricky and . . . oh, hell, what was the matter with him? He wasn't cut out to be a father or a husband. Seeing Beth and her kid had played havoc with his mind. Not that it mattered. He probably wasn't the kid's father, anyway.

Chapter Four

Max wanted to strangle his brother. Of all the low-life, stupid, selfish stunts Jenner had ever pulled, this was the worst. He leaned against the wall of his farmhouse, cradling the phone to his ear, imagining his mother wringing her hands.

"...so he didn't come home and heaven knows he shouldn't be driving," Virginia was saying. "I hate to bother you, Max, but I... Oh, Lord, I don't know what I'd do if anything happened to him."

Max shoved a hand through his hair and stared through the window as the first rays of sun began to spill over the horizon. His dog, Atlas, a half-grown Border collie, flushed a flock of quail from the brush bordering a thicket of pine trees. "If Jenner had been in an accident, he would have been taken to Dawson Memorial," Max said, glancing at the clock and scowling. It was only ten after six—way too early to be dealing with Jenner and his bad moods. "Skye's working in the emergency room. She would've called."

"Maybe he was life-flighted somewhere else." Virginia's voice quavered and Max silently cursed his brother again.

"Why did he leave?" Max asked as he propped the receiver between his shoulder and ear and began measuring coffee into the maker. Hell, what was Jenner up to now?

"He . . . he got into an argument with me. And Mavis."

"With Grandma?" That surprised Max. Jenner and the old woman had always been close. "Why?"

There was a hesitation on the other end, and Max experienced the first hazy sensation that there was more going on than Virginia was willing to say.

"Why'd he leave?" he repeated.

"You . . . you'll have to ask him. He just lost his temper—you know what a short fuse he has—and stormed out, claimed he might not be back. I'm afraid . . . well, I'm afraid he's gone for good."

"Gone where?"

"If I knew that, I wouldn't be calling you now, would I?" she snapped, then, as if hearing the anger in her tone, let out a long worried sigh. "I just don't know what to do. He . . . he said something about going back to his apartment."

"That's crazy."

"Tell him. I tried to call, but the phone was disconnected, and I couldn't imagine him negotiating the stairs to the second floor. I did leave a message on Skye's answering machine. Oh, Lord, Max, what if he had an accident and he's trapped in his truck. Or . . . or what if it wasn't an accident? Your father was forced off the road and the same thing could have happened to Jenner. Oh, God, Max—"

"Don't worry. I'll find him," Max cut in before Virginia's fertile imagination had Jenner murdered by the same madman who supposedly had killed Jonah and started the blaze in the stables. "Go to bed. Get some sleep." He hung up knowing she was about to break down into a crying jag and he felt rotten inside. His mother had always been a pillar of strength. For years, she'd held her head high, pre-

tending she hadn't known about Jonah's reckless affairs or
his shady business practices. She'd been his partner for life
and had supported him throughout every ordeal, ignoring
the calls from women, refusing to believe that the civil law-
suits against him and his company were anything more than
sour grapes. Loyal should have been her middle name.

Within fifteen minutes, Max had showered, shaved,
dressed and poured himself a cup of coffee. He shook some
dry dog food into a dish for Atlas, who greeted him by
jumping and barking and leaving dusty pawprints on his
jeans.

"Slow down. Eat some breakfast," Max insisted, but the
pup ignored his full dish and loped after him to the garage
where his pickup was parked. Atlas hopped into the cab of
the truck and Max didn't have the heart to shove him out.
"Just this once," he said as he backed out and drove along
the tree-lined lane leading to the edge of the McKee property and the county road.

He turned on the radio, listened to the sports scores and
then a report that predicted cooler weather, but his mind was
on his stubborn brother. It seemed that Jenner, born restless, had developed a bad case of impatience since nearly
being killed in the fire.

Not that Max really blamed him. Though Jenner had
improved to the point where he could walk with crutches,
the outlook wasn't all that great. Most of Jenner's doctors
had confided to Skye that Jenner would probably always
walk with a limp, maybe even be forced to use a cane, and
that his passion for riding wild rodeo broncs and Brahman
bulls was now a pipe dream.

Jenner didn't have to work, of course. He owned about
three hundred acres, and if that wasn't enough, there was
plenty of money in the old man's estate to go around. Since
Max was not only a lawyer but the executor, he could find
a way to set up a trust fund for Jenner so that he would be
comfortable for life. But he doubted that Jenner would ac-

cept the money. Ever since the fire, Jenner had been hell-bent not to accept charity or pity or anything that hinted at compassion for his plight.

"Idiot," Max growled as he pushed the speed limit. By the time he reached the outskirts of Rimrock, the street-lights had turned off and morning sunlight chased away a tiny hint of fog that lingered near the river. Max barreled over to the rooming house that Skye owned and felt a good measure of relief when he spied his brother's pickup, dent free, parked at the curb in front of the house. Leaving a whining Atlas in the cab, he wondered what the hell Jenner thought he was doing. He opened the front door with his key, climbed up the flight of stairs to the second-floor land-ing and banged on the door of Jenner's apartment.

There was no answer, but Max wasn't simply going to go away. He didn't care if Jenner was drunk, hung over or just plain dog tired. His brother had a lot of explaining to do. "Open up!" he yelled between bangs.

A door near the staircase opened and Mrs. Newby, in chenille robe and nightcap peered through the crack. "He's not in there," she said with the authority of a busybody used to checking up on her neighbors.

Max hooked his thumb toward the front door. "His truck is parked outside."

"He's in the basement."

"But it's not finished."

"I know," Mrs. Newby said, warming to her subject. "And I told Tina she was making a mistake by letting him stay down there, but he wouldn't take no for an answer and Tina, well, she just about melts every time she sees him. Sweet on him, she is and so...he ended up in the base-ment."

Max was already halfway down the stairs.

"When you see Skye," Mrs. Newby called after him, "would you be a dear and remind her about the security system I want installed?"

Max waved and hurried through the front door. In all his life he'd never been nor would he ever become anything closely resembling "a dear."

He took the outside steps two at a time and, once he was at the bottom of the stairwell, pounded on the door. It opened immediately and Jenner stood blocking the entry. Hair uncombed, jaw dark with stubble, shoulders hunched defensively as if he'd expected this fight, he balanced on his crutches.

"Don't tell me," Jenner growled with a sarcastic bite, "you've missed me."

"Mom's worried."

"I told her I wouldn't be home."

Max pushed past his bullheaded brother and into the unfinished room. His hands curled into fists of frustration. "She was up half the night worried sick. You know, Jenner, she doesn't need any more grief from you. She's got enough problems dealing with Dad's death and the murder investigation."

"Did she tell you why I left?"

"We didn't get into that."

Jenner's blue eyes sparked. "I didn't think so."

Max was suddenly wary. He sensed that something wasn't quite as it seemed. Just as he had during the telephone conversation with his mother. "Okay, I give up. Why did you drive off in one of your black rages?"

Jenner slammed the door shut. "Because I can't stand being a hypocrite for starters and I don't like anyone waiting on me hand and foot, watching my every move, hovering over me like a mother hen."

"She *is* a mother hen and you're supposed to be recuperating. Doctor's orders. 'No straining yourself, plenty of rest, exercise with a physical therapist, and—'"

"—and it's all a bunch of bull. You know it and I know it. The doctors aren't being straight with me. They don't think I'll ever be the same."

"No one really knows. A lot depends on you."

"More bull!" He glowered at his crutches. "Anyway, I've decided to recuperate on my own." Scowling fiercely, he rubbed his chin, and lines formed across his forehead as if he was thinking hard. Muttering a curse under his breath, he finally looked back at Max. "I don't suppose Mom told you what went on at the ranch last night."

"Just that you took off in some kind of blind rage."

"But not why."

Max couldn't help but smile. "I didn't think you needed a reason."

"I didn't. But I had one. A helluva reason," Jenner admitted. He hobbled over to the other side of the room where a hot plate, balanced on an old television tray, was plugged into the wall. An enamel coffeepot was warming on one of the burners, and the scent of brewing coffee overpowered the combined odors of Sheetrock, dust and varnish. Jenner found two chipped mugs, poured coffee, and motioned for Max to help himself. As they drank the bitter brew, Jenner settled into a folding chair and told Max some wild tale about Harriet Forrester's daughter, Beth Crandall, and Beth's contention that she'd borne Jenner a son. He also mentioned that somehow good ol' Jonah had found out about the kid, hushed it up, and managed to keep Beth from telling Jenner about the boy. Jenner didn't have all the details, but he was convinced that Mavis was behind Beth returning. What he didn't seem sure of was the paternity of the kid.

"...so the damned thing of it is, I don't really remember her, and believe me, she's a woman no one would forget in a hurry."

Max swirled the dregs of his coffee in thought. The story was incredible, but there was enough truth sprinkled into it to keep a person guessing. Max knew from personal experience that Jonah McKee was capable of manipulating his children's lives. Hadn't he forced Skye out of Rimrock years ago? Recently Max had gotten back with the woman he loved, and he and Skye were planning to marry in early December. Still, Beth Crandall's story seemed too pat. "You still think she's trying to scam you?"

"Don't know," Jenner admitted, his gaze clouding, "but if she is, she's good... damned good."

"You're buying into it and you don't even remember being with her?" Actually, Max liked the idea of Jenner being a father; it didn't even really matter if he'd sired the boy or not. Jenner needed some roots to tie him down, a reason to keep on living, and a kid would be just the ticket. Considering Jenner's accident, Max had some concern about his brother's ability to father children in the future, though no one had said anything aloud.

Max was lucky enough to have a five-year-old daughter from his first marriage. Hillary with her stubborn jaw and thick curls, was precocious, bullheaded and as cute as a bug's ear. He loved her more than he'd ever thought possible. Jenner could use a little of the joy and heartache that comes with being a parent. The feeling was like none other on earth. Since Skye would be unable to bear him any children, Max understood how precious each and every child was.

"I'm not buying into it," Jenner protested. "I'm just not sure. But I'll get to the bottom of it."

"How?" Max asked, setting his cup on the floor. "Are you going to go through blood tests? You know that would mean spending time at the hospital again—something you've stubbornly avoided."

Jenner snorted. "Before having any tests, I think I'll talk to our old friend, Rex Stone—see what he thinks."

"You're going to hire a private investigator to check her out?"

"Seems the logical thing to do." Jenner finished his coffee and set the cup on an old television tray.

"But you hate the guy, don't you?"

"Stone's a sleazeball, but I think he's good at what he does." Jenner's expression turned dark. "And I don't know anything about Miss Crandall." He concentrated on the middle distance past Max's shoulder. His jaw hardened defiantly as if he could see the woman in the room. "Before this is over," he vowed, "I'm going to know her better than she knows herself."

"What if you find out she's lying?"

"I'll make sure she regrets ever coming back to Rimrock."

"And if she's telling the truth?"

"I don't know," he admitted. "But I guess I'll cross that bridge when I come to it."

"You know there's always a need for medical help right here around Rimrock. I'm sure you could find a job if you looked. That way you could stay here, closer to me. And I could watch my grandson grow up." Harriet picked up the breakfast dishes as Beth wiped Cody's hands and face. Seated in an old high chair that Harriet had used when Beth was a toddler, Cody wriggled and protested, shaking his head vigorously.

"No!" Cody wailed. "Noooo!"

"He doesn't believe in the old connection between cleanliness and godliness," Beth said as she unsnapped the tray and placed Cody on the floor. Wiping her hands, she added, "I don't think a job this close to Jenner is such a good idea."

"I know, I know." Harriet rinsed the plates before putting them into the portable dishwasher. She looked about to say something, but thought better of it, and for the first time, Beth wondered if something was wrong. Before she could ask about it, Harriet said, "I don't trust those McKees, so don't get me wrong. But you can't run away forever, and even if you tried, there's no place on earth far enough away. If Jenner wants to be a father to his son, he will.''

"I don't think we have to worry about that." Beth wiped the table, then hung the dish towel over a metal bar near the sink. "But it would be difficult for Cody to grow up here and know that his father lived in town and didn't want him. . . ." She shook her head, her own painful memories assailing her.

"It's because of me, isn't it?" Harriet asked, her voice barely a whisper as she reached into a drawer for her carton of cigarettes. "It was hard on you growing up and you don't want your son to have to deal with all the questions and gossip you did." She flipped open the carton, extracted a new pack and tapped it against the counter. "You know, Beth, I was the best mother I knew how to be."

"I know," Beth said, a lump forming in her throat.

"And I realize that I was something of an embarrassment. I've heard the rumors, too. But most of it's just gossip. Idle tongues wagging and trying to stir up trouble." She unwound the cellophane wrapper, shook out a cigarette and struck a match. "It bothered me, of course, but the worst part was that the gossip, aimed to hurt me, probably cut you more deeply." She lit up and smoke filtered from her mouth as she sighed.

"I survived," Beth said.

"But I can't help feeling responsible."

"Mom, don't. It's over. Kids can be cruel, yes, and I hope Cody doesn't have to suffer the same things I did, but God knows I'm not the perfect parent and I don't know anyone who is. I'll make my share of mistakes." She winked at her mother, trying to jolly her out of her sadness. "Besides, all those teases and taunts made me tough—tougher than I would've been."

Harriet hesitated, then drew on her cigarette. "I hope that everything that happens here with Jenner won't make you think that you don't have any options, that you should just run off and marry the first man who asks you."

Beth stiffened. Her mother usually wasn't one to pry. "Are you talking about Stan? Don't you like him?"

"Of course I do. He's a wonderful man. I thought you should marry him, but ..." She hesitated. "But he's closer to my age than to yours." Folding her arms across her chest, Harriet ignored her cigarette and let the smoke curl in a wavering line to the ceiling. "I know what I said before but I guess I'm having second thoughts. Even if you do marry him and have a wonderful life together, who knows how long he'll be around. If you want Cody to have a father—"

"Stan's only fifty-eight. That's not ancient, Mom."

"No, but when Cody's fifteen and a hellion, which, judging by his genes, he probably will be, Stan will be over seventy. He might need some special care of his own—"

"I can manage. I'm a nurse, remember."

"A *young* nurse," Harriet reminded her. As if suddenly weary, she pulled out a kitchen chair and sat on the faded cushion.

"So what do you think I should do?" Beth asked as her mother smoked silently. "Try to find a way to make Jenner marry me?"

"Oh, God, no."

"Stay single? Let Cody grow up without a father?"

Harriet ground out her cigarette. "No," she said, "but if I were you, I certainly wouldn't marry a man just to give Cody a daddy. You might find this hard to believe, Beth, but every man I ever married, I married for love. And when I stood at the altar I really believed in till death do us part. That only happened once, thank God. Will was a special man, but cancer took him and ... oh, Lord, it was hard to watch him die." Her throat clogged and tears shimmered unshed in her eyes. "Do you remember him?"

"Not much, Mom," Beth admitted, placing her arm around her mother's shoulders. William Jones was little more than a hazy memory to her. "But I know he was a good man."

"The best," Harriet said as she wiped her eyes with her fingers and sniffed. "Until Zeke, he was the best." She blinked rapidly, and suddenly a smile stretched across her face. "Well, speak of the devil."

Zeke Forrester walked into the room in a gray-striped bathrobe and his slippers. A V-necked T-shirt was visible beneath the robe. Only five foot six, he had a blocky build and, before two cups of coffee in the morning, a sour disposition. "How ya doin'?" he said, pausing to buss his wife on the cheek.

Harriet scrambled out of her chair to pour him a cup of coffee, then went to open the refrigerator. "French toast?" she asked brightly.

"It's Saturday. You know I like bacon and eggs on Saturday." He shot Beth a dark look and took a quick gulp of the coffee. "Doctor won't let me eat eggs but twice a week," he said as some kind of explanation, then searched the tabletop and counters. "Where's the paper? Don't tell me the carrier didn't deliver it again!"

"I'll get it in a second," Harriet said. "And stop being so grumpy. Good Lord, you're a grouch in the morning."

"Cody and I will go out and get the paper." Glad for an excuse to escape, Beth carried Cody outside. She was still smarting from her mother's remarks about Stan, though she knew that Harriet's concerns only echoed her own. In the past few weeks, even before seeing Jenner again, she'd reconsidered her relationship with Stan. He was a good man. But he really wasn't interested in starting over with a young family.

Outside, the air was fresh, the sky a clear shade of blue. Beth breathed in a blend of fragrances from Harriet's flower garden and she watched birds flutter around a rusted feeder swinging from a low branch of an ornamental plum tree no longer in bloom.

"Well," she said, as she picked up the paper from the front porch, "how do you feel about meeting someone today?" Cody turned his blue eyes up to her.

"Who I meet?" Cody asked.

"Your fath—a man I knew a few years ago," she said, deciding it was better not to confuse her son. Not yet. Not until she knew how Jenner would react.

"A friend?" Cody asked innocently.

Beth rumpled her son's dark blond hair. "Well now, I don't know that I'd call him a friend," she admitted as she scanned the headlines. "But he's someone who wants to meet you." She winked at her boy and hurried back inside.

The phone jangled as Beth tossed Zeke's paper onto the table. Harriet grabbed the receiver on the second ring, then stretched the cord as she kept pronging pieces of bacon that were beginning to sizzle in a skillet on the stove.

"Oh, hello. Yes, she's here…no, don't worry about that. We're up with the chickens around here." Harriet's eyebrows rose as she handed the phone to Beth and mouthed, "It's Stan."

Beth's stomach clenched suddenly. She felt a jab of guilt and didn't know why, but she took the receiver from her mother's hand and tried to remain calm. After all, she'd done nothing wrong. Yet.

"Hello?" she said brightly as Zeke snapped his paper open and Harriet turned back to the stove. Cody investigated the back porch.

"Hi! Thought I might catch you." Stan's voice was friendly, and for an inexplicable reason Beth thought of her Uncle Jim with his pleasant smile and graying beard. Oh, Lord, this would never do.

"Hi! How are you, Stan? Didn't expect another call from you so soon," she said, easing around the corner for some privacy and drawing the coiled cord tight as a piano wire.

"I know, but I've been thinking." Then as an afterthought, he added, "You know, I really miss you."

"Oh, well—"

"I really do. It gets lonely here without you," he said, and she suddenly felt uncomfortable, as if a noose was tightening around her neck. "Listen, I had an idea. Maybe you could leave Cody with your mom for an extra few days and you and I could do something together."

"Without Cody," she said, her heart nearly dropping to the floor.

"Right. We need time alone. To be adults."

That was the problem. Always the problem. The noose tightened a little bit more.

"It's not that I don't love the little tyke, you know I do, but, well, frankly, Beth, he wears me out sometimes and I need a break. Besides, we never see each other without him. So... since you're there already, I thought leaving him for a few more days wouldn't be a big deal."

"I don't think that's possible, Stan," she said.

"Why not? It's not like your mother sees the kid all that often. She's his grandmother, for Pete's sake. You think she'd be thrilled to have him to herself for a few days."

"She works, Stan, and so does Zeke and... well, to tell you the truth, I don't want to leave him here alone."

"Why not? Don't you trust your mother?"

"Of course I do."

"Then I don't see why you couldn't spend a couple of days alone with me," he said in a tone that bordered on whining. Sighing patiently, he added, "You know, it wouldn't kill you to forget you're a mother once in a while."

"Never," she said, and then it occurred to her how far she and Stan were apart, at least on this issue. Stan was a kind, decent, loving man, but no matter how she tried to kid herself, she had to face the fact that he wasn't willing to be a father a second time around. He'd had his kids; he really didn't want hers.

"Beth, you know I think Cody's the greatest, but—"

"But you like him best when he's not around."

"That's not true!"

"Sure it is, Stan, and something else is true, as well. This—our relationship—isn't working. Not for me or for you." She waited and heard only stunned silence. "I've been thinking and—"

"You're seeing him again, aren't you?" Stan charged, his voice an angry whisper. "Cody's father. That's the problem." Stan jumped to the same conclusion he always did, whenever they argued—that Beth was still in love with the man who had sired Cody.

"I'm not seeing him. Not like you mean."

"But you'd like to. You're thinking that the three of you could be a cute little family unit, aren't you?"

"No, I—"

"Just remember how he reacted when you told him you were pregnant, will ya?"

"I never told him," Beth said, then held her tongue. This was a subject she and Stan had avoided in the year they'd been seeing each other. It only came up when they argued. He didn't know who Cody's father was and didn't really seem to care. She'd never confided the truth to him, only told him that her relationship with Cody's father hadn't worked out and that she'd wanted a baby and had moved away. It hadn't been a lie—not really—but she'd never felt close enough to Stan to share her most private secret. There had been a part of her that had always held back. Maybe it was because he didn't seem as close to Cody as she'd hoped he'd be or maybe it was because she didn't trust him. Not completely.

"Jeez, Beth, what do you want from me?" Stan asked, unable to hide a ring of anger in his words.

"Nothing." And that was the truth. "I don't want anything, Stan."

"So this is it? You're telling me it's over?"

She tried to swallow the lump in her throat. "I think it has to be, Stan, because Cody and I, we're a package deal. You don't get one of us without the other."

"For the love of God, Beth, listen to you! Have I ever said I don't want him? Have I?"

"Yeah, Stan, you did. Just a couple of minutes ago." Tears burned behind her eyes as she said a quick goodbye. She didn't need any more emotional turmoil in her life right now, didn't want to make any abrupt changes in her life. Yet she knew deep in her heart that Stan would never love Cody as his son. She'd rather never marry than put her own son through the hell of rejection that she'd felt because of her own father. Brushing aside her tears, she cleared her throat, walked back to the kitchen and hung up the phone.

As she speared crisp strips of bacon onto a plate, Harriet slid her a glance. "Oh, honey—"

"It's all right, Mom," she said.

Zeke didn't bother looking up from the sports page.

"You sure?"

"Positive."

As her mother cracked eggs into the skillet, Beth scooped up her son and held him as if she were afraid he might disappear. To think that she had contemplated marrying a man who didn't realize how wonderful Cody was. Again she fought tears. "Come on, kiddo," she said, forcing a smile as she kissed Cody's crown. "I think it's time we got outta here."

The apartment house wasn't as huge as Beth remembered, nor as imposing. For years she'd come to this old Victorian home on Pine Street with the basement clinic where Dr. Fletcher had had his practice before he'd moved to the modern facility on the next lot. Beth had always been intimidated by the size of the house, three full stories, and detested walking down the outside stairs to a small reception area. It had smelled of antiseptic and was guarded by a no-nonsense nurse with gray hair. She'd insisted that all the children who were patients of Doc Fletcher call her Nurse Hazel. A fleshy woman, she'd lied and told Beth that the shots wouldn't hurt, then handed out balloons when the ordeal of the examination was over. With kinky hair and big eyes magnified by the thick lenses of her glasses, she'd scared the life out of Beth.

It was a wonder she'd taken up nursing, she thought now, as she parked on the street and unbuckled Cody from his car seat.

So this was where Jenner lived. It didn't seem right somehow. She could see him in the sprawling ranch house at the Rocking M or imagine him throwing down a bedroll in a bunkhouse or under the stars. But an apartment in town? No way.

Carrying Cody, she walked up the front steps, opened the door to the foyer, and knocked on the door of the first-floor unit where she supposed the new owner lived.

The door swung open to reveal a tall blond woman who looked bone weary. Her hair was damp from a recent shower and she was wearing a pink-and-gray sweat suit. Without a trace of makeup, she was still beautiful. "Can I help you?"

"I—I'm looking for Jenner McKee."

The woman's eyes moved from Beth's face to Cody's and she managed a smile that didn't quite touch her eyes. "You must be Beth Crandall. I'm Skye Donahue." She extended her hand.

Juggling Cody, Beth took the long fingers in her own. "Should I know you?"

"I'm engaged to Max and—" She yawned and placed her hand over her mouth. "Forgive me, I spent the last twenty-four hours on my feet at the clinic and then worked the emergency room at Dawson Memorial Hospital. Jenner's downstairs in the basement. He doesn't know it yet, but I intend to evict him, at least until the place is finished. I think the board of health and the city wouldn't much like it if they knew he took up residence in a half-finished set of rooms." She let her eyes stray to Cody again. "So this is Jenner's boy?"

"You already know?" Beth asked, and something akin to fear stole through her heart.

Her concern must have registered on her face because Skye said, "Don't worry, it's not common knowledge—not yet. Except for the McKees. I don't think the rest of the town knows anything. But it will. It's just a matter of time. I only know because Max and Jenner spoke earlier today, and I talked to Max on the phone when I went off duty." She stretched and sighed, her gaze lingering on Cody, and a sadness seemed to come over her. "Go on downstairs—the door's over there on the other side of the foyer. I think Jenner's expecting you."

With Cody still in her arms, Beth steeled herself for another confrontation with Jenner and hurried down the stairs. Before she could knock, the door at the base of the steps was thrown open. Jenner stood in front of her, leaning against the wall. She watched his throat tighten when he gazed upon his son.

"So you're Cody," he said as she walked into the room. She felt Cody cling to her a little more tightly.

"He's a little...nervous about being here," Beth said. The apartment wasn't small, as it had once housed a reception area, an office and three examining rooms. But it had been gutted and now was one room devoid of any kind of flooring except old tile that showed the outlines of the former rooms.

"Don't blame you, Cody," Jenner said. "Makes me nervous, too."

"Who are you?" Cody asked, his face a mask of concentration, as if he, though only two, could feel the tension between his mother and this stranger. Jenner's eyes held Beth's an instant.

"A friend of your ma's. You can call me. . ." His brows drew over his eyes. "Just call me Jenner."

"Funny name."

Jenner's lips twisted into a smile. "That it is. Actually, my name's General, can you beat that? My dad. . ." He lost his train of thought again, but cleared his throat. "He gave me that god-awful handle, but Mom, she changed it to Jenner. Not much better, but I can live with it."

"General's in the army."

Jenner snorted. "What do you know about the army?"

"Television," Beth supplied as Cody, relaxing a little, wiggled to be let down.

"Don't watch too much of that," Jenner warned. "It'll rot your brain. A boy like you. . . well, you need to be out playing in the creek, building forts, riding ponies—"

"He's only two." Beth bristled a little. Jenner had no right whatsoever to insinuate that she was depriving her boy.

"Yeah, but he should start young."

"Cody and I live in an apartment, Jenner, not even as big as this one." She glanced around. "It does have more than one room and it is finished, but there's no yard or barn or creek. The nearest water is the Willamette River, where the water rushes over the falls in Oregon City, and when he needs to go outside we go to the park or over to his baby-sitter's house. She's got a fenced yard and—"

"Puppies!" Cody supplied. "Lots! A new one. Barney."

"Is that right?" Jenner's smile suddenly seemed tight. "You ever ridden a horse?"

Cody shook his head.

"Ever caught a tadpole?"

"I told you he's too young," Beth insisted, exasperated now.

"You know what a crawdad is?"

Cody's little lips pursed together in concentration. "No."

This was worse than Beth had expected. Jenner didn't bother to hide the censure in his gaze. "We live in the city," she explained.

"That's a problem."

"I don't think so. And it looks to me like you're in town now, too."

"It's only temporary."

"That's what I tell myself." She felt her blood begin to boil. Jenner McKee could be the most maddening man in the world. She knew that much about him. He lived by his own code, threw convention to the wind, and didn't give a damn about what anyone else thought about him. Including her.

His jaw muscles tightened and he shoved a hand into his back pocket. "You had breakfast?"

"Pancakes at Grandma's!"

"Well then, how about I buy you two some lunch? It's nearly noon."

"I don't know—"

"Hell, Beth, that's why you're here, isn't it? For us to get to know each other?"

"I'm here because I was threatened," she said, her voice barely a whisper.

"Oh, yeah, I forgot. My eighty-seven-year-old grandma scared the living hell out of you and you hightailed it right over here."

"No say hell," Cody said, and Jenner's gaze narrowed on his son.

"Seems your boy has himself some manners."

"I hope so."

"Maybe I can change that. Come on, Cody, let's have a hamburger and French fries and a milk shake, then we'll go out to the ranch and you can ride a horse."

"A what? No way!" Beth said.

Jenner turned and his eyes sparked with determination. "You gonna fight me on this, Beth?" he drawled.

"He's too little."

"Bullsh—" He caught Cody staring at him and bit off the rest of his curse. "I was in the saddle at his age."

"He's not you!"

Jenner's expression turned to granite. "Isn't he? Well, well, Ms. Crandall. You'd better make up your mind." He reached for his Stetson, which hung from a nail near one of the ground-level windows offering only a rodent's view of shrubbery. With a cold smile he added, "Either this here boy *is* mine, or he ain't, but I'm damn sure he isn't both. So, Lady, you'd better decide which it is and get your story straight."

Chapter Five

Beth couldn't decide whether to hate the man or love him.

From her side of the booth at the Shady Grove Café, she slid a glance in his direction. His hair was mussed, his hat hung on the post at the end of the bench seat. He still looked as hard and dangerous as the outcropping of red rock that rimmed the mountains surrounding the town.

She decided that hating him was a whole lot easier and safer than loving him. Ever since she'd shown up at the Rocking M, he'd berated and degraded her and she was getting fed up. She didn't need or want the abuse.

As for loving him—it was a fool's dream, an old, silly notion that she kept rekindling because of the stupid reason that he was Cody's father. Big deal. So he'd sired her boy; that was no reason for childish fantasies about him.

An ancient air-conditioning unit rattled and wheezed, losing the battle with the smoke and heat that wafted from the kitchen. Beth swirled a straw in her diet soda and watched as Cody, his little face beaming with delight, wiggled happily in a booster seat set on the worn Naugahyde. He alternately sipped from his strawberry milk shake and dunked French fries in a glob of catsup Jenner had plopped onto his plate.

For Cody's sake, Beth managed a tight smile, but her nerves were stretched as tight as newly strung barbed wire. Jenner, one long leg stretched into the aisle, regarded his son with an amicable enough expression, outwardly seeming to enjoy himself. But his cold blue eyes betrayed him. He regarded the boy carefully as if looking for flaws, and studied Cody's facial features as if trying to find clues to the boy's parentage.

Only when Jenner glanced at Beth, when his gaze pierced hers, did she see the anger, the accusations, the repressed fury that boiled inside.

Beth ignored the hostile glare even though Jenner seemed to be silently warning her that if Cody did prove to be his son, she was in for the battle of her life. Playing idly with her straw, she worried that it was a battle she might lose. Her heart shredded a little when she noticed how easily Cody responded to this man he'd never met before.

Jenner taught Cody how to blow the paper off his straw and make a foam mustache by drinking the milk shake right from the glass. He even let Cody wear his cowboy hat.

"That's right, Cody," Jenner said, his eyes moving from the boy to Beth. "Maybe I'll take you riding, and someday we can even go camping out by the stream at the ranch."

"Don't," Beth said under her breath as Cody picked up his child-size burger. "There are no maybes when you're two years old. Either you make a promise you intend to keep or you hold your tongue."

"I keep all my promises." His voice was low and steady, his eyes so intense that her stomach seemed to be suddenly filled with a swarm of restless butterflies.

"Do you?" she asked.

"Every last one." His jaw was set, his lips a thin line of determination, and Beth was swept away as the memory of making love to him flashed into her mind.

She remembered the heat, the raw passion that seemed to surge through his blood, the way he'd made their mating an urgent, savage event that still, even three years later, sucked the breath from her lungs. She glanced away and cleared her throat. "Then I guess that makes you a hero," she said sarcastically.

His eyes narrowed and he reached across the table, knocking over the catsup bottle as he grabbed her arm. "Let's get one thing straight, okay? I am *not* a hero. Got it?"

"Oh, that's not what I heard," Sarah, the heavyset waitress with a crown of frizzy curls, interrupted as she refilled Jenner's coffee cup. "The way I heard it, you saved your brother's little kid, and if it wasn't for you, the Rocking M would've lost all its livestock. Without you, Dani Stewart might not have made it. That girl has had a string of bad luck, let me tell you—not like her sister at all—but she lucked out this time."

Irritation pinched the corners of Jenner's mouth and the fingers of steel that had tightened over Beth's arm loosened their grip. "You've been talking to Max," he said as he let go.

"No way. Heard it from the fire chief, himself. Fred has breakfast here every morning and he thinks you saved lives. Course he's cussin' you, too, 'cause you and Max got in the way. Max wouldn't do what he was told, and you, you nearly ended up dyin' just to save some horses."

Jenner glowered up at the waitress. "It wasn't a big deal."

Sarah shrugged a hefty shoulder. "Whatever you say." She righted the bottle of catsup as she eyed Cody. "This your boy?" Beth's heart nearly stopped until she realized the woman was speaking to her.

"Uh, yes. Cody." She whispered in her son's ear, "Say hello."

"'Lo," Cody replied, staring warily at the friendly waitress.

"He's sure a looker." Sarah grinned at him and reached into her pocket. She found a mint and set in on the table in front of Cody. "You're gonna break your share of hearts, son, believe you me."

"Thank you," Beth said, feeling a lump form in her throat. Jenner hadn't said a word, just leaned back against the seat and watched the exchange.

"Is there anything else I can get you?"

"Not for me," Beth said.

"Thanks, anyway, Sarah," Jenner drawled.

Sarah's gaze sharpened just a tad. "Is it true what I've been hearin' around here—that your pa might've been murdered?"

"Looks that way," Jenner admitted with a scowl.

"Good Lord A'mighty. Why, no one's been murdered in Rimrock before—I mean, unless you count Elvin Green runnin' down Indian Joe ten years ago, but that was just an accident, I guess."

"That's the way I heard it."

"Anyway, I don't s'pose they have any idea who's behind it."

"Not that I know," Jenner said, wishing the nosy waitress would just disappear and leave him alone. He wasn't going to confide that Rex Stone had at first come up with the brainstorm that someone in the family might be responsible. He seemed to have given up on that ludicrous assumption, and if he had any other suspects, he hadn't shared his suspicions with Jenner.

Sarah moved closer to the table and whispered, "I hear your family's offering a reward."

"A what?" Jenner's head snapped up and he saw a gleam of greed in the waitress's gaze.

"Twenty-five thousand dollars for information leading to the arrest of the person responsible for your dad's death and the fire at the ranch."

"I don't know a thing about it."

"Heard it this mornin'. Two deputies were talkin' about it while eatin' breakfast."

"This is the first I've heard of it," Jenner said, hoping to hide the fact that he was furious. It was all he could do to remain at the table. Why hadn't anyone told him? Then he remembered. Mavis and Virginia had been at a meeting with Rex Stone last night. They must've made the decision at that time and never bothered to tell him—not that they had the chance, really, considering the conversation. But Max hadn't said a word this morning. It looked as if his family was still trying to protect him—keep him calm so that he could heal—or they were holding out on him. Either way, he was going to find out the truth. His jaw clamped so hard it hurt.

"Hey, how about a refill, Sarah?" At a table on the other side of the entrance, Cyrus Kellogg held up his empty coffee cup. He caught Jenner's attention and gave a sketchy wave. "Glad to see ya up and around, McKee. Helluva thing, that fire."

Jenner nodded to the weathered rancher who owned the spread just north of the Rocking M. Cyrus, smoking a cigarette, was seated with three other men from around the area. One was Ned Jansen, who once owned the old copper mine in the hills surrounding the town. Jenner's father, Jonah, had bought the mine for a song a few years back when Ned had needed the cash to pay back alimony to his two ex-wives. The mine was rumored to be worthless, but Jonah had taken a chance and eventually found a mother lode. Wouldn't you know? The old man had been blessed—or cursed—with the Midas touch.

Len Marchant sat with his back to Jenner. A short, lively man, Len, too, had done business with Jonah. Once the town baker, Len had sold out at a loss to Jonah, who had remodeled and converted the old bakery into a minimall that now supported five small shops. The third man was Otis Purcell, a rancher with a mean streak whose single claim to fame was that he raised wolf pups and, to Jenner's knowledge, had never been swindled by Jonah McKee. That alone was some kind of record.

"Come on, let's go," Jenner said. He realized that he'd run out of conversation with Beth and didn't like the sidelong glances cast in his direction from the other patrons. The Shady Grove was half-filled with customers looking for a simple, cheap meal. Most of the people tucked into the booths and seated at the tables were ranchers and townspeople Jenner had known most of his life. But there were a few strangers, as well. His gut clutched into a tight knot as his thoughts ran in a new and frightening path. What if Rex Stone was right? What if Jonah had been murdered? And what if whoever was behind the murder *and* the arson at the stables wasn't satisfied? What if he wanted to do more damage? What if, instead of holding a grudge against Jonah, the psycho behind the crimes wanted to get back at Max . . . or Jenner?

He sliced a look at Cody innocently sipping his shake. Beth was dabbing at the corners of his little face with a cloth, completely unaware of any danger.

Using the crutches for support, Jenner climbed to his feet just as Beth gathered Cody into her arms. What if the kid really was his and whoever was gunning for the McKees found out about him? Jenner's throat turned to dust. Cody could unwittingly become a target—as could Beth.

Cold sweat beaded on his forehead, and for the first time in his life, Jenner McKee felt vulnerable.

Beth expected Jenner to take her back to his apartment where she'd parked her car. When he'd insisted on driving his truck earlier, she'd argued, remembering how his pickup had careered down the street the night before. Eventually, after extracting a promise from Jenner that he'd be careful, she'd given in, and they'd survived, though the ride to the Shady Grove had been a little harrowing as Jenner had been forced to work gas, clutch and brake with his right leg. She hadn't complained, only held on to the armrest in a death grip with her other arm tightly wrapped around Cody. The toddler had only laughed when the truck had lurched into slow-moving traffic.

"I thought you might want to meet my grandmother," Jenner explained as he drove north and passed the city limits.

"That's not necessary."

"Sure it is, Beth," he said, looking over Cody's head to capture her in his cynical gaze before turning his attention back to the road. "You started this, so you're going to play it out."

"*We* started this," she said, unable to hold her tongue a minute longer. "You and I both. I'm sick of women always having to take the blame as well as the responsibility for their kids." She wanted to add that without men there would be no children, but she managed to swallow her words for Cody's sake. She never wanted him to hear anything that might suggest that he was unwanted or that she considered him a mistake. Because that wasn't true. She loved him more than life itself, and if given the choice again, she would gladly go through the pregnancy alone and accept the hard choices that followed. Smiling, she grabbed one of his chubby hands in hers.

"We go to Grandma's?" Cody asked, all innocence and smiles.

That was a tough one. "Not to Grandma Harriet's, honey. We're going to Mr. McKee's—"

"Jenner."

"Jenner's ranch."

"I see horses?"

"You bet you will," Jenner said.

"I ride one?"

Beth cleared her throat. "I don't think that would be such a good idea—"

"Of course you can. Got a little pony that would be perfect."

Beth shot Jenner a warning glance silently telling him to back off, but if he noticed her aggravation, he ignored it and reached into the glove compartment for a pair of aviator sunglasses. He slipped them over his nose and now he seemed more remote than ever, the dark shades hiding his eyes, his mouth set in a harsh, uncompromising line.

He seemed to be getting the hang of driving with only one leg. He managed to work the clutch smoothly enough and the old Dodge hummed over the county road that rose along the contour of the hill, but always followed the winding path of Wildcat Creek as it slashed through the land a hundred feet below. Beth rolled down the window, smelled the dust and dry grass and felt the sun warm her shoulder as the wind streamed through her hair.

How many times had she ridden this very road, listening to the radio, laughing and thinking of Jenner McKee? All those years ago, she'd never met him, but he'd been a local legend, a rebel son rebuffing his father by turning his nose up at the old man's money and striking out on his own.

She ran her fingers along the edge of the window that peaked up from the door. Yes, she'd dreamed about him, never daring to guess that someday she'd run into him, that she'd let him buy her a couple of glasses of wine and she'd end up sleeping with him and bearing his son. She chanced a look at her boy, but he'd fallen asleep in the warm cab of the truck and was blissfully unaware of the reasons she'd been forced back to Rimrock.

Jenner pulled off at a narrow spot in the road where the old guardrail had been hit and given way completely. A new piece had been fitted between two posts right at a sharp curve, nearly a hundred feet above the canyon. Beth didn't have to be told that this was where Jonah McKee had lost his life.

He stopped the truck and killed the engine. Cody stirred but didn't open his eyes, not even when Jenner opened the cab door and hopped to the ground. Using the pickup for support, he edged around the truck, leaned a jean-clad hip against the fender and gazed down the cliff face to the swift waters of the creek.

Beth eased out of the truck and joined him. The sun was warm against her crown, the hood of the old Dodge hot and grimy with dust and dead insects.

"I haven't been here," Jenner said, "not since it happened." He rubbed the back of his neck impatiently and his brow furrowed above the frames of his sunglasses. "You know, I was never close to the old man. In fact, I professed to hate his guts. I did everything I could to irritate the hell out of him." He kicked at some loose gravel and the stones rolled off the shoulder and past a few dry blades of grass to tumble freely into the canyon. "I didn't like the way he treated people, especially me and my sister. Max—" Jenner shrugged "—he was Dad's favorite, and for years Max turned a blind eye on what the old man was doing. But he found out. Damn, did he find out." Jenner turned his gaze up to the cloudless sky as if he could discover the answers to his questions in the vast heavens. "Even though my father was a liar and a cheat, even though he manipulated people, he didn't deserve to die. Not like this."

She didn't know what to say. Did he want comfort? Or was he talking not so much to her as to himself? She reached forward, her fingers touching his bare arm where he'd rolled up his sleeve.

He didn't move, just glanced down at her small white hand resting against the bronzed skin and gold hair of his forearm. He lifted his head, and from behind his dark glasses, he stared straight at her, causing the pulse at her throat to throb. For a second, she thought he might draw her into his arms, might kiss her until the breath left her body, might hold her so close she could feel every hard contour of his muscles.

Her throat worked. His lips flattened and he turned away. "Come on. We're wastin' time."

By the time they reached the ranch it was early afternoon. Trucks and cars, most covered in a haze of dust, were parked in the yard, and ranch hands could be seen working with the livestock.

Jenner guided his pickup into a vacant spot near the garage. As he climbed out of the cab, he waved to a few of the men and stared at the rubble and ash still piled where Beth assumed the stables had once stood. Yellow tape, announcing a crime scene, was stretched around the charred concrete and blackened debris, while the odors of dust and ash mingled in the breeze with those of cattle and bleached grass.

Hundreds of heads of cattle had been herded into a series of pens surrounding a large barn. Calves bawled and men shouted as the animals were inoculated, their ears notched and tagged, before they were forced into a chute leading to another field.

"Cow," Cody said, blinking and yawning as he woke up. Beth got out first, then set him on the ground.

"Many cows," Beth corrected.

"Many cows, bulls, steers and calves. You want to see?" Jenner asked, starting to hobble toward the nearest fence.

"I don't know..." she said, regarding the beasts with their dusty red, black, gray and ocher hides. Most of the animals were huge, some had humps at their shoulders and wicked-looking horns sprouting from their heads. Flies swarmed and the smell of manure permeated the air.

"Lighten up, Beth," Jenner called out as he limped swiftly toward the melee and left Beth in the shade of a solitary pine tree. "The boy's not made of glass."

"I know, but—" *But he's all I've got, and if anything happened to him...* She released Cody's hand and he ran to keep up with the man on crutches. Beth felt something inside her die as she watched her son run so confidently to Jenner and reach for his hand.

Maybe Cody wasn't made of glass, but it seemed as if her heart was.

Grasshoppers flew out of his path and flies buzzed over his head and his sneakers were dustier than they'd ever been in his short life, but there was a joy about him that brought tears to her eyes. She was losing something by introducing Cody to Jenner. Until now, she'd been everything to her son—provider, mother, friend, the sun, the moon and the stars. But Cody was gaining something—something precious—if Jenner would accept him as his son.

Something inside her seemed to tear. She blinked hard and told herself she was being a fool. Didn't she want Cody to know his father? Didn't she want him to feel the warmth of a father's love—that special warmth she'd never known? Her throat was so thick she could barely breathe as she watched Jenner, balancing precariously on his crutches, lift Cody onto the third rail of the fence so he could rest his arms on the top rail and gain a better view. His little feet shifted, but Jenner's hand, tanned and weathered, was splayed firmly against the child's back, and Beth knew Jenner would fall himself before allowing any harm to come to Cody.

"Oh, God," Beth whispered, "please let him be all right."

As if in answer, Cody let out a whoop when a rangy calf drew close enough so that he could bend over the fence and pat the animal's head.

Beth bit back a warning for him to be careful when she saw Jenner's arm surround his son's waist. Her heart twisted at the sight. Father and son. Together. A picture she thought she'd never witness.

Jenner said something and Cody laughed so loud the calf started and backed away. A few men came over and Jenner talked to them, keeping his hand on Cody all the while. More than one interested glance was cast in her direction, but she couldn't hear their conversation over the noise of the herd.

Eventually the men went back to work and Jenner peeled a reluctant Cody from the fence. Together they walked back to the truck.

"I seen lots of cows!" Cody announced, obviously pleased with himself as he climbed into her arms and managed to smudge dirt all over her blouse.

"Did you?"

"Millions of 'em."

Jenner chuckled, and together they headed toward the front door. "Brace yourself," Jenner whispered to her as they reached the porch. "I'm not in good graces with my mother just now."

"Oh, great."

"Nor with my grandmother."

"What are we doing here then?"

He slid her a glance. "Not getting cold feet, are ya? After all, this is your party." He shoved open the door and stepped inside.

Sharp footsteps echoed through the rooms as Casey half ran down the hallway. "Where the hell have you been?" she said, her hazel eyes spitting fire. "Mom and Grandma are both fit to be tied..." Her voice trailed off as she realized that she wasn't alone with her brother. "Uh...well...I didn't mean... Damn it, I don't care, Jenner, you're—"

"Irresponsible and going to roast in hell. I know. Now, maybe you'd like to simmer down and meet these people.

This is Beth Crandall and her son, Cody. My sister, Casey. As you probably noticed, she's the calm one in the family.''

"Very funny," Casey muttered, her eyebrows drawing angrily together. Somehow she managed a smile when she shook Beth's hand. "I remember you. You were in the class ahead of me in school."

"That's right."

"And this is your little boy?" Casey grinned widely at Cody.

"Yes," Beth said, her insides beginning to twist. "Cody."

"Isn't he a doll?" All of Casey's anger with her brother seemed to fade as she reached out and grabbed Cody into her arms. "Well, what're you doin', big fella? Did you come out to the ranch to rope some steers or ride some broncs bareback?"

Cody didn't say a word, but his eyes rounded in wonder.

"Beth's here because Grandma wrote to her," Jenner explained, his gaze locking with Beth's. She narrowed her eyes at him to warn him, but one side of his mouth twisted upward in a sarcastic smile.

"Grandma?" Casey repeated.

"Mmm. Seems she and Beth have quite a correspondence going."

"Is that so? How do you know our grandmother?"

Bristling, Beth said, "She wrote and asked me to come back to Rimrock because she thought it would do Jenner a world of good to see me and Cody. We've known each other a few years."

Storm clouds gathered in Casey's usually clear eyes. "Oh." She slid a glance at Cody and her face suddenly paled.

"Beth's here to clear up a few things."

Casey's throat worked and Beth felt her cheeks grow hot as embarrassment stole over her face. "That's right," she admitted, wondering how much Jenner intended to confide in his sister.

"Jenner? Is that you?" Over the staccato tap of heels on hardwood, Virginia McKee's voice carried through the hall. She appeared suddenly through an archway and stopped dead in her tracks when her gaze landed on Beth. "Oh...well, I see you've brought a guest." Her practiced smile fell perfectly into place, though she didn't seem pleased and her eyes remained frosty, even when she looked at her grandson for the first time. "Come in. Please." She led them into a spacious sunken living room decorated with pine walls, rock fireplace and heavy furniture in shades of forest green and tan. Along the back wall, windows offered a view of a ridge of mountains reflecting in the clear waters of a lake. "Please, sit," Virginia invited.

Jenner propped his crutches against the fireplace and settled onto the raised hearth. "I'd hoped Mavis would be around."

"She's resting."

"I am not!" Mavis's voice rang clearly through the living room as she entered. "What's going on— Oh!" Her gaze landed on Cody and Beth. "Well, it's about time you showed up around here." Using her cane, she crossed the room and smiled at Cody. "So this is the boy. I believe it. Just look at him, Virginia. He's the spitting image of—"

"Mavis!" Virginia hissed. "I don't think this is the time or the place—"

"Sure it is. We all know what's going on here."

"Not all of us," Beth said quickly, holding on to her boy. "Cody—"

"Won't really understand what's going on, but it's time he did. That's what you want, isn't it, Mavis? You're lookin' to find yourself a great-grandson." Jenner's words were harsh and cut to the quick.

The old lady took a seat in an armchair and sighed. "I told you why I wrote to Beth, Jenner, but it was only part of the truth. I thought that seeing the boy would be good for you, yes, and good for the entire family, but I also thought that it was time to right a wrong. Lord knows I loved Jonah. He was my only child and I adored him, but . . . I'm afraid his father and I spoiled him and let him believe that he could take everything he wanted from life. He was a good man. I believe that with all of my heart, but sometimes he made mistakes and he . . ." She sighed again and looked down at her hands, where age spots mottled the once-clear skin. "Well, I didn't think it was right when he broke up Max and Skye, twisting the truth as he did, but I didn't interfere.

"As for you and Beth, things were different. You weren't in love like Max and Skye, but you became involved and you fathered a child, a child you never knew about. Jonah thought it was for the best and I disagreed with him, but I couldn't dissuade him. Once again, I let him have his way. But now he's gone and I can't help thinking he made a terrible mistake."

"That bastard!" Casey said.

Virginia's face turned the color of chalk. "He was your father and a good father and I won't have you speak ill of him, Casey Maureen McKee!"

"Enough, Mom," Jenner cut in. "Casey's just surprised. We all know what kind of a man Jonah was."

Mavis wound her fingers nervously over the handle of her cane. "He only did what he thought was best."

"Best!" Jenner snorted disdainfully, but held his tongue. Leaning back against the smooth stones of the fireplace, his arms crossed over his chest, his jean-clad legs stretched out in front of him, he watched Beth through eyes opened at half mast, as if expecting her to say something, anything, that might somehow prove she was lying.

"This is all just conjecture," Virginia said pointedly to Mavis, "and I don't think you should go around maligning your own son. Jonah, rest his soul, may have made mistakes in his life, but we all do, and we have no proof that the boy is Jenner's."

"Beth is here because I insisted she come," Mavis said, her mouth pursing.

"Why didn't she ever contact Jenner?" Virginia turned her attention to the woman who dared challenge her son.

Beth raised her chin up a notch. "He was already gone when I found out. Back on the rodeo circuit. He'd never tried to contact me since . . . since we were together, and afterward I heard rumors that he was engaged to Nora Bateman."

"That was over," Jenner said sharply.

"Not according to your father."

Jenner swore roundly.

"I'll not have you speak that way about your father," Virginia admonished, her eyes narrowing. "He was a good—"

"Stop kidding yourself, Mom! Open your eyes. Jonah P. McKee did whatever he wanted, whenever he wanted, to whomever he damn well pleased."

"Jenner—"

"Jonah McKee was a lousy husband. Why you pretend that you didn't know that he ran around on you is beyond me." Mavis gasped and Casey shook her head vigorously, trying silently to stop her brother's tirade, but Jenner wasn't finished. He was just beginning to warm to his subject. Pushing himself upright, he said, "As for his being a good father, Mom, he was a complete failure."

Mavis let out a small groan of protest but didn't attempt to stop her grandson.

"You and I and Casey and Max and even you, Mavis, we all know the kind of man he was. Jonah's kids weren't people—at least not to him. They were just things, possessions like everything else around here. Trophies when they were good, embarrassments when they were bad. I guess I win the award for being the worst." Shoving himself forward, Jenner refused to use his crutches and half stumbled over to the couch where Virginia was sitting, clutching her hands over her heart, her eyes brimming with tears. "It's time to stop deluding ourselves. All of us."

"You didn't even know him," Virginia whispered.

Jenner snorted. "We all knew him, but we just made excuses. Mavis here, she blamed herself for spoiling him. You...I guess you figured you were lucky to catch the richest man in the county and turned a blind eye to his faults. Max believed in Dad to the point where he was almost corrupted himself, and I... Well, I spent a lot of time trying to prove that I didn't want or need him, just the way he treated me."

"He loved you!" Mavis interjected.

"He loved himself."

Beth couldn't stand any more. Gathering Cody into her arms, she said, "I think I'd better go."

"What?" Jenner turned too quickly, nearly fell over, but caught himself. "Already? Just when things are getting interesting?"

"I did what I had to do. Now I think it would be best if—"

"If what?" he roared. "We all went back to our same little lives? If we all acted as if you hadn't appeared with your son and your claims about his heritage? Is that what you expect?"

Her spine stiffened and she stared him straight in the eye. "What I expect, Jenner, is respect. That's all I want from anyone, including you!"

"Don't go!" Mavis pleaded, her lips quivering. "Jenner will apologize."

"Like hell!"

"Why did you bring me here?" she demanded, and Jenner's grin was as cold as a blue norther raging through the mountains.

"I wanted you to see what it was like to be a McKee. You know, a lot of people in town envy us, think we've got the perfect lives, but they aren't privileged enough to see deeper than the surface into the flaws."

"What Jenner is trying to say," Casey cut in, "is that he's being a class-A jerk to scare you off because he's afraid of what you and your son represent."

"Which is?" Jenner asked.

"Responsibility and stability."

"One psych course in college and now you know all about me."

"You're classic, Jenner."

"And you all wonder why I moved out."

"No, we all know why," Casey snapped back, her temper rising along with his. "It's because you can't face yourself in the mirror, brother. It's because you're scared to death that you're never going to be able to do the things you love. It's because you're... you're..."

"Go ahead and say it," Jenner snarled, his face flushing an angry shade of red. "A cripple. That's the word you were looking for."

"I was going to say a coward."

Virginia shook her head. "That's not true! He saved Hillary's life and Dani Stewart's, as well."

"Oh, hell, let's not forget the horses, shall we?" Jenner said sarcastically. "Don't you know, Casey? Haven't you heard? I'm some kind of hero. A goddamned, crippled hero!"

That was enough. Holding Cody close, Beth headed for the front door. "Thanks... thanks for the hospitality," she blurted out, though, considering the situation, it hardly seemed sincere. She walked through the door and headed for Jenner's pickup. Oh, Lord, why hadn't she brought her own car? She could call her mother, she supposed, but Harriet was working the afternoon shift at the Pancake Hutt and Zeke was probably getting ready to head out for the swing shift at the mill. Short of walking the nearly ten miles back to town, she had no recourse but to wait for Jenner.

"Damn! Damn! Damn!" she said, rolling her eyes to the blue sky and wishing she hadn't been such a fool. Coming back to Rimrock had been a mistake of the highest order. The more she was around the McKees, the more certain she was that she'd made an irrevocable error, one that would affect her son for the rest of his life.

"You mad?" Cody asked, his eyes round with worry.

"No . . . well, yes."

"At me?"

"Oh, no, pumpkin." She wrapped her arms around her son more tightly and wondered how much of the conversation in the ranch house he'd understood. She should never have subjected him to such a horrid and painful scene.

She heard the front door open and listened for Jenner's uneven gait. "Jenner's coming!" Cody obviously spied Jenner over her shoulder. Wriggling to the ground, he raced up to the cowboy who had sired him.

Jenner managed to balance on his good leg and hoist the boy into the air. Cody giggled in sheer joy and Beth's heart tore a little with the sound.

"I ride horse now!"

"Well, pardner, not right now."

"When?" Cody demanded as Jenner set him on his feet.

"Maybe later."

"When?"

"Tomorrow."

"I told you—don't make promises you can't keep," Beth warned as Cody, intrigued with the old crossbred retriever lying in the shade of an old apple tree, ran eagerly to the dog.

"Be careful," Beth warned.

Jenner snorted a laugh. "Careful of old Reuben? He wouldn't hurt a flea. Isn't much of a watchdog for that matter."

"Look, would you just give me a ride back into town?" she asked, not wanting to share any small talk with him. It was better when she hated him, when she didn't trust him, when her heart was hard where he was concerned.

"You don't want to stay at the Rocking M—even with the red-carpet treatment?"

"I need to get back."

Casey, half-running, hurried out of the house. "Oh, Beth, I'm glad I caught you," she said, crossing the yard. "I just wanted to apologize for my brother. He can be one helluva bastard when he wants to be."

"Now wait a minute—" Jenner cut in.

"Rude, obnoxious, self-indulgent, arrogant, a real jerk."

"Thanks," Jenner muttered.

"I'm not telling Beth anything she hasn't already figured out." Casey shot her brother a furious glare. "I don't really understand everything that went on in the house, but I heard enough to put two and two together, and it looks like I've got myself a nephew." She smiled as she cast Cody a loving glance. "I can't tell you how thrilled I am, and if... well, this sounds really hokey I know, but if you ever need anything, especially a baby-sitter, I'm available."

"Hey, hold your horses!" Jenner objected. "We don't even know—"

"Know what? That the kid's yours?" Casey whirled on him. "I heard the whole story from Grandma just now. Of course Cody's yours. Look at him, for crying out loud. He's got McKee stamped all over him."

Despite the tension straining the air, Beth almost laughed.

"How can you tell? He's just a kid!" Jenner said.

"Ever see any pictures of you as a toddler? Go look in Mom and Dad's bedroom. Cody's a dead ringer for you." She shook her head and met Beth's amused gaze. "I'd better warn you of something. All the men in this family are muleheaded. Maybe there's still time with Cody, but the rest of them are beyond help."

"Thank you, Dr. Freud," Jenner muttered.

"I'll send you a bill," Casey quipped back, then rolled her eyes at Beth. "I'm serious," she affirmed. "Anytime you need anything."

"How about a ride into town?"

Jenner stepped between the two women. "Wait a minute. I'll give you a ride home."

"Don't bother. If Casey would—"

"I said I'd do it." He grabbed her arm possessively.

"Don't you understand, Jenner?" she said, angling her face to his. "I'm giving you an out."

"Well maybe I'm not asking for one."

Casey lifted both palms skyward. "Hey, I'm not going to get in the middle of this. I'm outta here. You two work it out and you—" she pointed a finger at Jenner "—be smart for once in your life!" Flipping her hair away from her face, Casey climbed into an imported sports car of some kind and roared down the lane.

"My sister neglected to mention that the women in the family have some of the same unique and endearing traits as the men." Jenner's fingers still surrounded Beth's wrist. He blew out a sigh and watched Reuben lick Cody's chubby little hands. "About what happened in the house—"

"Let's just forget it, shall we?" A dry gust of wind caught her hair, blowing the dark strands over her face. Just as she was brushing them aside, Jenner touched the edge of her cheek with a callused finger.

"I just wanted you to see what you were getting yourself into. What kind of family we are."

"It doesn't alter the facts, does it? Or were you just trying to test my mettle and scare me off?"

His fingers traced the line of her jaw, his gaze suddenly warm, and the harsh edges of his face seemed to soften a little. "You've given me a shock. I just want you to realize all the ramifications of what you're doing." His hand dropped back to his side and he leaned a hip against the fender of the truck.

"I can't turn back now," she said, and he watched the breeze play with her hair again. Sunlight glinted off the red-brown curls and her cheeks were high with color, probably from embarrassment.

Suddenly Jenner felt like a heel. "Do you want to...turn back?"

"I don't know," she admitted, her jaw jutting forward in defiance. "I thought this was the perfect opportunity for Cody to meet his father. Maybe I was wrong." Before he could answer, she called to her son. "Come on, Cody. It's time to go."

"Dog come, too?" Cody asked.

"No, but—"

"Sure. Come on, Reuben." Jenner whistled to the old retriever who loped over to the truck, then upon command leaped into the bed.

"I ride with him."

Beth was horrified. "No way."

"You're up in the cab, pardner," Jenner said.

"But I want doggy."

"Who's gonna steer the truck?"

Beth let out a little squeak of protest.

"I drive?"

"You bet." He winked broadly at Beth as he yanked on the door of the old Dodge.

"God help us," Beth whispered as Cody, with Jenner's help, scrambled into the driver's side. She was climbing into an ancient pickup that was going to be driven by a man with the use of one leg and a two-year-old. "Crazy, that's what this is," she muttered under her breath.

Jenner shoved the truck into reverse, and Cody, sitting next to him in the car seat reached over and honked the horn loudly. From the bed, the dog let out a sharp bark and they were off, leaving a plume of dust in their wake.

Beth glanced at father and son, both grinning widely as if they were having the time of their lives. She couldn't help but wonder just how long it would last.

Chapter Six

Jenner smelled trouble. The kind of trouble that reeked of problems and clung to a guy for the rest of his life. Not only was that little imp of a kid getting to him, but the mother, as well.

They'd spent the rest of the day together. Though Beth had come up with a hundred reasons to return to her mother's house, he'd managed to convince her to stick around. They'd gone to the park, a dippy kid's movie in Dawson City and out to dinner at an Italian restaurant. Eventually, with Reuben still in the back of the truck and Cody falling asleep leaning against his mother, Jenner had taken her home to the cottage on Buckskin Drive. The house was nearly dark, soft light coming from only one window near the back and a single bulb burning on the front porch.

He pulled into the driveway and cut the engine. Tapping his fingers against the wheel, he squinted through the grimy windshield. "You're not what I expected," he admitted.

"I hope not. You thought I was some kind of con artist, I think."

"That about sums it up."

"Not quite. You thought I'd do anything, even jeopardize my child's emotional well-being and security, to get at a few McKee dollars."

He rubbed the stubble on his chin. "You make it sound like Monopoly money."

"You're the one who suggested I was playing a game."

He leaned back against the seat and studied this woman who just twenty-four hours ago he hadn't known existed. Resting against the door, her son sleeping in the car seat, illumination from the porch lamp highlighting her features, she kissed the top of Cody's head by instinct, and Jenner watched the movement, his gut tightening at the familiarity and warmth of this simple act. For a split second, he considered kissing her, just as he had earlier today when they were overlooking Stardust Canyon and she'd touched his arm.

Her lips were pliant and now devoid of lipstick, her arms protectively wrapped around her child. Her hair was mussed, thick mahogany curls tangled from the wind as they'd pushed Cody on a swing, or balanced together on a teeter-totter, or spun slowly on a merry-go-round. Beth had raced her son to a slide, then slid down with him when the child had protested that the contraption was too high.

"It's supposed to be high, silly," she'd explained with a gentle nudge. "Otherwise it would be flat and we would have to push ourselves along. Let me hold you first and see if you like it, okay?"

"'Kay," Cody had said reluctantly, but had soon been whooping in glorious excitement as they'd slipped down the slick piece of equipment. "Do again! Do again!" he'd insisted when they'd landed.

Beth's generous smiles and laughter had touched a dark part of Jenner's soul that was better left locked away.

Cody's little feet hadn't been able to race fast enough back to the ladder, and the second time he'd needed no prodding from his mother. "You do, too!" he'd cried, pointing at Jenner, who had been forced to decline rather than stumble up the metal steps with his one good leg.

His back teeth ground together as he thought of a lifetime of missed opportunities. A lifetime that, despite the encouraging words from surgeons, would never be the same. He stared at her long and hard. "You've never said what it is that you want from me."

"I wish I knew," she admitted, a line forming between her arched eyebrows. "I . . . well, when I first found out I was pregnant, I had this silly fantasy that you and I would . . . oh, well, you know . . ." Her voice trailed off in embarrassment.

"What? Get married?"

He noticed the dark stain that washed up the front of her neck. "Something like that," she admitted, her voice rough. "I knew it was out of the question, that we really didn't know each other, but I had this Norman Rockwell vision of what a family should be."

He snorted. "Not my family."

"Nor mine," she said, shifting a sighing Cody in her arms. "Anyway, I made the mistake of trying to locate you and instead I ran into a brick wall named—"

"Let me guess. Jonah McKee."

"Right. I don't know how he found out, but I suspect it was through Ralph Fletcher. They had some business dealings, I believe. Anyway, your father set me straight right away. Told me that you weren't the marrying kind and when you were you'd probably settle down with Nora Bateman. He acted as if she was the typical girl-next-door and said you two had been involved in some kind of on-and-off-again romance since high school."

Jenner scowled. "It was off when I met you."

"Was it?" She let her chin rest on the top of her son's head.

"Been off ever since."

"Then I guess Jonah didn't like me or the thought of a bastard grandchild."

Jenner's gaze skated down Cody's dozing face. A bastard? Would someone—his own father—actually look upon this dynamo of short legs, curly hair and bright eyes as a bastard? The thought brought a vile taste up the back of his throat and he realized with sudden clarity that no matter how much he protested the fact that he'd sired this boy, the kid was really getting under his skin. He experienced a strange sense of caring for this little two-year-old scamp. Funny, he'd never liked kids much. Except for Hillary, his niece, he didn't have much use for children and thought most of them were brats. He sure as hell had been one.

"I can't explain Jonah," Jenner finally said. "I don't think anyone can."

"Anyway, I think I was telling you all about my stupid fantasies." She stared through the windshield and into the night. "Once your father shattered my illusions, I left Rimrock and finished nursing school. I decided that neither Cody nor I needed you, that we could get along just fine. And we have. Until your grandmother wrote me."

Jenner still wasn't absolutely convinced. Though Beth looked as if she was telling the God's honest truth, he didn't know her. She could be the world's most accomplished liar for all he knew. "So now what do you expect of me?"

"I don't know. Recognition maybe. I, um, grew up not knowing my dad and it would've been nice to put a face with a name occasionally."

"You never saw him."

"Not much. Once in a while he'd show up, or he'd call, but it was pretty much hit-or-miss."

"And that bothered you?"

She opened her mouth as if to give a quick answer, a lie maybe, then shut it quickly. "Yeah," she admitted, "it bothered me a lot."

His gut tightened when he saw the tip of her tongue skim her lips nervously. He didn't want to feel any empathy for her, didn't want to feel anything. So she had a rotten childhood. Lots of people did and they survived.

"Well, look, it's late. Cody's already asleep and I'd better get going." She reached for the handle of the door, but he grabbed her shoulder, surprising himself.

"Wait—" His body just seemed to react on its own as he dragged her close, boy and all, and let his lips touch the wet trail her tongue had left only moments before. Her mouth was soft, pliant and brought back dusty memories as she sighed softly. She smelled and tasted familiar, but that could have been his imagination playing tricks on him. The way her body seemed to melt into his... Warmth, hot and urgent, invaded his limbs, caused his heartbeat to thunder in his ears.

Cody, caught between them, moved and made sucking noises with his mouth, but Jenner didn't mind. In fact, as his arms drew her closer, the child was wedged between them and it felt right somehow.

His heart was still pounding when Beth lifted her head to gaze at him for a second. "Stop," she said, her voice breathless. "This isn't necessary—"

"Has nothing to do with necessity."

"You don't need to prove that... Damn it all, just because you and I... Just forget it, okay?" She pushed away quickly as if suddenly afraid. Her fingers scrabbled for the handle of the door.

The latch opened. A rush of cool air swept into the cab, dispersing some of the condensation that had collected on the windows. But Jenner wasn't quite finished. He reached for her again and tightened his fingers into a firm, angry grip. "There's something you'd better understand about me," he said unevenly. "I don't *have* to do anything and I know it."

"Of course not. You're a McKee, aren't you?"

Growling a curse, he yanked her close to him again and his lips were no longer gentle, but came down with a punishing anger that was hot and wild and way out of control. She took a swift intake of breath and he pressed his advantage, his tongue delving deep into the warm, sweet recesses of her mouth.

Cody let out a squeal and Jenner let go, suddenly realizing what he was doing. Shooting a hard glare in his direction, Beth held Cody more tightly and slid from the seat of the cab. As her feet touched the pavement, she sent him a scathing look. "You made your point, Jenner," she said, taking deep gulps of air between words. "I've done my duty by coming here and you've done yours by meeting Cody. You don't owe him or me anything." Tossing her hair out of her face, she said, "Let's call it even."

"Even?"

Back stiff as sun-dried leather, she marched up the walk and disappeared inside.

"Hell," Jenner muttered. He reached across the seat and grabbed the door. A jolt of pain shot up his leg, raging like a prairie fire as it raced from his knee to his hip. Slamming the door, he straightened, ignored the throbbing and tore away from the curb.

Who was that woman? And why the hell did she get to him?

"It's pointless to stay any longer," Beth said as she eyed the small bedroom where she'd laid Cody in his playpen. Snuggled under a blanket, thumb firmly in his mouth, he'd barely awakened when Jenner had squeezed him during their kiss. She turned off the light and, with her mother following her, headed back to the kitchen. She needed a drink. Something stronger than coffee. Oh, for God's sake, who was she kidding? She reached the kitchen, grabbed a wineglass, then shoved it back into the cupboard. Instead, she paused at the sink and splashed some water on her face. Her lips still felt the warm impressions of Jenner's mouth and her blood was still running hot. Too hot.

"But you just got here. Just because things didn't go so great with Jenner McKee is no reason to turn tail and run." Harriet reached for a pack of cigarettes on the counter.

"I'm *not* running!" Good Lord, she was protesting much too loudly.

"I thought you were staying for a week."

"I was, but—"

"But now, just like that—" Harriet snapped her fingers loudly "—you're heading back to the city."

"I belong in the city."

With a flick of her lighter, Harriet lit up and drew in a lungful of smoke. "If you say so." Her eyes darkened a second as if with a private pain, then she sighed.

"Mom…I only came back because of Mavis's letter. I felt coerced into seeing Jenner again."

"Did you?" Harriet leaned a hip against the counter, crossed her arms over her waist, and let her cigarette burn between her fingers as she studied her daughter. "I wasn't going to say anything. Lord knows I hate a meddling mother. But I feel it's only right to speak my mind.

"You've got your life all neatly planned out. Get another job working at a hospital, marry Stan and hope that he'll be the father to Cody that he doesn't have now. You'd like to pretend that Jenner McKee doesn't exist, that you don't give two cents about him, but the truth of the matter is that you're not over him. Probably never will be."

Beth dried her face on a towel hanging near the window. "I thought you didn't like the McKees."

"I don't. Don't trust 'em, neither."

"But—"

"But you'd better listen to your heart, girl, or you're going to end up in a whole lot more trouble than you're already in. Marrying Stan because he's stable, because he's nice, because he's financially secure won't make you forget Jenner."

"I already broke up with Stan and I don't know what you're—"

"You're too smart not to know. Face it, Beth. I see the way your eyes light up at the mention of Jenner. He stirs your blood, and don't tell me he doesn't. I've known enough men to recognize when one's got hold of my daughter's heart. I hoped that you'd forget him, that when you saw him again you'd see that he's not the man for you, but unless I miss my guess, that little plan backfired."

Harriet's words echoed Beth's own worrisome suspicions, but she wouldn't acknowledge them. "Jenner and I have a history, that's all."

"Not quite," Harriet reminded her. "The two of you have a son."

"Let's not talk about it now." Beth glanced out the window. "I left my car at the apartment. How about helping me retrieve it?"

Harriet grabbed her keys and purse. "All right, but just remember Jenner McKee has done nothing but hurt you."

The Black Anvil was one cut up from a dive. The bar had seen better years, the floor was made of worn oak slats polished by spilled beers, broken glass, dirt from unwiped boots and even occasional drops of blood from nosebleeds, the result of infrequent but angry fistfights.

Several of the regulars had bellied up to the bar. Jenner recognized Jeb Peterson, a big bear of a man who owned a sawmill in Dawson City and whose affinity for ale bulged over his belt. Slim Purcell was perched on the end stool and Jimmy Rickert was shooting pool. A cigarette hung limply from the corner of Jimmy's mouth as he concentrated on his game against Barry White who was somehow related to Ned Jansen. Rimrock was a small town—lots of people related to each other, everyone knowing everyone else's business.

Maybe it was time to move on.

But where? Sure as hell not back to the rodeo circuit, and he could never again hire on as a hand at a ranch. The owner would take one look at his leg and... Damn it all, he needed a drink. A stiff one.

Forcing his bad leg up to the bar, Jenner settled on a stool. "The usual," he said to the bartender.

Swiping the bar with a wet towel, Jake glanced down at Jenner's leg. "Actin' up again?"

"It's a pain in the butt. Literally."

Within seconds, a frosty mug and an open bottle sat in front of him. "Maybe you'd better get a second opinion on that knee and hip." Jake poured the brew into the mug.

"For what?"

"See if a little surgery will fix 'er up. Maybe then you could join the circuit again."

Jenner shook his head. "That's over for me," he said.

"Doesn't have to be."

"I've had enough surgeries. More'n my share."

The beer was cold and wet. Jenner sipped slowly and saw his reflection in the mirror—a broken-down, crippled cowboy who liked liquor a little too much.

His attention was drawn to the end of the bar where Wanda Tully, the waitress, was waiting for an order. Her pale blond hair looked silver in the dim light and she flashed Jenner her thousand-watt smile. Returning it with a sketchy wave, he wondered why he had no interest in Wanda. Twice divorced and working two jobs, she was a good woman who flirted with him just about every time he came through the door. Her legs were long, her breasts high, and though she was a little worn around the edges, she was still pretty. Wanda was a simple woman, one who would never place any demands on him, and right now he didn't need complications the likes of which he felt every time he was with Beth.

Yet, even here, nursing his beer, feeling Wanda's interested gaze sliding in his direction, he couldn't shake Beth's image from his mind. Her hair, a rich shade somewhere between dark brown and red, was long and full, and her cheekbones flared becomingly above hollow cheeks and full lips able to ease into a wide, sincere smile that seemed meant only for him.

"Son of a bitch," he growled, reaching for a handful of salty peanuts. Things weren't going as he'd planned. The pain in his leg was a constant reminder that his life had changed, and Beth, now that she was here, made it worse.

"Yep," Jake said, pouring a drink for a kid who looked barely twenty at the end of the bar, "if I were you, Jenner, I wouldn't give up working with the rodeo stock."

Jenner didn't argue. Gritting his teeth, he told himself that he could handle every stumbling block fate cast his way. He'd always believed that a man had to accept the cards that lady luck dealt him and make the best of any situation. Even though Jenner had been born to wealth, he'd shunned the old man's money as well as the trappings and responsibilities that came with a huge bank account.

From years riding rodeo, he'd broken more bones than he could count, been thrown, trampled and dragged by more horses than he cared to remember. Each time he'd climbed on the back of a range-tough rodeo bronc, he'd taken his life in his hands. There had always been the chance that he could have been killed or severely injured, so this...this useless leg shouldn't come as any big shock. He'd either get better or he wouldn't. But, deep down, it scared him. It scared the living hell out of him.

"Say, McKee—" a harsh voice broke into his thoughts "—I hear your family's offerin' a reward for information on the guy who started the fire in your stables and maybe had somethin' to do with your old man's accident."

Jenner bristled. He twisted on his stool and saw three men huddled around a nearby table.

Fred Donner sniffed, then rubbed the edge of his sleeve under his nose. He'd posed the question. "Is that right?"

"I don't know anything about it."

The men exchanged glances. "I heard it was ten thousand dollars."

"Twenty-five," Ned Jansen said. He crushed out his cigarette. "That's what I heard. Ain't that what you heard, Steve?" he yelled at his son who was one of the men playing pool near the back room.

"Yep." Tall and rangy, Steve nodded but didn't break his concentration on the game. Money was riding on his ability to slam the next few balls into the pockets, and Steve Jansen had a reputation for knowing the value of a buck—even if his father didn't.

"Wasn't it thirty grand?" the third man at the table, Cyrus Kellogg, asked. "That's one helluva pile of money." Cyrus finished his drink and eyed Jenner. Near sixty, Cyrus owned the property on the other side of a stand of timber owned by the McKees.

"Could be just a rumor." Ned scowled.

"Nope," Fred insisted, his weathered face looking grim.

Years ago, he'd lost the water rights to his ranch because of dealing with Jonah and he'd never gotten over the sting of the loss. Fred had been one of the men living around Rimrock who'd counted Jonah as a friend. And he'd been stabbed in the back, Jenner thought. By the master of backstabbing, good ol' Jonah Phineas McKee.

"I heard it from Ada Patterson, and she knows everything that goes on 'round here."

"Sometimes before it happens," Jenner agreed with a half smile. Besides being a gossiping busybody, Ada owned and was the editor of *The Rimrock Review*. Jenner finished his beer and set the mug back on the counter. A trace of foam settled back inside. "But, as I said, I don't know anything about it." Which wasn't all that surprising. It seemed that everything going on in the family these days was happening behind his back. He hadn't known about Mavis and her damned letter to Beth; nor had he been privy to some of the conversations with doctors about his...condition. Max and Skye had handled that while he was recuperating in the hospital. The insurance investigation was an ongoing battle that Max was handling while his mother was dealing with Rex Stone concerning his father's death.

Well, that's the way he'd always said he wanted it. He'd never shouldered any responsibility for McKee Enterprises while his father had been alive and he certainly wasn't going to take on any more obligations now.

Except maybe for Beth. Mavis might have started the business with Beth Crandall, but he sure as hell would be expected to finish it.

"Jeez, Jenner, you've always been a straight shooter. Jonah, well, he was one to talk in circles, tryin' to make things sound good for you when they were really good for him, and Max, hell, he's too much like your old man to do much better. But you—"

"I said I don't know anything and I don't. The rest of the family doesn't always tell me what's going on. Matter of fact, that's the way I like it!" Jenner stood. The men at the table turned back to their drinks, but he felt the weight of more than one interested gaze following him as he grabbed his crutches with jerky movements and made his way out of the building.

He didn't feel any better than he had when he'd swung into the bar and had been determined to drive Beth out of his mind. But the country music, clink of glasses and murmur of conversation hadn't stopped his thoughts from returning to her. The smoky atmosphere and thin odor of grease from a deep fryer hadn't overridden the fragrance of her perfume that still lingered in his nostrils. Nor had the malty flavor of his favorite brew washed away the taste of her lips.

"Damn it all, anyway." He tossed his crutches into the cab and whistled to Reuben. "You can ride up front," he told the old dog, who gladly bounded out of the truck bed and hopped through the open door.

Dogs were just so much easier to deal with than women.

"What the hell does this mean?" Jenner wagged the morning edition of *The Rimrock Review* under his brother's nose. Upon seeing the first edition and the story about the reward offered for the arrest and conviction of the culprit involved in Jonah's murder and/or the fire at the stables, Jenner had driven to the ranch and found his mother and brother in the kitchen, drinking coffee and sampling Kiki's sourdough biscuits as if they had nothing better to do. Jenner slapped the newspaper onto the top of the table where he'd eaten for a good part of his life.

"Want some coffee?" Kiki asked. A gray-haired, skinny woman with a sour disposition that didn't quite hide her heart of gold, she stared at Jenner as she always had, with steady disapproval.

"No, I don't want any coffee! I want answers."

"Kiki, please," Virginia said. "Jenner could use a cup."

"Maybe it should be decaf," Max suggested.

"Very funny!" Jenner pinned his brother with a hard glare. "You're all just full of surprises, aren't you?"

Max leaned back in his chair. "I take it you disapprove of the reward."

"Hell, yes, I disapprove. It's the single most foolhardy thing you've done yet. You're going to get every piece of slime in the county crawling out from under his rock to come out and try to collect."

"And we just might find the killer," his mother said as Kiki set a cup of black coffee in front of an empty chair. "Come on, Jenner, sit down and—"

"For the love of Mike, Mom, don't you see what you've done?"

Virginia's gaze hardened. "Why don't you enlighten me?"

"You've drawn attention, Mom. Attention to the Rocking M. Attention to the family."

"And attention to you," Max said, pouring a thin stream of cream into his cup.

"That's right."

"And you don't like it."

"Damned straight." Placated somewhat, he shoved his crutches up against the wall near the bay window and dropped into one of the old kitchen chairs, which had the audacity to creak against his weight.

"You know, Jenner, this is a surprise. For years, you've worked hard to be in the limelight—riding rodeo and all, rebelling against Dad, getting your butt thrown in jail." His eyes narrowed as he took a gulp and watched his brother over the rim of his cup. "Seems to me, you've had a change of heart."

"I'm a cripple, or don't you remember?"

His mother gasped, but Max didn't so much as flinch. "But that's not it, is it?" Max guessed. "This has something to do with Beth Crandall and the boy."

Jenner hated it when Max could read his mind. He wanted to reach across the table and wrestle Max to the ground as he had when they were boys. He also wanted to lie. To say that Beth and her impish son meant nothing to him. But Jenner was through with lies. "I don't want them dragged into this."

"Because of the scandal," Virginia said.

"That's not it," Max said, and one side of his mouth lifted. "Jenner cares about them, doesn't want them hurt." His smile stretched even wider. "Hell, you think that boy is really yours, don't you?"

Virginia shook her head. "Oh, no—"

"Could be." Jenner grabbed a biscuit and slathered it with butter and blackberry jelly. "Whether he is or isn't, I don't want anyone from the *Review* or any damned news reporters from any other paper or magazine botherin' 'em."

"Or putting them in danger," Max surmised.

Jenner felt every muscle in his body tense with the thought of Cody or Beth being in jeopardy because of him. "That's right," he said, realizing that if anyone was going to protect them, it had to be him. From the corner of his eye, he caught a glimpse of his crutches. Some bodyguard he'd be. He couldn't even walk normally. His fingers clenched the handle of the cup. "I need to talk to Rex Stone."

"So you don't trust her."

"Do you?"

Max didn't say a word, but it was Virginia's turn to read his mind. "You'd use Rex to find out if Beth's telling the truth about the boy?" Clearing her throat, she set down her cup to stare at her second son. "Don't tell me you're falling for her story... or for her?"

"Course not," he said quickly, maybe too quickly, because Max, damn him, barked out a short laugh that called him a liar. Changing the subject, Jenner said, "There's something else we need to discuss."

"Shoot," Max said.

"I need to get back to work."

"You're not ready."

"I may never be ready." Jenner glared across the table. "I'm tired of being a hard-luck case."

"Jenner, you're not anything of the kind," Virginia whispered. "You're injured."

"And I can't stay cooped up another minute. Either I get my old job back helping Chester manage this place, or I go hunting for another."

There was silence. Aside from the click of a timer on the stove and the swish of Kiki's broom across the floor, no one dared breathe a word.

"Don't you think it would be better if you gave yourself a rest and came back when you're a hundred percent?" Max asked.

"That may never happen." Jenner drained his cup. "You know it and I know it."

"Skye seems to think it's just a matter of time and maybe another surgery or two."

"I'm done being under the knife and recuperating!" Jenner growled, banging his fist on the table and making the spoons jump and cups rattle. Even fastidious Kiki gave up pushing her broom. "I need to get on with my life!"

Virginia tried to lay placating fingers on his, but he jerked back his hand as if her touch had burned him. "For the love of God, Mother, quit treating me like I'm a kid with a terminal illness!" He managed to pull himself to his feet with every bit of dignity he could muster and braced his hands on the tall back of the caned chair. "I'll be back tomorrow," he said to Max. "I either still have a job or I don't. You figure it out!"

Snatching his crutches savagely, he shoved them under his arms and plunged through the kitchen door.

"It's that Beth woman!" his mother whispered to Max. Jenner kept right on going as if he couldn't hear. "She's making him crazy, trying to pawn off that kid—"

"Cody could be his, Ma."

"Max, really! Don't even say it. Jenner would never get involved with Harriet Forrester's daughter!"

"Like hell," Jenner mumbled under his breath as he reached the front door and yanked it open. Fresh, cool autumn air, swept into the house. The door banged shut behind him.

It didn't really matter what Max or his mother thought, but one way or another, Jenner was going to get to the bottom of Beth's story and sort out truth from fiction. While he was at it, he'd have to make sure that the press—and the damned culprit whoever he was—didn't discover that Cody might have McKee blood running through his veins.

"Right here—look for yourself!" Harriet wagged the morning edition of the *Review* under Beth's nose.

"What's so important it can't wait until after Cody's bath?" Beth glanced at the section of newspaper Harriet held out and caught sight of a bold headline for the want ads.

"'Wanted for full- or part-time position: Registered Nurse. Inquire at Post Office Box 762 in care of *The Rimrock Review.*' Didn't I tell you? I'll bet it's a job at the clinic or maybe over at Dawson Memorial Hospital."

"Great," Beth said, wrinkling her nose as Cody, his blue eyes gleaming mischievously, splashed water over the front of her blouse. "Then I could work with Dr. Donahue, who's supposed to soon become Dr. McKee. Max's fiancée." She grabbed a thick, rose-colored towel and pulled Cody, kicking and protesting loudly, out of the old tub. "Why don't I just find someone to torture me slowly? You know, sticks under my fingernails, or water dripped on my forehead, or—"

"Why you say that?" Cody asked, and Beth sighed.

"I'm just making jokes. I was trying to be funny."

Cody looked puzzled.

"It wasn't funny," Harriet assured her grandson. "Sometimes your mother has a very sick sense of humor."

Beth laughed and fluffed her son's hair with the towel. "So does your grandmother," she said with a wink.

"I don't know why it would be so bad to live here close to us—"

"Mom, we've been over this a hundred times on the phone."

Harriet threw up her hands and let the newspaper drop onto the floor. "Fine, then there's no use arguing, is there?" she said and huffed out of the tiny bathroom. Beth's gaze fell to the front page of the *Review,* which had slid away from the classified advertising section. Her heart jolted as she read the headline: MCKEE FAMILY OFFERS REWARD

A picture of Jonah McKee, dressed in a western-cut business suit and shaking hands with the mayor a few years back, graced one side of the column. Beth couldn't help feeling a tiny speck of anger at the man who had rejected his grandson and bilked the citizens of Rimrock of their hard-earned cash and property. She didn't wish him dead, but she wouldn't miss him, and only felt a stab of guilt when she realized that her son would never know his grandfather, nor would Jenner ever see his father again.

Skimming the article, she learned that Virginia McKee was offering twenty-five thousand dollars for information leading to the arrest and conviction of a suspect involved in the arson at the ranch or connected with Jonah's death. There were quotes from the sheriff's department and a private investigator named Rex Stone, all sounding overly confident, all assuring the community that justice eventually would be served.

"Splash Mommy 'gain," Cody said, reaching into the tub and thrusting another small handful of water at her.

"No more splashing." She dropped the paper. "Come on, sport, let's get you out of here." She tried to wrap Cody in the towel, but he squealed and ran down the hall.

"I naked!" he proclaimed, his damp little feet slapping against the bare floors. "Can't catch Cody!"

Harriet poked her head into the bathroom. "What in heaven's name—?"

"It's a game we play," Beth said, giving chase. Cody was already in the living room and opening the front door.

"No, Cody, not outside!"

"Outside!" he insisted with glee. Shoving the door open, he hurtled through.

"Stop!" Beth commanded just as Cody laughed at her sorry attempt to catch him and his slippery little body collided with the long, jean-clad legs of his father.

Chapter Seven

"What's this?" Jenner asked, trying to keep his balance while he picked up the kid, who was as naked as a jaybird. "You're in your birthday suit!"

"I not!" Cody insisted. He wriggled to get away from Jenner's arms, but Jenner wouldn't let go. "I naked," he asserted, thrusting out his little chin.

"You sure are." Warm and wet and smelling of soap, the boy had a way of wedging himself into Jenner's heart, and for a second he wondered if it really mattered whether his blood was flowing in this kid's veins or not.

"I want down!" Cody said, squirming.

Beth came to the doorway and offered him a tentative smile. "Sorry. One of the convicts escaped."

"By boat, it looks like." Jenner couldn't help noticing the water on her blouse, which made the fabric more sheer and gave him a view of the edge of her bra and a tantalizing glimpse of the darker disk of her nipple. A strange knot began to unravel in his gut and he drew his eyes upward again.

She let out a soft laugh. "It's true. A person could drown trying to get this guy clean." She wrapped the towel around her son's wriggling, slick body and lifted him from Jenner's arms. "Bathing Cody is aerobic exercise. It's how I get my daily workout, isn't it?" she asked, sticking her nose into his damp hair.

The kid had left a wet impression on Jenner's shirt, and the scents of baby shampoo, soap and a fragrance he was beginning to associate with Beth lingered in his nostrils for a fleeting second.

"So what are you doing here?"

"I thought we should talk."

She hesitated a second, then smiled, "Come on in," she invited, holding the door open with her backside as Cody squirmed in her arms. Her hair was pulled into a ponytail that fell in wild curls past her shoulders and seemed to catch fire in the morning light.

Grabbing his damned crutches, he hoisted himself through the doorway and into the house. The furniture was worn but clean, the pictures on the walls colorful reproductions. Plants in bright pots were placed near the windows, and hand-crocheted afghans were tossed haphazardly over cushions that had seen better days.

Harriet Forrester was brushing away a speck of dust on an old Formica tabletop near the fireplace and trying to hide a surprised grin that bugged the hell out of Jenner. Dealing with Beth was difficult enough; he didn't want to have to face her mother.

"I think you know Mom."

He inclined his head. "We've met."

Harriet's lips twitched with undisguised pride. "Well, Jenner, what do you think of our boy?"

"Mom!"

Jenner bristled inside. Why did she want to put him on the spot? With a shrug, he said, "Seems like an okay kid."

"Oh, he's way beyond okay. He's downright phenomenal, aren't you, baby?" she said, her gaze resting on her grandson for a second before her expression changed and her smile faded. Her lips pinched a little at the corners and she cleared her throat. "You know, I was wondering what it was that you and your grandmother want."

"Excuse me?"

"Mom, I don't think this is the time or place—" Beth interjected.

"What *I* want," he clarified.

"Mmm. And Mavis. She's in on this, too."

"Mom, don't—"

"We're talking about my grandson, Beth, my *only* grandson and we're in my house, so I think I'm entitled to a few answers. Now, Mavis wrote you, asking about Cody, demanding you come here and let Jenner meet him, on the excuse of his accident, but I want to know where we all stand." She lifted her chin a notch and looked over at Jenner again. "My family and yours run in different social circles and I've never hidden the fact that I'm not fond of anyone named McKee, but I'm willing to put the past aside for the sake of the child. However, I don't expect to be run over roughshod just because—"

"Please, Mom, for God's sake—"

"It's all right." Jenner held up a hand to stop Beth's protest, then turned his attention back to Harriet. "I don't blame you for wanting to know what's up. I didn't know anything about my grandmother's letter, just like I didn't know anything about Cody until Beth showed up at the Rocking M a few days ago. To be honest, I'm not even sure what's truth and what's fiction around here. I'm trying to sort it out."

"You still think I'm lying," Beth accused, her green eyes snapping with fury.

He didn't bother answering.

Harriet snorted, and Beth, holding a swaddled Cody, said coldly, "I don't need to be a part of this. You two, with all your built-in predjudices about each other, work this out. You can inform me later. Right now, I'm going to get my son dressed before he freezes to death."

"Or escapes again," Jenner said.

Beth turned on her heel, and walking smartly through an archway that led down a hall to the bedroom, she disappeared. He itched to follow her, to have it out with her once and for all, to hold her in his arms and...oh, hell, what was he thinking?

"You have a lotta nerve," Harriet said quietly. She hardly looked old enough to be Beth's mother.

"So I've been told."

"Do you honestly think Beth would come back here and put her heart and pride and child on the line all for the sake of a lie? Think about it!"

"Depends on how much money is involved, I suspect."

She reached for a partially smoked pack of cigarettes and shook one out. Her fingers seemed to tremble slightly as she placed the fliter tip into her mouth. "Money! Always money with you people."

"With most people."

Harriet struck a match and held the flame to the tip of her cigarette. "You sure think you can run things, don't you? Just like your father." A shadow crossed her eyes as she waved out her match and drew on her cigarette. "He took the cake, that one. You know, I have half a mind to call up Mavis and tell her to back off."

Despite his anger, Jenner felt the corner of his mouth lift a little as he thought about Harriet and Mavis squaring off. Kind of a battle of the grandmothers. "I've already tried. It didn't work."

Harriet didn't see an ounce of humor in the situation. "You be careful, Jenner McKee," she advised as she shot an angry plume of smoke from the corner of her mouth.

"Don't think you can do the kind of fast shuffle your dad was so good at."

"I'm not like my dad," he said evenly, and Harriet, through a haze of smoke, gave him the once-over.

"Aren't you?"

"No way." His eyes narrowed as he studied the woman whom he'd heard rumors about all his life. Rumors that linked her to just about every available male in Rimrock. Harriet Winward Crandall Something-or-other Forrester. There had been other names he'd heard, too. Floozy. Whore. Bimbo. You name it and Harriet had been called it. Though she'd never been linked to any married men, Jenner couldn't help but wonder if she'd been involved with his father. Maybe it was the way she'd nearly sneered when she'd brought Jonah up, as if she'd been familiar with him. That thought made him uneasy as he watched her take a seat on a worn couch and motion for him to sit, as well.

"So what're your plans?"

"Haven't got any."

"McKees always have plans."

He'd been polite long enough. "Let's be straight with each other, Mrs. Forrester—"

"Harriet. Just call me Harriet."

"Okay. Ever since I walked through the door you've been using me for a punching bag." Wielding his crutches, he moved so that he was standing directly over her. "So why don't you give me your best shot and tell me what it is you don't like about me?"

"You mean other than the fact that you used my daughter—got her pregnant—then left without a backward glance? Or if that's not good enough, let's take ridiculing her when she gathered the nerve to come and tell you about Cody."

"*After* the letter from Mavis."

"Whatever." She waved impatiently, and smoke swirled around the hand holding her cigarette. "The point is, it took guts to come back here and face you."

"It would've taken more a couple of years ago."

"Back then she came up against Jonah. You do remember your father, don't you? How he tried to manipulate everyone in this town?" With a final drag, she shook her head, then jabbed out her cigarette in a glass ashtray. "He didn't want you tied down to my daughter and he wouldn't accept the fact that Cody was his grandson. Prince of a fella, your old man."

"She should have talked to me."

"You should've stuck around. Loving 'em and leaving 'em isn't exactly admirable."

"I think that's enough, Mom," Beth said, her cheeks flushed slightly, as if she'd heard more than she should have when she walked back into the room.

Jenner offered a lazy smile. "Your mother was only expressing her opinon about my family. No harm done."

Cody ran pell-mell into the living room, his feet in new sneakers pounding loudly. His hair was combed and he was wearing a pair of stiff new Levi's. Grabbing a book from a basket near the fireplace, he crawled onto the couch and smiled up at his grandmother. "You read?" he asked her, his eyes glinting as if he knew how adorable he was.

"Of course I will."

"I think you and I should talk," Beth said to Jenner, then shot her mother a meaningful glance. "Alone."

"Fine with me," Harriet said. "I was hoping to take Cody into town later anyway."

"That would probably be a good idea."

This was gonna be trouble. If Jenner stuck around, Beth was going to mess up his mind, sure as shootin'. But he couldn't very well just walk out on her. Besides, a part of him was curious to know what she had up her sleeve this time.

"All right," he drawled.

"Then you and I," Harriet said, giving her grandson a wink, "will go down to the Pancake Hutt where Grandma works. Since it's my day off, we'll splurge on lunch and I'll show you off to some of my friends. I'll buy you a Belgian waffle with strawberry jam and whipped cream. How would you like that?"

"Mommy come?" Cody said, and his brow furrowed.

"Not this time."

"Mommy come!" This time it was a command.

"I'll be back soon, sweetheart," Beth promised.

"Noo!" He started to wail and Beth picked him up. He let his picture book fall to the floor. "You stay! Mommy, you stay!"

Beth bit her lip, obviously torn. "We'll be back soon," she said to the boy, and Cody, clinging even more tenaciously to his mother, glared up at Jenner.

"No!"

"It'll be all right, honey," Beth whispered, holding the boy close. "I'll bring you a surprise."

"You stay with me!"

"I can't, honey, really."

"Let me take him. You two run along." Harriet peeled her distraught grandson from Beth. "We'll be fine. The minute you leave this'll be over."

Beth didn't look convinced as she grabbed a jean jacket from the coat tree standing guard near the front door. "I can drive—"

"No!" he snapped quickly as he pushed his crutches out in front of him and concentrated on limping as little as possible. "I'll drive." Cody's wails followed them to the front porch and Beth cast a guilty look behind her as she crawled into the cab of his truck and he threw his damned crutches in the back. Now what?

Trying to ignore the sounds of her son's cries, Beth eyed Jenner and wished she didn't care for him. Not at all. It wasn't as if she was in love with him or anything, but there was still a part of her that found him fascinating—on a purely sensual level. She tried to convince herself that her feelings existed simply because he was the father of her child, that of course she should care for him, but deep inside she worried that she still might harbor a little seed of the old crush she'd had on him. It was silly, really, but there it was, buried deep in the back of her mind, ready to sprout if given the least bit of encouragement.

Which she wouldn't get from Jenner, so she was safe. Out of habit, she checked her watch.

"You have to be somewhere?" he asked, braking for a red light.

"It's just that Cody…he doesn't like it when I leave him. I really shouldn't be away a long time."

"What about when you work?"

She shrugged a shoulder. "He adjusts. I've got a wonderful baby-sitter who treats him like he's one of her own grandkids."

"You mean she spoils him."

"You can't spoil a two-year-old," she said defensively. She felt her maternal talons beginning to show.

"You spoil him, too."

"As I said—"

"Yeah, yeah, I heard. 'You can't spoil a two-year-old.' Well, that's a pile of B.S. and we both know it." He slid her a glance that could cut through steel, then shifted into first gear as the light changed.

"So now you're the expert on child rearing?" she asked, arching a dubious eyebrow as he worked gas, brake and clutch with relative ease.

"Nope, just an expert on being spoiled rotten. My father thought you could buy a kid's affection and my mother always worked under the assumption that being a slave to your husband and your kids would assure you a place in heaven or some such crap. Sometimes she played the mar-

tyr so well I was certain she'd be cannonized." He snorted
and his hands seemed to grip the wheel a little tighter. "It
doesn't take a genius to see where my folks screwed up."

"You all seemed to survive."

"If that's what you want to call it." He was driving north
where the highway cut through the foothills of the mountains. The sun was shining, but thin clouds had appeared on
the horizon. "Max did everything he could to please Dad.
Became a damned yes-man for a while. And Mom, hell, she
knew Dad cheated on her, but she pretended that it didn't
happen, that he was faithful. She still goes around acting as
if he were some kind of saint. Casey's a hothead, always
runnin' off at the mouth and getting herself in trouble.
Doesn't seem to know what she wants out of life. Like I
said, I know spoiled."

"And what about you?" Beth asked as he drove past the
tree-lined lane leading to the ranch house.

"Spoiled rotten." His smile turned cynical. "I did everything I could to be a pain in the old man's backside. It
seemed to work, too," he admitted, though he didn't seem
pleased with himself.

Giving the wheel a sharp turn, he drove off the main road
and onto an overgrown gravel drive that was barely more
than two ruts cutting through a stand of pine. A gate with a
No Trespassing sign nailed to the top rail warned them off
the property, but Jenner ignored the faded red lettering as
he climbed out of the truck, grabbed his crutches and hobbled to the fence. After extracting a ring of keys from his
pocket, he tried several in the rusted lock before the latch
gave way and the chain fell to the ground.

"Drive through," he yelled, pushing the gate. It opened
with a squeal of seldom-used hinges.

Beth slid behind the wheel and shoved the pickup into
first. Barely able to reach the pedals, she eased the truck
through the opening and Jenner closed the gate. A second

later, he was back in the truck and she was sliding across the
seat. "Mind telling me where we're going?"

"To my place."

"Your place," she repeated. "But I thought you lived in
the apartment."

"Temporary accommodations." He angled the nose of
the pickup up a steep slope. The truck bucked as it hit unseen rocks, and long, dry grass and thistles scraped the un-
dercarriage. "I wanted you to see something."

"What?"

He cast her a glance that nearly melted her bones. Her
breath stalled somewhere above her lungs and her heart began to beat more quickly.

They were nearly at the crest of a hill when the road
seemed to give out altogether. Jenner didn't even slow down,
just kept driving through the openings in the trees until the
pines gave way to a meadow. He cut the engine, then
climbed out of the cab. Cursing his crutches, he managed to
climb the short distance to the crest of the hill with its view
of the valley below.

"What is this place?" She saw the John Day River, little
more than a blue-green thread weaving along the bottom of
the canyon, and the ridges of red rock that she'd always
viewed from the valley floor were now huge bolders that felt
the sun's warming rays.

The town of Rimrock was visible, a webbing of streets and
buildings spreading around the bend in the river.

"This was the original homestead of the McKee family."
He pointed to a cabin standing near the edge of the clearing. It was small, barely more than one room from the looks
of it, the porch sagging, the roof caved in. Other nearby
buildings, sunbleached and tumbling down, were covered in
brambles. Farther away was a graveyard, fenced and overgrown, the last resting place of McKee pioneers, Beth
guessed.

"Over there—" Jenner motioned beyond the edge of a cliff "—is a parcel that used to be Ned Jansen's copper mine—well, at least the back of it. The main entrance is half a mile west of here." He leaned against one of the boulders and set his crutches beside him. With one hand shading his eyes against the sunlight, he pointed to the south. "That bit over there is still part of the Rocking M. It's kept separate from the homestead, but I guess this could all be considered part of it because McKee Enterprises owns the old copper mine."

"The mine is abandoned, though, isn't it?" Beth asked. She was standing so close to him she could see the small creases in his skin caused by hours of squinting against the sun. His scent drifted on the breeze. All male and clean, it made her insides shiver in anticipation.

"*Was* abandoned. Jansen had just about given up on it— thought he'd mined all the copper out of it. His team of geologists agreed."

"So why did your father buy it?" she asked, dreading the question, dreading the answer more.

"Well, Ned got himself into some trouble. He's been married a couple of times and divorced. The divorces were expensive. When the mine seemed worthless, he had to borrow money somewhere and the banks turned him down." He leaned back and studied her, his gaze lingering on her face. "But he was in luck. Good ol' Jonah P. McKee was more than willing to help bail an old friend out of trouble. He loaned Ned enough money to get his wives off his back and pay off some overdue child support and alimony. Took the mine as collateral. Ned could never repay him, of course, and Jonah ended up with the mine. And lo and behold, guess what?"

A knot of tension had been tightening in Beth's stomach. She hardly dared breathe because she knew the answer. "The mine was valuable."

"Give the lady a prize!" Jenner mocked. "It was valuable, all right, probably worth millions in copper and silver."

"But why would Ned's own team of geologists lie to him?"

Shrugging his shoulders, Jenner stared into the distance. "I don't have any proof, but my guess is that they were bought off—paid more money than they would ever see in their lives—to fudge their reports."

"You're saying that your father had his eye on the mine all along?"

"Of course he did! Don't you understand? Haven't you figured the old man out yet? Jonah never got involved in any deal unless it would make him money. That was the bottom line. Always. No exceptions." Pain seemed to flicker in his blue gaze.

"What did Ned do?"

"When he found out?" Jenner shrugged. "Nothin'. He couldn't do a thing. Jonah hadn't done anything illegal."

"Except bribe the experts."

"But that couldn't be proven, could it? And Ned tried to sue everyone involved, but his geologists had moved out of state, dissolved their partnership. Ned had no recourse because he couldn't prove criminal intent. Even geologists make mistakes now and again."

The wind crept up the hillside and goose bumps rose on Beth's skin. She rubbed her arms and wondered about the man Jenner had called father, the man who had rejected her son as his grandchild. She remembered him as imposing, with thick white hair that ruffled in the breeze. She'd gone to the ranch to find Jenner, and instead had come face-to-face with his father. Jonah had just dismounted. A cigar had been clamped between his teeth, a rifle clenched firmly in his hands. Seven or eight squirrel carcasses were tethered to his saddle, little, bloody scraps of brown fur that were his trophies for the day.

"You're here lookin' for Jenner, unless I miss my guess." His smile had almost seemed sincere as he'd closed the gate behind him and motioned for one of the hands to deal with his horse. "You just missed him. He took off two days ago for some rodeo in Canada, I think. Alberta or British Columbia, I b'lieve."

"I need to talk to him."

"Because of the baby." She'd been stunned, had felt her skin go white. "This is a small town—bad news travels fast."

"But no one knows. Just me and Dr.—" Her words had nearly strangled in her throat when she'd seen the flicker in Jonah's eyes.

"Oh, hell, there's plenty of people who work in the clinic. Word's bound to get out."

"But not about the father."

Jonah had shrugged, struck a match against the fence post, and puffed on his cigar. "Doesn't matter. Jenner'll never claim the kid and Doc Fletcher can arrange to have the whole business dealt with. There's a physician in Dawson City who'll—"

"No!" she wrapped her arms protectively around her middle. Jonah's eyes had narrowed; he wasn't used to people disagreeing with him. "I'm not going to get rid of this baby."

"It's not a child yet."

"It's your grandchild, Mr. McKee."

His face had turned to stone. "It's a bastard—nothing more. Things would be different if you and Jenner were dating seriously, but you aren't. He's about to become engaged to Nora Bateman and I won't have you ruining his life, or hers."

"I just want to talk to him."

"Why?" He rolled the cigar between his teeth. "Do you think he even remembers you? He and Nora, they broke up a few months back and Jenner decided to sow a few wild oats, kick up his heels, but now he and Nora are planning to get married and you're just one of a dozen or so women he's had a fling with.''

She swallowed hard and felt like being sick.

"What?'' Jonah asked, smoke sailing into the sky. "You didn't think you were special to him, did ya?'' He barked out a laugh that rattled her to the bone. "Jenner's not the settlin' down kind. If it wasn't that he's been in love with Nora since he was sixteen, I wouldn't believe he'd ever get married. But he loves that gal. Always has. Always will.''

There was more than a trace of truth in Jonah's words. Beth had seen Jenner and Nora together years before. They'd dated in high school and even later when he was on the road. Then Nora had gone off to college and Beth had assumed they'd broken up. It had been a long time ago.

"It just took Jenner a long time to grow up, but now he's ready to take a wife.'' His smile was brittle. "Nora, now she's a good girl, comes from a good family in town. The Batemans have been in Rimrock nearly as long as the McKees. Nora's parents have been married nearly thirty years and they're strong, upstanding citizens who've worked hard and increased their land.'' He chuckled and puffed on the cigar. "Nora, she's just the girl for Jenner.''

Beth had eventually believed him and, she realized now with a guilty conscience, accepted his bribe—money to help her start a new life far away from Rimrock and his son. Jonah had convinced her that Jenner didn't want her or her child in his life, and she'd turned heel and ran, never trying to contact Jenner again.

"Are you all right?''

Jenner's voice brought her crashing back to the present, and she shoved the image of Jonah from her mind. "Fine,'' she lied. "But you didn't bring me up here to tell me about your father's business dealings.''

"That's true," he admitted, rubbing his hand around the back of his neck. "We should have that talk you wanted and I thought we should get some things straight about Cody."

Here it comes, she thought, bracing herself. "Something other than the fact that I'm spoiling him?"

He studied her so intently she wanted to step back. Instead, she held her ground and wrapped her arms around her middle. "You *are* spoiling him, but I'm not too worried about that—"

"You shouldn't be."

"But I am concerned about his safety."

"Safety?" she repeated. "Look, Jenner, I take good care of him! You're the one who's talking about letting him catch crawdads and ride horses and—oh!" Suddenly Jenner reached out, curled his fingers over her arm and yanked her hard against him—so hard he nearly fell over.

"This isn't about keeping little fingers away from hot stoves," he said through lips that barely moved.

"Then . . . what?" She tried to keep her mind on the conversation because he was telling her something important, but she couldn't ignore the feel of his hands, rough and possessive, surrounding her wrist, nor could she force her gaze away from the blue depths of his. She licked her lips and thought she heard him groan, but it could have been the soft sigh of the wind rushing through the canyon.

"All this business with my father—his supposed murder."

"That has nothing to do with Cody." Fear, stark and piercing, drove a stake into her heart.

"Maybe, maybe not. There was also the fire in the stables. The fire chief is calling it arson. People seem to think that the same person was probably involved—someone with an ax to grind against the McKees."

"But—"

"Some sicko's got it in for my family. A maniac with a helluva grudge. No one seems to know which way he'll turn, but the sheriff doesn't think he's gonna stop—not until he gets his vengeance, whatever the hell that is."

"I still don't understand."

"If this sleazeball heard you claiming that Cody's my boy," he said, his skin stretched tight over his face, "you could be placing your son in danger."

"What?" Beth shook her head. She refused to hear any of this craziness. But a chill as cold as death crept through her blood. "I can't believe—"

"You'd better," he insisted, his fingers digging more deeply into her flesh. "Max's worried about Hillary. He never lets her out of his sight when she's visiting him and he's warned Hillary's mother, but Colleen has her hands full with twin girls about Cody's age and doesn't always have time."

"But no one knows about Cody."

"Except you and me and everyone at the ranch and whoever else your mother or my grandmother wants to know. Look, I'm not trying to scare you, Beth—"

"But you are!"

"I just want you to be careful."

She swallowed with difficulty. If anything ever happened to her son... "Maybe we should get back," she said, her voice the barest of whispers.

"That's a good idea." But he didn't make any move to release her. He studied her mouth for a heartbeat before lowering his head and brushing his lips slowly across her own. Beth told herself to pull away from him, to fight this stupid attraction she felt for him, but instead she opened her mouth to him and felt his tongue slide easily between her teeth.

Don't! For God's sake, Beth, don't do this! her mind was screaming, but her body was all too willing.

The voice in her head was silenced as his arms surrounded her, dragging her roughly against the straining contours of his body. Whether he planned to tumble to the ground or whether Jenner simply lost his balance, she never knew, but soon they fell onto the dry grass, kissing hungrily, hearts beating a savage rhythm. His mouth was warm and anxious, his fingers strong, as he pressed against the small of her back, forcing her against him with an urgency that caused her blood to heat as it had only once before— with Jenner on the night that Cody had been conceived.

His hands tangled in her hair and he kissed her as if he would never stop, his lips hard and demanding, his tongue supple, his body straining for release. Somewhere in the back of her mind, she knew she should stop him, that kissing him was dangerous, that she would never recover from the mistake of making love with him. Yet she couldn't force the words of denial over her tongue.

Her skin was on fire, and she felt the bulge beneath his jeans, the rough denim straining against the seams. Slowly, as if giving her time to tell him to stop, he reached beneath her jacket, found the hem of her sweater, and inched his fingers up her ribs. She gasped as his hand shoved the cup of her bra aside to grasp her breast. His thumb moved restlessly over her nipple and she arched beneath him.

"That's it," he whispered, kissing her hungrily as he shoved the jacket from her shoulders and pulled the sweater over her head. Then she was nearly naked, her bra twisted beneath one breast. While looking deep into her eyes, he traced the edge of her nipple with a finger and watched as her abdomen sucked in. "God, you're incredible," he said, then held her breast and slowly lowered his head to brush the tip with his lips.

A jolt shot through her the moment his tongue traced the path his finger had taken earlier. Grabbing the back of his head, she held him close to her, and he eagerly took her breast in his mouth, sucking as if thirsty for all of her.

Heat swirled deep in her innermost core. Wet and hot and dark, the want uncurled through her blood. She felt him shift, knew that he'd unhooked her bra and dropped it somewhere in the grass as he'd rolled her on top of him so that he could bury his face in her breasts, tasting of one succulent nipple before turning to the other.

When he finally looked up at her, his face was flushed, his eyes a deep, dangerous blue. Without a word, he slipped his hand beneath the waistband of her jeans, popping the top button. Her throat turned to sand. He moved his hand. Fingers grazed her skin and another button popped, the sound seeming to ricochet off the surrounding hills. Pop. Pop. Pop. His hand was beneath her underpants, parting the nest of curls, delving deep inside her.

"Is this what you want?"

Breaking through the haze of their lovemaking, his voice shocked her.

Yes! She tried to clear her mind, but his hands were still tantalizing her, and he breathed hotly across her nipple, causing it to grow harder still. The hollow ache within her begged to be filled. "I . . ."

"What, Beth? Tell me." His fingers moved and she moaned, tossing back her head, letting her hair fall down her back.

"Jenner," she whispered hoarsely.

"Is this what you want? Is this why you came to me?"

"Yes. No. I don't know."

He froze and his eyes focused. "Damn it all." Angrily, he rolled away from her, apparently disgusted with himself as well as her. "Look, let's get out of here before we do something we'll both regret later." He saw her sweater, picked it up and tossed it to her. Then he hitched himself over to where his crutches lay and hauled himself onto his feet.

Beth felt like she'd been slapped in the face. He'd wanted her; she'd responded to his desire, noticed the swelling in his jeans. And yet he'd rejected her, acted as if she'd planned to seduce him. Mortified, Beth struggled into her clothes, fastening her bra and pulling her sweater over her head with lightning speed. She felt the heat in her cheeks, knew she was blushing, and wondered what in the world she'd been doing kissing Jenner, holding Jenner, letting him touch her in the most intimate of places. "I didn't mean to—"

"Neither did I."

"But—"

"Let's just go, okay? No need to talk about it." He planted his crutches firmly in front of him and, with jerking movements, plunged toward the truck. "I should never have brought you here."

"Don't blame yourself."

"Oh, and who should I blame?"

Anger and frustration building in her blood, she shook the grass from her hair and started after him. "Don't blame anyone, okay? There's no reason to try to lay blame."

"Hell," he muttered.

"We both just made a mistake. No big deal," she said, feeling the lie trip on her tongue. It was a big deal and she should never have let it happen. But it was over...or was it? How could she have been so stupid? Hadn't she already learned her lesson where Jenner McKee was concerned?

Stomping after him, she saw his crutch slip just before he reached the pickup. He swore and fell to the ground with a thud. As his bad leg crumpled beneath him, he let out a cry.

"Jenner!" Beth quickly ran to his aid and dropped to her knees next to him.

"Leave me alone!"

"Let me see."

He grabbed her then and his eyes flared in pain. "I said leave me alone, for God's sake. It'll be fine!"

"Let me be the judge of that."

"You can't judge anything." He tried to move, his face paled, and his breath hissed between his teeth. "Son of a—!"

"Come on, let me help you—" She tried to touch his arm, but he yanked it away.

His nostrils flared. "I said—"

"I heard you. Loud and clear. But I'm just trying to help. I'm a nurse, for crying out loud."

"Big deal. I don't want or need any help!" he asserted as he found one crutch that had fallen into a clump of sage-brush. Gritting his teeth, he hauled himself upright.

The second crutch was farther down the hillside, and though he grumbled at her, Beth retrieved it. "You could let people help you, you know. It's not a sign of weakness."

"I said I don't want any help. Hell, you're as bad as my family!" His face was a ghastly shade of white and he winced as he plunged the crutches ahead of him and tried to walk, but he didn't say another word, only hobbled to the driver's side of the truck and slammed his crutches into the bed. "You gettin' in?" he demanded, shooting her a glance that was so hostile she nearly backed up a step. "I'd hold the door for you, but—"

"Don't!" Her temper ignited. His head snapped up and she held his gaze. "Don't you ever patronize me, and for God's sake, don't act like I'm pitying you just because I want to help you! I'm a medical professional and I think we should immobilize your leg, stretch you out in the back, and run you into the nearest emergency room."

"No way."

"But—"

"I said I'm fine, Beth. Just get in the damned truck."

"Only if you let me drive."

"Forget it."

"You're hurt, for crying out loud!"

"And I'm not gettin' any better waitin' on you!"

With renewed determination, she stalked to the driver's side and waited. "For once in your life, Jenner McKee, let someone do you a favor. Quit being so damned bullheaded and let me drive so that you don't kill us both."

"I said no."

She crossed her arms firmly under her breasts and shot him an authoritative glare that she'd practiced on her most recalcitrant patients. "I'm not about to risk my neck just because you're reckless with yours. I'm a mother and Cody's counting on me coming home in one piece, which I fully intend to do, even if his father is a muleheaded, stubborn jerk who doesn't know a helping hand or an olive branch when he sees one!"

"Oh, hell." Grumbling all the way, he climbed into the cab and slid over to the passenger side. Beth noticed the way he winced as he dragged his bad leg across the seat, swung it under the dash, then slumped against the door. She climbed behind the wheel and managed to start the old truck. She caught a glimpse of the weathered cabin and the grass that had been flattened during their lovemaking and she felt like a fool all over again.

Why had she let him kiss her? Why couldn't she resist him?

From the corner of her eye, she caught him watching her, his eyelids at half-mast, and she felt an uneasy fluttering in her stomach, the way she always did when he stared at her intently.

She drove slowly down the hillside, paused and let the truck idle on the far side of the gate, then swung it shut and climbed back in. Jenner didn't say a word. In fact, he spent the entire ride back to town in brooding silence.

When she turned onto the street where his apartment house was located, he roused. "You can take me to your place."

"I'll walk," she insisted. "It's less than a mile."

"I'll drive you."

"I *want* to walk, Jenner," she insisted and parked the truck near the curb.

"For the love of God, woman," he grumbled, but didn't protest any further. She let him get out of the truck by himself, but he had no choice but to accept her help getting downstairs. He slung his arm over her shoulders and used a single crutch. By the time he was unlocking the door to his apartment, he was sweating and gritting his teeth against the pain.

"Let me get Skye—"

"Don't even think about it, Beth." He yanked out the key and shouldered open the door. Once inside, she frowned. There wasn't a bed to stretch him out on, only a bedroll on the cracked tile floor. "Maybe I'd better take you to the Rocking M."

He let out a humorless laugh. "Not on your life."

"But you need a bed. And how're you going to get to the bathroom?"

"I'll manage," he said as he settled onto the bedroll and groaned.

She wasn't convinced and decided that she couldn't leave him to fend for himself. She knew he wasn't going to like what she planned, but she had an obligation to him, didn't she? She couldn't just leave him lying on the floor in agony. "Okay, Jenner, I want to look at your leg, so I'm going to ask you to take off your boots and jeans. I'll help—"

"Like hell!"

"It's either that or I call your mother or the clinic."

His fists clenched. "For God's sake, woman, just leave me alone."

"Can't do it," she said, determined to win this battle. "Now, are you going to help me, or am I going to have to strip you myself?"

"You really don't know when to quit, do you?" Jenner glared up at her as she knelt next to him. "Or is it that you just want a peek at what I've got in my pants?"

"Don't try to intimidate me." Beth was already kneeling at the end of the bedroll, ready to help remove his boots.

"This is—"

"Necessary," she supplied crisply and reached for the heel of his boot. She thought he might wrest his foot away, but he didn't.

"Damn it all, anyway," he growled but slid out of first one, then the other.

"Good. Now the jeans."

"My God," he muttered, but undid his belt. She looked away, but her back stiffened as she heard the buttons of his fly pop in rapid succession—like her own had done only an hour before.

Cursing under his breath, he tried to struggle out of his jeans, and Beth, telling herself that he was now just a patient, helped him squirm away from the denim. Her breath caught as she saw his legs, white from lack of sun, sprinkled with dark hair and firmly muscled, though his left leg was thinner than the right. A bruise and swelling had already formed at his ankle and she examined it carefully, fingers probing gently against the discolored flesh. "Can you move it?"

"Couldn't much before."

"Tell me if this hurts." Gently rotating his foot, she watched him and saw the pain flare in his eyes.

His breath whistled over his teeth. "Hell, yes, it hurts," he said.

"Looks like you've sprained it...maybe more." Carefully she let go of his foot and tried not to notice that the front of his Jockey shorts was straining over a large swelling. "I think you should see a doctor."

"Why doesn't that surprise me?" He was lying faceup, his hands beneath his head so that he could study her. "The thing is that doctors can't do anything for me. They've already tried, or can't you see the scars?"

She'd noticed them, of course.

"I've got more plastic and metal in that leg than I've got bone and muscle."

"I doubt that. But it's all the more reason for you to see a—"

"Come here," he said in a voice so low she could barely hear him.

"What?" she said, then caught his gaze. Cloudy like blue smoke, filled with desire.

"Come here, Beth."

"I'm here...."

"Closer."

"Jenner, I don't think that—"

"Don't think, Beth," he said, lowering his hands and reaching for her. Strong arms surrounded her and he pulled her steadily closer, so that she was lying half on top of him. He dragged her head to his, and hard, anxious lips claimed hers with a hunger that touched a forbidden spot in her heart. "You want to make me feel better, don't you?"

She'd told herself that she wouldn't get involved with him, that she wouldn't touch him, that she wouldn't fall for him, and yet here she was kissing him and feeling the strength of his body in hers.

His tongue pressed against her teeth and she opened her mouth to him like a flower to the sun, with no resistance. His hands slid beneath her sweater and pressed warmly against her back.

Thoughts of denial seeped from her mind as he touched her, his fingers drawing lines along her spine, his lips warm and wet as he kissed her lips, her eyes, her throat. A low moan escaped her throat as he unhooked her bra and his fingers found her breasts.

"Damn," he whispered hoarsely. "I know that I said we should stop, but I can't." His hands kneaded her breasts and she seemed to melt into him. The same deep, moist warmth that she'd felt before uncoiled inside her. Desire, forbidden and dark, slid through her blood.

He pushed the sweater and bra over her head, then pressed moist kisses to her throat and collarbone. She cradled his head as he touched her, teasing her nipples with his fingers before tasting them with his lips.

Beth sighed as he held her close and suckled and she didn't stop him when he found the waistband of her jeans and quickly removed them from her. Anxious fingers pushed her legs apart to delve into her. She quivered, for it had been so long, but his probing was gentle, at first slowly exploring, then touching that most vital spot in faster and faster strokes until she gasped his name and convulsed before falling atop him.

He kissed her again and gazed into her eyes, silently asking. Without words, begging.

Still drenched in her own sweat, she swallowed against a suddenly dry throat and kissed him. Hard. Without a trace of guilt. Her fingers found the buttons of his shirt and she pushed the soft flannel over his shoulders and down his arms. The smell of fresh air and grass still clung to him and he tasted of salt as she kissed his neck, his shoulders, and then slid down to press her mouth against his flat nipples.

"Oh, baby," he whispered, his fingers tangling in her hair as she teased him and felt him strain upward. "Beth, please..."

Her fingers found the waistband of his shorts and he groaned, whether in agony or pleasure she couldn't tell. "Whatever you want," she whispered against his skin and licked his abdomen.

He shuddered. "I don't know—I'm not sure that I can..."

Stripping him quickly, she lay beside him, naked body next to naked body. "Just lie there," she whispered, her fingers reaching forward to touch him and bring him to a release. "I'll do all the work."

His fingers twined in her hair as he dragged her head closer and his lips found hers. With slow, firm strokes she found a way to ease his pain.

Chapter Eight

Good Lord, what had she done? Nearly made love to Jenner McKee—just like before. As she lay in his arms, listening to his gentle breathing, she wanted to snuggle against him, pretend that everything was right with the world, but she couldn't. She had a son to think about, a life to live. A life that didn't include Jenner.

She reached for her clothes and the strong arm surrounding her tightened. Hand clasped firmly over her breast, Jenner cradled her close.

"I think I'd better go," she said, rolling over to gaze into slumberous blue eyes.

He managed a crooked smile. "So soon?" He shoved a strand of hair from her eyes. "I can think of other things we could do."

She blushed at the turn of her thoughts. "Any more things you come up with, cowboy, can only spell trouble."

"What's wrong with trouble?" He shifted, half-rolling atop her and wincing a little as he moved. His skin was tight over well-defined muscles and his scars from battles with onery rodeo broncs and bulls were barely visible.

"Jenner..."

He dipped his head and, still looking at her, touched the tip of his tongue to her nipple. It hardened immediately, puckering as he gently sawed his teeth against her flesh.

"Please..."

"Please what, love?" he asked, and the endearment tore her apart inside. He didn't love her; never had. In fact, he hadn't even remembered her. Love was just a word he used when he was in bed with a woman. Any woman.

"I have to get back to Cody. You mentioned that there might be danger." She really didn't believe it, but she couldn't take any chances and she needed an excuse to get away.

At the mention of the boy, his muscles flexed and he lifted his head. "I've been thinking about him."

Her heart started to gallop: "And...?"

"I want to see more of him."

Where was this going? She didn't know whether to be elated or worried sick. "Why?"

He snorted. "*If* he is my son—"

"We've been through this before."

"Then I think he and I should spend more time together. What do they call it? Quality time. Yeah, that's it."

She glanced around the unfinished room. "You want me to bring him here?"

"Or the Rocking M." He gazed at her and his smile slid off his face. Hostility flickered in his expression as he, too, took in the bare floor and meager furnishings. "What? This isn't good enough for you?"

"I didn't say that."

"But you thought it."

She reached for her clothes again, but he ripped the sweater from her hands and threw it across the room.

"What is it, Beth? Not what you planned? What did you expect—that after Jonah died, I'd be rich?"

"I didn't expect anything. Your grandmother threatened—"

"Yeah, yeah, I know. But still, when you decided to return, you thought you'd be visiting a wealthy man with a big house and bank account instead of a broken-down, crippled rodeo rider."

"That's not true!" she said angrily as she slipped her arms through the straps of her bra and clasped it into place. "I knew what you were and who you were, Jenner. I had no expectations, not after I talked to your father and found out that you'd just used me for the weekend." She pulled on her sweater, tugging her hair through the boat neck.

"I didn't use you."

"You were still hung up on Nora Bateman, intended to marry her, the way I heard it."

"From Jonah."

"He tipped me off, yeah," she said as she walked to the corner and retrieved her jacket. "But afterward, I listened to the town gossip and discovered that you'd been dating her off and on for years."

"At the time I met you, if in fact we did meet—"

"You still doubt me?" she whispered, flabbergasted. After what they'd just shared, he still didn't believe her?

His brows slammed together and he looked suddenly savage as he reached for his faded Levi's. "To tell you the truth, I don't know what to think. It seems damned convenient that after one weekend together that I can't remember, you end up pregnant, don't bother to tell me because of Jonah, and then once the old man's gone, show up, whether my grandmother wrote you or not." Some of his hostility seemed to fade a little as he wrestled with his jeans. Every time he moved his bad leg, he sucked in his breath and swore roundly. Beads of sweat dotted his brow and his face contorted with the effort.

"Let me help you," she offered, but he sent her a look that could have sliced through granite.

"I can handle it."

"So I've heard. Over and over again. You're so damned set on being independent that you don't care about injuring yourself again."

"Last I checked, it was *my* body. And *my* problem."

"I was only trying to help, Jenner, but obviously you don't want it, so I'll leave." She glanced around the room and shook her head as she reached for the door. "If you want to see Cody again, call."

Heart pounding with anger and some other emotion she didn't dare name, Beth marched outside, pulled the door shut and took several long, deep breaths. She knew she shouldn't leave him—he was in no condition to take care of himself—but she couldn't take any more of his verbal abuse.

Though she'd seen his kind of frustration in patients before, none of those she'd been caring for had been endowed with the ability to wound her as Jenner was doing. She'd been able to fend off their hostility and bad manners and harsh language with a smile or a fast quip. But Jenner was different.

She'd climbed the stairs and started for home, thinking the long walk would do her good, when she decided that there was another option. Turning abruptly, she hurried along a path at the side of the house that turned past a laurel hedge near the back porch and led to the clinic.

A bell sounded as she entered, and a stern-looking receptionist with a name tag reading Madge Bateman looked up from a computer. At the sight of the woman's last name, Beth nearly stumbled. This woman was Nora's aunt.

"You have an appointment?" Madge asked.

"No, but I'd like to see Dr. Donahue."

Madge's no-nonsense expression didn't change. "It'll be awhile. We got patients stacked up for nearly an hour."

"That'll be fine. Tell her Beth Crandall would like to see her."

"Crandall?" Madge's eyes narrowed and she pulled on the glasses that held by a glittery cord were resting against her ample bosom.

"It's personal."

"Personal." Madge, ever unflappable, wrote the message on a pink slip of paper, and with lips pinched a little at the corners, she waved Beth into one of the worn chairs in the waiting area. "I'll let Doctor know you're here."

"Good. Could I use your phone? It's a local call."

With a put-upon expression, Madge turned her phone around. "Dial nine first," she said. Once she connected with Harriet and found out that everything was all right and Cody was napping, Beth felt relieved. Jenner's conversation about danger to her son had worried Beth. Harriet said she had a few errands to run when Cody woke up, but that everything was fine.

After she hung up the phone, Beth thanked Madge, then settled into a chair near a planter and, while trying to stem thoughts of Jenner lying on the floor of his apartment, thumbed through some old newsmagazines.

In less than fifteen minutes, Beth was called to Skye's office. "Come in, come in," the doctor said, waving from her seat behind the desk. A smile stretched across her face. "What's going on?"

Madge closed the door and Beth dropped into a chair. "It's about Jenner."

"Oh." Skye leaned back in her chair and worried a pencil between her fingers. "What's he done?"

"It's what he won't do, which is seek medical attention. He reinjured his leg today and I think you or an orthopedic specialist should have a look at his ankle—maybe his knee— again. I don't know what the ankle looked like before, but, well, I examined it this afternoon and it's definitely swollen and black-and-blue. He's in a lot of pain that he won't own up to and he refuses to have anyone fussing over him."

"Sounds like Jenner." Skye rubbed her jaw thoughtfully. "*You* examined him?"

"I'm a nurse, Dr. Donahue—"

"Call me Skye."

"Okay. I've seen my share of wrenched knees, sprains, torn ligaments and broken bones. Without X rays or an MRI, I wouldn't even hazard a guess as to how bad it is. The leg still supports him—barely—but something's not right. I thought maybe you could take a look at him."

"If he lets me." She chewed on the end of her pencil. "But don't worry about that right now. I'm sure I can find a way to convince him."

"Thanks." Beth stood. "I appreciate it."

"Not at all. Someone's got to take that hardheaded cowboy and tell him what's good for him." She flashed Beth a smile. "It may as well be me!"

Jenner felt like hell. His leg was so stiff, he could barely move, his head throbbed, and he couldn't get Beth out of his mind. She'd left him feeling empty and disgusted with himself. Because of his damned leg, he hadn't been able to get her on her back and make love to her as he'd wanted to. Well, maybe this was better. Maybe now he didn't have to feel so guilty because they hadn't made love. Damned close, but they hadn't really done the deed, though the memory of her caused a tingling deep inside and a want for more. Much more.

It was dark now and he looked around his austere apartment with new eyes. He realized what she saw when she came here. A large, unfinished room in the basement of an old house. No carpet. Not much in the way of appliances or furniture. Hell, he didn't even have a bed he could take her to.

He ran his tongue around his teeth and decided he needed
a drink. A stiff one. Because he had to make some deci-
sions. He struggled to his feet, then flipped on the light and
saw the telephone. Well, it was now or never.

He reached for the receiver and punched out the num-
bers for one Mr. Rex Stone, private investigator. Though it
bothered him more than he wanted to admit, Jenner knew
he had to check out Beth—discover what her plans were,
who she was. For all he knew, she could have a husband or
a boyfriend back in Portland or Oregon City or wherever
the hell it was she called home.

Head throbbing, he waited until the phone was answered
and Rex Stone's too-smooth voice came over the line. But
it wasn't the man himself. Jenner was listening to a damned
tape recorder. He had just left his message and hung up
when he heard light footsteps on the stairs and his stupid
heart kicked a little at the thought that Beth had returned.
A jab of guilt cut through him when he remembered his
message to Rex Stone, but he ignored the pangs.

"It's open," he yelled at the sound of knuckles banging
on the door. Bracing himself against the far wall, he felt a
wave of disappointment when Skye, dressed in her lab coat,
walked into the room.

"Well, well, well," she said. "Rumor has it you reinjured yourself."

"I'm fine."

"Prove it. Walk over here." She stood in the doorway, her
arms crossed, defiance in her eyes.

"What is this?"

"Concern, Jenner. I got a call from Beth. She says you
might need medical attention."

He let out a string of cusswords guaranteed to turn a
sailor's face red, but Skye didn't budge.

"Max is on his way. Either you let us help you into the
clinic where I can examine you, or we'll do it the hard way

and call an ambulance, but let me tell you, you're going to get the help you need.''

"I don't need—"

"Stop it! I'm tired of you telling me how to treat you. *I'm* the doctor here, remember?''

"What I don't remember is calling for one.''

"You're as stubborn as your brother. Probably worse.'' She eyed him up and down, her gaze landing squarely on the leg he favored. ''Now, Jenner, it's either my way or the hard way. What's it going to be?''

"All right, Skye, you can get a thrill and look me over, but I'm *not* going back to any damned hospital, so you'd better be ready to give me a brace and some pills for the pain. I can't be laid up right now.''

"You might not have a choice.''

"That's where you're wrong,'' he said, planting his crutches and dragging himself closer to her although his leg hurt like hell. ''I'm still calling the shots when it comes to my body!''

No one was home when Beth returned to her mother's house, and Beth couldn't sit in the living room alone with her thoughts of Jenner and how easily she could have made love to him. When she remembered their intimacy, how passionate their lovemaking had been, she felt herself blush.

Ever since her weekend with Jenner three years ago, she'd told herself that she'd imagined the heat they'd shared, that the force of their lovemaking had been something she'd created in her mind. But she'd been wrong. Dead wrong.

Even now, at the thought of his hands and mouth touching her, she quivered inside, and a deep longing brought erotic images to her mind. Their hunger and desire three years ago had been real. The lust had been strong. But they hadn't loved each other, just as they didn't love each other now. And that was the root of Beth's problem, for she found it impossible to believe in passion without love. Oh, sure, she knew it existed. All the time. But not for her.

Rather than watch the day settle into night, she found her purse and keys and climbed into her car. She'd drive around Rimrock, reacquaint herself with some of her old haunts, and try like hell to force Jenner McKee from her head.

"You need to see an orthopedist." Skye continued to cluck over him like an old mother hen. In some ways, because of her medical license, she was as bad as his family, always telling him what to do. "Your ankle's probably just sprained, but the knee isn't good."

"That much I know."

"Do something about it, Jenner, or it won't get any better. Call Dr.—"

"Yeah, yeah, I know. Kendrick. The man with all the answers."

"Has anyone ever mentioned that you've got a bad attitude?"

"A few times."

"Okay, so set up an appointment with Kendrick."

"I will," he said with a cocky grin, making a promise that neither one of them believed.

A new leg brace had been fitted over his bum knee as well as another one for his ankle. Although Skye thought both joints were only sprained, that the X rays showed no sign of bone breakage, and that it didn't seem as if any of his ligaments had been torn, she wasn't completely convinced. "The pain pills won't last forever," she warned.

Jenner scowled. "I don't plan to get hooked on any medication, Doc."

"Good. Because if you don't go see Dr. Kendrick at his clinic in Dawson City, I won't give you any more."

"Kendrick's a stuffed shirt."

Skye shook her head and rolled her eyes skyward. "Ron Kendrick's one of the best. Okay, I'll admit his bedside manner isn't particularly kind—"

"It stinks," Jenner said flatly. "The guy's got no sense of humor."

"The important thing is he knows his stuff. You can't find a more capable surgeon anywhere around."

"Thanks, but I'm not looking." Jenner turned toward the door, the edge of his pain dulled by one of the sample tablets Skye had given him. He'd started into the hallway when her voice arrested him.

"Jenner, for your family's sake, take care of yourself."

His jaw tightened as he made his way out of the clinic on the crutches. Damn, he hated anything to do with medicine. Hospitals and clinics, they were too sterile, too cold, too unfeeling. He couldn't imagine Beth working in that kind of environment.

Beth. He couldn't shake her image from his mind—the way she'd gently caressed him, the feel of her tongue against his nipple, the smell of her hair as she'd found a way to pleasure him. He'd wondered over the past few months if he'd ever be able to make love again. She'd shown him that his manhood seemed to be functioning normally. In fact, ever since she'd returned to Rimrock, his hormones had been on overload.

Once outside, he determined to see Beth again and pin her down.

He couldn't leave things the way they were.

The last thing Beth needed was to see Stan's Chrysler parked in the driveway, but there it was, big as life, sitting in the shade of a spruce tree and blocking the view of her mother's flower bed.

A weight settled over her shoulders as she edged her trusty Nova next to the curb, twisted the key in the ignition, and felt the little car's engine shudder to a stop. "I don't think

I'm ready for this," Beth said with a frown. She really didn't want to deal with Stan, not after changing the course of her life forever by becoming intimate with Jenner.

In a few short days, she had let Jenner touch her where Stan had never dared; he was too much a gentleman. The opposite of Jenner McKee. "Come on, Crandall," she told herself. "You can't put this off." With a new sense of determination, she tossed her keys into her purse and headed out.

Inside the house, Harriet sat cross-legged on the floor working a puzzle with Cody. Stan was leaning back in the rocker, one leg propped on a footstool, reading glasses perched on the end of his nose as he perused the local paper. Beth didn't bother closing the door.

Scrambling to his feet, Cody spied her first and cried, "Mommy! Mommy!" He hurled his sturdy little body into her arms. "I ate a waffle this—" he held his arms as wide as they would stretch "—big!"

"Good for you," she said, holding him tightly, her throat suddenly clogged as she remembered Jenner's worries about his safety. Surely there was no reason to think her son was in danger.

Carrying Cody on her hip, she walked into the living room and offered a smile to Stan, who was watching her over the top of his reading glasses. "Hi," she said. "I was surprised to see your car outside."

"I know. I probably should have called but, well, for once I thought what the hell and just took off."

"I couldn't eat it all," Cody said, casting Stan a dark glare.

"What? Oh, the waffle. Well, that's all right. Hey, tell me, did you meet some of Grandma's friends?" she whispered into her son's ear.

"Lots and lots!"

"They thought he was absolutely adorable," Harriet boasted. "Oh, look, here's the duck's beak."

"Me do!" Cody squirmed out of Beth's arms and dashed back to squat near the puzzle and shove the yellow piece firmly into place. "All done!"

"And well done," Harriet said.

"Do 'gain!"

A furrow deepened between Stan's eyesbrows. "Now, Cody, your grandmother's already helped you with it three times since I've been here. Maybe you can think of something else to do."

Harriet laughed as Cody, ignoring Stan, dumped the pieces onto the floor.

"Do 'gain, Gramma."

"Why not?"

"Cody—" Stan began to reproach him in a gentle but firm tone.

"It's all right, Stan." Beth tossed her purse into a corner of the couch and hung her jacket on the coat tree. She wondered how she looked, if she showed any signs that she'd spent the better part of the day with Jenner, most of which was involved in lovemaking.

"You know, Beth, I was worried about you. After the phone call the other morning, I thought I'd better drive over here and see what was wrong."

"Nothing's wrong."

"Nothing? But—" He stopped and cast a glance at Harriet and Cody.

"I guess that's our cue to leave, sport," Harriet said. "Besides, we've got work to do. There's some apples that need to be picked before dark if we're gonna make that pie."

Cody was on his feet in an instant. "Like pie," he said.

"Then come on, we'd better get shakin'." Harriet took his hand and, leaving the puzzle pieces in the middle of the floor, headed through the kitchen and out the back door.

Beth waited to hear the door slam before she let out her breath. This wasn't going to be easy, but she knew, as she'd suspected for a long time, that Stan wasn't the man for her.

And Jenner McKee is?

No! Maybe there was never going to be a man for her.

"Come here," Stan said, and when she didn't move, he walked across the room and took her into his strong arms. Though he was nearing sixty, he kept himself in good shape and could have passed for forty-five. "You scared me, Beth. When you said it was over."

Her heart softened a little. "It scared me, too, Stan," she admitted, carefully sliding out of his arms. "But I think it's for the best."

"The best? Are you out of your mind? I'm crazy about you." He ran a hand through his graying hair. "I . . . I can't imagine what it would be like living without you."

"You did it before."

"And it was hell."

She told herself to be strong, that though she cared for Stan, it wasn't enough. She didn't love him, not as he wanted or needed or ought to be loved. Then there was his problem with Cody. "I'm sorry, Stan," she said, her throat clogging, "but I've thought about it and I can't keep seeing you."

"Why not? Don't you hear me, Beth? Aren't you listening? I love you, I want to marry you, to take care of you and your son."

At one time those words would have been music to her ears, but she'd learned that she could stand on her own, take care of herself, be both mother and father to Cody. She could juggle a job and single motherhood; in fact, she was damned good at it. Her mother was right. She couldn't settle. "I—I've been doing a lot of thinking since I got here, Stan, and it's not working, not for me. And I don't think it's working for you, either."

"You're wrong," he protested, but she noticed the doubt in his eyes.

"What you and I want are worlds apart."

"How can you say that?"

"Please," she said, steeling herself, "let me finish. I want more kids, Stan."

"Good Lord, *why?*"

"It's just the way I feel. Cody needs a sister or a brother and I . . . I would like to be a mother again."

The corners of Stan's mouth pinched, the way they did when Cody made too much noise or demanded too much attention or got in the way when Stan wanted to take her to a movie or a ball game or a restaurant alone. "There's more, isn't there?" he said, his voice suddenly cold, his nostrils twitching as if encountering a bad smell. "You're trying to take up with Cody's father again, aren't you?"

She wanted to lie, to tell him that she didn't care for the man who had sired Cody, that she was willing to turn her back on him. But the truth of the matter was that, if she examined her feelings for Jenner more closely, they were a lot more complicated than she would ever admit. To Stan. Or to herself.

"Oh, God, Beth. Do you know what you're throwing away? All for a man who didn't want you and didn't want his boy."

Beth didn't have time to respond because at that moment she heard the distinctive roar of an old pickup's engine and knew that Jenner had just rounded the corner of the street. Her stomach clenched when she heard the engine die, the slam of a heavy door and the uneven tread of boots hitching up the front walk. Her throat worked for a second. "I'm sorry, Stan," she said with more than a little regret. She had pinned so many hopes on this man, probably been blind to his flaws because she wanted the security of a stable, rock-solid man's love.

A father figure. Not for Cody—but for myself!

Deep inside her, something broke free.

A heavy hand knocked boldly on the frame of the door.

"It's open," she called over her shoulder, and Jenner, crutches thrust out ahead of him, a thunderous expression as dark as the mountains in winter, filled the doorway.

"I didn't think we were finished…" Jenner's voice trailed off and his gaze collided with Stan's for a second, and then, as if he thought the older man was a friend of Harriet's, he forced a grin. "Jenner McKee," he said, hobbling up and extending a hand, even though he was balancing on his crutches.

Stan's eyes narrowed and his gaze slid from the tips of Jenner's dusty boots, up his worn jeans, past his flannel shirt and shadow of a beard, to his eyes—blue as the Oregon sky in June. Stan's nostrils flared as if he smelled something unpleasant, but he extended his hand. "Stanley Cole. I'm a friend of Beth's."

One of Jenner's eyebrows arched. "Of Beth's."

Stan slipped his wallet out of his back pocket and withdrew one of his business cards. "That's right." He handed the embossed card to Jenner. "I'm with the National Insurance Company."

Jenner glanced at Beth as if to ask if this guy was for real.

She didn't move a muscle, just prayed that this whole thing would soon be over. Her palms began to sweat as Jenner flipped the card over once, then lifted his eyes to meet Stan's again. This time his gaze was dark and serious. "I'm a friend of Beth's, too."

"Just a friend?"

"A close friend."

"Jenner, don't—"

"Why not?" Jenner demanded. "Who is this guy?"

"Before she came back here to see you—I assume this is the guy—" he hooked his thumb in Jenner's direction and glanced at Beth who nodded "—Beth and I were planning to get married."

Jenner's mouth flattened into a harsh line.

"That's not true, Stan," Beth interjected. "We'd discussed it, yes, but it wasn't as if we'd even gotten engaged."

"Because of *him*," Stan accused, his furious gaze raking down Jenner again, one finger jabbing the air near Jenner's chest. "Because you never got over him, even though the only thing he did was get you pregnant and dump you."

Jenner moved fast, too fast for a man on crutches, but he kept his balance and swung himself closer to Stan. His eyes were mere slits. "You don't know anything about what happened," he said, his lips barely moving, his eyes bright with anger.

"I know she ended up in Oregon City—*alone.* Had a kid there. And I know that before she came here to see you, she was different."

That much was true. In the days she'd been in Rimrock, she'd changed, become more independent, realized more fully what she wanted out of life. She'd thought once that she could be content with Stan, that she shouldn't expect more out of life than contentment and security. But then she'd met Jenner again and realized there was more. If nothing else, she owed Jenner McKee for making her face up to her own needs and wants as a woman.

"You mixed her up, McKee," Stan charged.

"I'm not mixed up," Beth interjected.

"Maybe you never really knew her," Jenner drawled.

"I think I know her better than some punk cowboy who's..."

"Who's what?" Jenner demanded. "Go ahead and say it. A cripple. That's what you were thinking."

Stan had the decency to close his mouth.

Jenner swung around and faced Beth. "You want this guy?" he asked, pointing a crutch at Stan.

"Jenner I—he's my friend."

"Sure. Well, lady, it's your choice. If you want to marry the insurance man, no one's going to stop you." His eyes narrowed on her, but the blue flames of anger were still visible.

"I'm not marrying anyone," she said firmly. "I don't need a man—"

"Then why'd you come back here?" Jenner asked, cutting her off.

"For God's sake, Beth, he can't talk to you like that."

"Maybe it would be better," she said, more calmly than she felt as her insides were quivering in rage, "if you both left."

The back door squeaked, and Cody, an apple with a tiny bite out of it in one hand, streaked into the room. He saw Jenner and slid to a stop. "You here 'gain?"

Stan stiffened. Beth, sending both men a glare meant to keep them quiet, bent down on one knee. "It's polite to say hello," she said, her heart thudding wildly.

"'Lo."

"He doesn't know?" Stan asked. This time Jenner's harsh glare shut him up.

"Know what?" Cody asked innocently.

"That Stan's leaving, honey." Beth picked her son off the floor and tried to paste a composed, friendly smile on her face, though she seethed inside. "Say goodbye."

"Bye-bye." Cody moved the fingers of his free hand up and down in a wave.

Stan sent Beth a withering look. "All right. You've made your decision. But when it doesn't work out with the local yokel and you fall into a million pieces, don't expect me to pick them up again."

"I won't," she answered quietly and flinched as Stan stormed out of the house, the door banging shut behind him.

"He mad," Cody observed.

"Very."

Jenner hooked an insolent thumb in the direction Stan had taken. "*That's* the kind of man you've been dating?"

"The only man," she said, still holding Cody so tightly that her son squirmed in her arms. Every other man who'd shown interest in her hadn't accepted Cody and looked upon her son as extra baggage. She hadn't expected the same from Stan.

"Sheesh." He watched through the window as Stan slid into a shiny new Chrysler, started the engine and pulled a U-turn on his way out of town. "That guy's old enough to be—"

"Don't say it," she snapped. "He's a good man. This wasn't one of his better days."

"I hope not." Jenner's gaze lingered on Beth's face for a second longer than necessary before sliding over to Cody's. "How ya doin', sport?" he asked. Cody tilted up his face to stare at Jenner.

"Why you got those?" He pointed at the crutches. "You hurt?"

"A little bit."

"And that." Cody eyed the brace quizzically, dropping the apple in his curiosity. He poked at the straps and padding. "I wear."

Jenner snorted a humorless laugh. "Believe me, you wouldn't want to."

"It wouldn't fit, anyway," Beth said as she stood and straightened her sweater—the same sweater that Jenner had pulled over her head and tossed into the corner of his apartment. At that particular thought, her throat turned to sand and she couldn't find her tongue for a second.

Jenner turned his intense gaze on her again and she hazarded a quick glance at his face. What she saw there caught her breath, for the look he sent her was all male and sensuous, as if what had happened between them this afternoon was just a sample of what would happen, if she let it. She cleared her throat and said, "Well, since you didn't take my advice and leave, I guess I could offer you something cold to drink."

Cody, oblivious to the silent message between his mother and his new friend, said, "We ride horses?"

"Wh-what?" Beth said.

"Horses," Cody repeated, his brows knitting in frustration. "Ride."

"Oh, I don't think—"

"Sure," Jenner cut in. "How about tomorrow?"

"Jenner, it's not a good idea. He's too young."

"I was riding by myself by the time I was three."

"Yeah, but he's only two and you're certifiable, remember?"

"Come on, Beth. This is what you wanted, wasn't it?" he asked, the mockery in his face undisguised.

She couldn't answer. For the first time in a long while, Beth Crandall wasn't sure what she wanted.

Chapter Nine

"I didn't expect anything so soon," Jenner said as Rex Stone slid a manila envelope across the polished mahogany top of his desk. They were seated in the private investigator's office in Dawson City. His back to the only window, Rex was wedged into a tufted leather chair positioned behind the desk. Jenner was on the far side, in a smaller, less-imposing chair. He picked up the envelope and fingered the corners, feeling an unexpected ton of guilt settle squarely on his shoulders.

"It's just preliminary. A little background on Ms. Crandall. I can dig deeper, but I thought we'd start here and you could tell me if you wanted more. Didn't want to waste your money."

Jenner doubted that. He was certain that Rex had no qualms whatsoever of spending anyone else's cash. Nonetheless, he ripped open the envelope with his finger and slipped out the contents: copies of report cards from Rimrock High School, transcripts from Eastern Oregon College, several pictures of Beth as a student and later as she recieved her R.N. degree at the University of Oregon Nursing School. He also saw copies of her birth certificate, driver's license, social security card and a résumé of her employment record. But the document that fascinated him most was Cody Crandall's birth certificate. Beth's name was listed in full, but the space for his father's name was blank, as if the man had never existed.

Jenner's fist closed over the papers. He felt like a goddamned Peeping Tom, peering into Beth's private life behind her back. He might as well be standing on the dark side of a window, peering through the blinds, watching her undress.

"The thing that I found interesting," Rex said as he picked up a letter opener and began cleaning his thumbnail, "is that the blood type fits. The kid could be your son. But unless you want to go through all that DNA garbage, you only have her word." He flicked off a bit of smut that he'd dislodged from his nail. "So... what do you want me to do? I also did a little checking to see if she was involved with any man three years ago, just in case there was an obvious boyfriend that we could pin the kid's paternity on. No such luck."

"Good." Jenner's gut twisted.

Was Cody really his son? Did it even matter?

Jenner rubbed the new growth of beard shading his jaw.

"Good? You want the kid to be yours?"

Good question. "I don't know," he said, but deep down he knew the truth. He wanted to claim that fair-haired piece of mischief as his own, and the thought of Beth being with any other man disgusted him.

Rex leaned forward, placing his elbows on the desk. "I can keep digging, you know. It's fascinating how some people appear so ordinary and normal on the surface, but underneath they're entirely different people. I followed one woman—a schoolteacher, no less. Came from a good family, had a loving husband, two kids, even a dog. Ended up she'd been having not one affair but *two* for years. Just to spice up her life. The husband was the last to know."

Jenner thought he might be sick. "This is enough," he said, pushing himself upright and balancing on his good leg. He shoved the papers back into the envelope, folded the packet and tucked it into an inner pocket of his jacket.

"Have you talked to your brother lately?" Rex asked.

Jenner pinned the P.I. with his intense stare. The only conversation he'd had with Max was about him going to the hospital. It hadn't ended well. "Why? What's up?"

Rex smiled, his pudgy face stretching like kid's clay. "That reward we offered is generating a lot of interest."

"I'll bet. Every two-bit con artist in the state is probably coming up with stories just to get his hands on it."

"We'll have to weed through the fakes. That's not so hard, but we might just get ourselves a concrete lead or two." He rubbed his fleshy hands together in anticipation. "Even Hammond Polk thinks we might flush out a suspect or two."

"Sure he does—he's up for reelection soon and doesn't want to lose his cushy sheriff's job."

Nodding goodbye to the P.I., Jenner left the tiny suite of offices on the third floor. The entire conversation with Stone settled like lead in his gut. First there was the matter of the reward; Jenner was against it. The last thing his family or the Rocking M needed was a crowd of near criminals trying to find ways to get to the reward money. His mother, grandmother and Casey were alone in the ranch house every night, miles from town, with only Jonah's old Winchester and an ancient dog for protection—not that those women usually needed any.

Then there was the matter with Beth. Rex Stone, because of Jenner's request to find out the truth about Beth had just assumed Jenner wanted to prove that she was a self-serving gold digger willing to use her child to get a little fast cash from the McKee bank. But Jenner, who had once assumed the same wasn't so certain now. She seemed to love that kid so much; it couldn't be an act. Or could it? Or could she love the kid enough to do anything, including pawning him off on some unsuspecting cowboy, to assure the kid a secure future?

Hadn't the old man—Stan Whatever—said that he and Beth had planned to be married? He seemed to believe it even if Beth had denied it up and down. Would she have sold herself to a man more than twice her age just to provide for her little boy? The thought of Stan and Beth together made Jenner's blood run cold, but, if he was honest with himself, it wasn't so much Stan or his age that got to him, it was the fact that Beth had been involved with another man. Any man. "You're an ass, McKee," he grumbled, and a slim woman standing next to him in the elevator glanced his way.

"Pardon me?" she asked, her perfume hanging on the air, her blond hair sweeping her shoulders.

"Sorry. Talkin' to myself."

She favored him with a smile that would have, at one time, ignited something within him. "I do it, too. More often than I'd like to admit."

He shrugged and turned away. The attractive woman held no interest for him—not like she would have a few weeks ago. Not like she would have before Beth Crandall had marched into the den of the Rocking M and announced they'd had a brief, hot, one-night stand and now were the parents of a two-year-old scamp named Cody.

Could the kid really be his? He was starting to believe it. Otherwise, Beth was taking a helluva risk, including scandal, because these days it was pretty easy to prove paternity. Hell, what a mess. What a goddamned, no-easy-way-out, gut-churning mess!

The elevator stopped and he maneuvered his way through a crowd who'd been waiting for the car. Most people gave him the right-of-way because of his crutches, and he didn't know which he minded worse, the do-gooders who stepped aside and offered tentative, pitying smiles, or the hard-nosed, self-important jerks who took no heed of his . . . his what? *Disability?*

His stomach soured. Surely he wouldn't be disabled for life. His blood congealed at the thought and he shoved it aside. Maybe Skye and Beth and his whole damned family was right. Maybe he should go back to that orthopedic snob and sign himself up for the physical therapy he'd signed himself out of.

"Here you go." An old lady walking a dog no bigger than a rat held the door for him and he cringed inside.

He wanted to shout out that he could damned well handle the door himself, but instead he forced a cold grin and tipped his head. "Thanks."

"No trouble. Come along, Felix," she said with a winning seventy-year-old's grin as she tugged on the rat's leash. With a yip it headed into the building.

Outside, the day had turned cloudy with gusts of wind blowing down from the north. Any hint of summer seemed to have fled with the dry leaves scurrying across the street and the smell of rain in the air. Jenner climbed into his truck and glanced up at the offices of Rex Stone. The guy gave him the creeps. Stone seemed to *enjoy* digging into the dirt surrounding a person. But he wasn't just interested. No his fascination stemmed from some kind of deep need to prove that other people had failings—big-time failings.

Jabbing the key into the ignition and pumping the gas pedal, Jenner glanced in the rearview mirror and caught a glimpse of himself. Unshaven and weathered, squinting hard, he wasn't a pretty sight, and not much better than Rex Stone. Hadn't he ordered the investigation of Beth Crandall?

"Damn it all, anyway," he muttered as he eased the truck into the uneven flow of traffic in downtown Dawson City.

Shrugging his shoulders—as if he could shake the feeling of being akin to a snake like Stone—didn't help, and the investigator's report felt like a dead weight in his pocket. He'd never liked this slimy little P.I., but Rex was necessary it seemed to find out who was behind his father's death.

He pushed the speed limit and chewed on his lower lip. What if this mess about the murder was true? What if someone was really after the McKees? What if they'd stop at nothing to get their revenge or whatever it was they wanted? What if Cody and Beth were in danger?

"You promised!" Cody insisted, his lower lip protruding petulantly.

"I said I'd think about it. That's not a promise."

"But I want horse ride!"

Beth gritted her teeth. Sometimes her boy could be so stubborn. *Just like his father!* The father who was definitely to blame in this case for offering to teach Cody to ride. A two-year-old! While the orthopedist was checking out his leg, Jenner McKee should have a neurosurgeon examine his head. "Look, I said we'd go out to the ranch this afternoon and I'll take you, but it's not time yet."

"When?"

"In a couple of hours."

"Now!" Cody protested. Beth decided he needed a nap. It was barely noon, but he was showing all the classic signs of being overly tired. He rubbed his eyes and stuck out his lower lip, looking more like Jenner than ever.

Jenner. Beth's heart seemed to clench each time she thought of him. He was the reason she was sticking around. By all rights, she should be returning to Oregon City and starting to look seriously for a new job. The little bit of savings she'd put away wouldn't last forever and she needed to get on with her life. She'd done her duty by the McKees; now it was time to start over.

Except she couldn't. Not until things were settled with Jenner and Cody. She carried her son into the back bedroom but when he saw the playpen, he balked. "Nooo!" he wailed, sounding like a siren. "No. No. No!"

"Come on, sweetheart," she cajoled, grateful that they were alone in the house. Her mother, bless her, had infinite patience with her headstrong grandson, but Zeke wasn't as understanding. He'd made a couple of comments and glared at Cody enough times to let Beth know they were about to wear out their welcome.

"Nonsense," her mother had insisted when Beth had mentioned it, but her smile hadn't been quite as wide as usual and Beth knew that Harriet, though she protested, was feeling the strain, as well. Yep, soon it would be time to go home.

Home. And where was that? The tiny apartment overlooking the Willamette River, where the sound of traffic was steady all night long? Or here in Rimrock, where the sky seemed to stretch forever and the moutains loomed like craggy sentinels and she knew many of the townspeople on a first-name basis.

Was home Oregon City, where she was anonymous and her son would grow up without a father, without many questions being asked, where many of his friends would also have single mothers?

Or here. Where everyone would know that he was Jenner McKee's bastard son? That his mother had been unmarried when she'd given birth? Would he grow up knowing that his mother and father had never really been in love and that his conception was just a mistake of white-hot lovemaking for a single weekend? What if Jenner married and had other children?

"Read!" Cody demanded, and Beth was grateful to turn her thoughts away from Jenner and concentrate on the worn pages of a collection of fairy tales, the same book that her mother had read to her. The pages were smudged, the cloth-bound cover ripped, crayon marks scattered throughout and corners of the most loved passages torn. She'd grown up with these fairy tales, believing her mother's soothing voice as she'd read about castles and princesses and enchanted frogs who, with a single kiss, could be changed into the handsome, rich son of a king.

They were silly, childish stories and still they rested deep in her heart. Didn't she, a grown woman, still believe? Wouldn't she always?

Jenner parked his truck near the garage and glanced past the barn to the dry fields where the horses turned their noses to the wind, ears flicking, as they smelled the approach of the storm. A few anxious nickers rippled on the breeze and the younger colts, tails aloft, raced along the fence line, bucking and rearing and feeling the energy in the air.

He felt the storm approaching, too. The wind was picking up, tossing the branches of a pine tree near the garage and shifting the old weather vane on the roof of the barn. He'd always liked the excitement a thunderstorm brought with it and he anticipated the sizzle of lightning streaking across the sky, looked forward to the crack of thunder rolling over the valley.

Hired hands on horseback sorted through paddocks of cattle, separating the heifers from the young bulls. A couple of other men were among the hands—new cowboys he didn't recognize. One sat atop the fence, another leaned against the barn. Both seemed vigilant, but not all that interested in working with the stock.

He felt a drip of apprehension in his spine. Something wasn't right and it wasn't just the approaching storm that caused the hairs on the back of his neck to raise.

In the near paddock, Dani Stewart, Skye's younger sister, was working with Max's daughter. The fiesty five-year old was astride a docile gelding named Cambridge. Over the protests of his ex-wife, Colleen, Max had presented the palomino to Hillary on her fifth birthday. The stirrups were so high they looked comical, but Hillary was serious about riding. Even though she'd had a terrorizing experience during the fire, when she'd been trapped in the stables with Dani as they'd brushed Cambridge after a lesson, Hillary was persistent and claimed that she wanted to be a trick rider someday, just as Dani had once been.

Jenner climbed out of his truck, smelled the scent of ash and charred wood that still lingered after the fire, and pocketed his keys.

Dani's voice carried on the wind. "That's it, Hillary. Show him who's boss." With a quick little kick, the girl urged the horse into a trot. "Take control. There ya go."

Again Hillary gave a nudge of her heels. Flicking his tail, the horse broke into a slow gallop much to Hillary's delight. "Faster!" she cried, her brown curls bouncing in the brisk breeze. "Come on, faster!"

"I don't think so." Dani watched her small charge carefully. "Come on, slow him down. Pull back on the reins easy now. Don't hurt him. I swear, Hillary, someday you're going to be the best cowgirl in the county!"

Hillary giggled at the praise, then reluctantly obeyed and slowed Cambridge into a trot, then a walk.

"That's about it," Dani said, and Hillary's face fell.

"One more time," she begged. "Please."

Dani checked her watch and shook her head. "I can't, hon, really. I'm supposed to be at the Purcell place in fifteen minutes and it'll take me twenty to get there. So come on, you help me with the saddle and bridle." She looked up as Jenner hobbled to the fence. At the sight of his crutches, she winced. She, too, had nearly lost her life in the fire.

"Jeez, are you still on those?" she asked as she uncinched the saddle.

"For a while yet. Here, let me help you—"

Her gaze stopped him cold. "I can handle it," she assured him as she swung the saddle from the horse's back and plopped it onto the top rail of the fence. "I do this for a living, y'know."

"So I've heard," he drawled.

"Just because I'm a woman—"

"It has nothing to do with that, Dani. Okay? Give it a rest. I only wanted to help."

She lifted a shoulder. "Well, I don't need it, but thanks, anyway." She yanked the blanket from Cambridge's back and told Hillary to run into the barn and fetch a curry-comb.

A pretty woman with curly red-blond hair and eyes the color of whiskey, she had a temper that was legendary. Years before, there had been rumors about her. She'd been wild. A party girl. Someone you could call for a good time. Or so the town gossip mill had insisted, though Jenner didn't know anyone who'd actually taken her out.

Now, she was a strong woman who, in Jenner's opinion, married the wrong man. Jeff Stewart was one year younger than Jenner and seemed to spend more than his share of time on a bar stool at the Black Anvil flirting with the single women who happened in.

Jenner knew. He'd been there himself.

Hillary returned with brush and comb and both she and Dani started working on the gelding. "That's it," Dani encouraged as Hillary, tongue angled out of her mouth, tried her best to groom the horse. Jenner leaned against the top rail of the fence, watching his niece wrestle with a knot in Cambridge's tail.

"Be careful," Dani said. "He's even-tempered, but even the best horses have been known to kick."

The knot gave way and Hillary dropped her brush onto the ground. "All done," she announced.

"Good job." Dani was still brushing the palomino's hide. She glanced up at Jenner. "I don't know if I ever really thanked you for—"

Jenner waved off her words. "It was nothing."

She rolled her eyes to the darkening heavens. "Hear that, Hillary? He thinks saving our lives was nothing."

"That's because Uncle Jenner's full of B.S."

"Says who?" Jenner asked, and reached over the fence to swing the little girl into the air. She gave out a whoop of delight while he tried to ignore the shaft of pain that sliced down his leg. The screen door banged, and from the corner of his eye, Jenner watched Max stride across the parking lot. His face was stern and set, his mouth an angry line.

"Mommy says."

It figured. These days Colleen Smith didn't have anything good to day about the McKee family. "Well, tell your mommy that I think—"

"Don't say anything," Max warned his brother as he approached. He winked at his daughter. "When you go back to Mommy's, you tell her that you had a nice time and that you were safe, okay?" Max shot his brother a look that warned him not to argue.

Jenner wasn't having any of it. He gave Hillary a hug. "You tell your mom that you're a brave girl and that you can handle a horse as good as the best of 'em. And you tell her Uncle Jenner said so."

"I will," Hillary pronounced with a mischievous grin cast in her father's direction.

Jenner couldn't let it go. "And let her know she's right. I am full of B.S."

"He means hot air," Max said quickly, "but since you're relaying messages, Hillary, tell Mommy that Uncle Jenner's a troublemaker who doesn't know when to keep his big mouth shut... No, on second thought, just tell her you had a great time while you were here at the ranch. She doesn't need to know all the details." Max lifted Hillary from his brother's arms and squeezed her in a gentle hug. "So, how'd the lesson go?"

"Great. Hillary's a natural," Dani said as she unbuckled the bridle, and Cambridge, glad to be rid of the straps of leather, snorted, tossed his head, and took off, bucking and running to the far side of the corral. Hanging the bridle on a fence post, Dani sighed. "I guess he's glad the lesson's over."

"How about you?" Max asked.

"Me? Naw. I could do this all day." Dani climbed over the fence, dusted her hands on her jeans, and pulled a set of keys from her pocket. "I'll be back next week." She managed a smile for her enthusiastic student. "Practice if you can and when you're done, you put Cambridge away. Make sure that he's taken care of. Cooled off and brushed. Don't let your dad do it for you." With a wave she climbed into her dusty Bronco.

As Dani drove off, Max set Hillary on the ground and rumpled her wild curls. "Why don't you see if you can wangle a piece of Kiki's pie from her?"

"She made pie?"

"Apple and blackberry."

"I want both."

"Good luck," Max said, and Jenner smothered a smile. Kiki was outwardly gruff, complaining about kids these days being spoiled, but the old cook had a soft spot in her heart for all the McKee children and grandchildren—she'd even done her share of the spoiling. Jenner guessed that with one sly little look, Hillary would have all the pie she wanted.

Hillary took off in a cloud of dust, her tiny red boots pounding the dry earth, her hair streaming behind her, Max followed her with his eyes, his grin suddenly wide and proud, and Jenner understood, really understood, the bond between father and child for the first time in his life.

Because he might just have a child of his own.

He shoved his hands into the front pockets of his jeans. "I'm here about work," he said.

Max eyed his crutches, and the smile that he'd had on his face for Hillary, disappeared. "You can't—"

"I damned well can, Max. I told you I'm tired of being a charity case." That much was true. He wanted to work, needed to feel his hands doing something, anything, to get rid of the restless energy in his blood. There was another problem, as well. He wanted to be closer to the Rocking M, to the investigation into his father's murder because of the worries that gnawed at the back of his brain—worries about Beth and Cody's safety. "Just because I'm on crutches doesn't mean I'm useless."

"I know, but you should take your doctor's advice and—"

"To hell with my doctors! I want to work, and I'm gonna do it. Either here or someplace else." That was stretching the truth a bit, but he didn't care. "I already told you—"

"Okay," Max said, his eyes narrowing. "You can have your old job at the ranch back. You know it's waiting for you, anyway, but you've got to agree to keep seeing the physical therapist and the doctor."

"You can't tell me—"

"I can and I will. As long as you work for the Rocking M—" Max bit back the words. "Oh, hell, Jenner, just use your head for something other than a spot to hang your hat." He ran stiff fingers through his hair and cast a wary glance toward the dark-bellied clouds moving slowly across the sky. "Besides, I need you around. We got problems."

"That much I know."

"All of a sudden we've got more witnesses than we can handle—witnesses who claim they know who killed Dad and started the fire."

Jenner's muscles tensed. "You believe 'em?"

"None so far. All just fortune hunters."

"Big surprise."

"But we're generating a helluva lot of interest."

Jenner's mouth curved into a cynical smile. "Ain't it amazing what a few dollars can do?"

"I'm not taking any chances. I hired a couple of security guards to keep an eye on things. Chester's not too happy about it, but I think they'll work out."

Jenner glanced back at the two cowboys who didn't quite fit in, undoubtedly the men who were supposed to guard the ranch. From whom? Who was out to get the McKees?

So Max was concerned enough to take some extra precautions. That worried Jenner. It worried him a lot.

The first drops of rain plopped against the Nova's windshield as Beth parked her car next to Jenner's truck. The sky was slate gray, the clouds shifting in the rain. Any plans for Cody to go riding would have to be postponed now. She didn't like thinking about arguing with her two-year-old, who wouldn't understand that sometimes promises had to be altered. No, she thought as she glanced at her son asleep in the car seat, Cody would give her a hard time when she tried to explain about the weather.

Great.

He barely roused as she unbuckled his seat belt, pulled up the hood on his sweatshirt and dashed through the raindrops to the front porch. With her free hand, she rang the bell as Cody yawned and settled against her shoulder.

The door opened and Jenner stood framed in the doorway. Backlit by the lights in the hall, he seemed as rugged as the rocky gorge of Wildcat Creek. For a brief second, they stared at each other, gazes touching, Beth remembering what it was like for his work-roughened hands to caress her skin. Her throat was suddenly dry and she licked her lips nervously as he stood aside.

"Come on in." He held the door for her and she walked into the fortress of the Rocking M. "Great day for a ride, eh?"

"You explain it to him."

"Thanks a lot," he said sarcastically. "Everyone's in the den."

Beth wasn't sure she was ready for 'everyone,' but she took a deep breath and walked into the room. A fire crackled against pitchy wood and gave the room warmth against the coming storm. Beth's spine stiffened when she saw Virginia, huddled in a corner of the couch, her face without a trace of warmth. Max was seated behind the desk and Mavis rocked in a chair near the fire. At the sight of Cody, the little old lady found her cane, stood stiffly, and made her way across the room. "Well, here he is," she said as Cody's eyes blinked against the soft lights. "Been sleeping, haven't you?"

"He's usually a little grouchy when he wakes up," Beth cautioned.

"Am not!" Cody's expression was dark and mistrusting. "Not grouchy!" He clung to her.

"It's all right." But she felt as if she was lying because the hostility in the room fairly sizzled.

Mavis knew when to retreat. "Well, when you wake up, dumpling, come on over and see me. I think we have a book to read or—"

"No!"

"It'll just be a few minutes," Beth apologized, embarrassed at Cody's behavior. He was only two, but she wanted him to show his best side, to be the adorable little boy she loved, to prove to the whole McKee family that he was as special and bright as she thought he was.

But why? So they would accept him? Part of her heart squeezed as she saw the censure in Virginia's features. She would never love this boy, nor would she ever believe that he was her grandson. And Beth would never put Cody in a position where he was judged by a bitter woman who couldn't face the truth.

"He just needs some time to wake up," she explained to Mavis, who, diametrically opposed to her daughter-in-law, seemed anxious to welcome the boy into her family.

Mavis crackled a laugh. "Don't we all? Sometimes I'm a little grumpy when I first wake up. So was that son of mine, rest his soul."

The room turned suddenly quiet at the mention of Jonah, as if his ghost had entered the room.

"Oh, Lord," Virginia whispered.

Jenner, shifting his body so that he stood between Beth and his mother, ruffled Cody's head. "I think I promised you a horseback ride."

Beth's stomach clenched. "But it's raining."

"Never stopped a good cowboy."

Cody managed a shy smile. "I ride?"

"Right now, if you want to."

Beth felt everyone's gaze rest on her. "I don't—"

Jenner grabbed her arm and turned her toward the door. "We'll discuss it in the barn." With a glance over his shoulder, he said to his brother. "We'll be back in a little while. Beth and Cody are staying for dinner."

"Oh, no—" Beth protested.

"Of course you are." Resting both hands on her cane, Mavis beamed while Virginia's eyes slid away to stare out the window at the darkening countryside.

"Glad to have you," Max said, though his smile seemed a little forced.

Outside, Jenner moved quickly, and Beth, protecting Cody's face with her body, dashed across the parking lot. Rain splattered against the pavement and pounded on her head as she ducked into the barn. Jenner switched on the lights and the fresh scent of rainwater was overcome by the odors of horses, dung and dust.

"We used to let the cattle in here, but until the new stables are built, Max keeps only the most valuable horses inside." Where there had once been a large area for the cattle to mingle and feed, there were now new stalls constructed out of fresh lumber, individual boxes that broke up the large space. Horses snorted and hooves rustled in the straw.

"Lots of horses!" Cody said, his eyes round with wonder.

Jenner paused near a small box with a palomino gelding. "This guy—" he hooked a thumb at the horse "—isn't worth all that much, but he belongs to Hillary, Max's daughter. Docile as a lamb. Come on, fella, let's give you a thrill."

Rather than protest, Beth relinquished her baby to the strong arms of his father and watched as Jenner, without his crutches, opened the stall gate, braced himself on the rails and limped through. He placed a beaming Cody on the palomino's bare back and was rewarded with a grin that stretched across Cody's face.

"Hang on . . . and be careful." Jenner kept a firm grip on his son's back. "Now, don't kick old Cambridge."

"I ride, Mommy!" Cody announced proudly.

"You sure are."

"Take a handful of his mane—this stuff—so you won't fall off. There ya go."

"I not fall!"

"I've said that before and been wrong. Got the scars to prove it."

All of Beth's apprehensions fell away. Jenner's hands were always on the boy, and the horse was calmer than any she'd ever seen. Cambridge's eyelids nearly drooped and one back leg cocked as Cody sat, short legs barely able to straddle the gelding.

"What you need is a pony," Jenner said.

"And a puppy!"

"That, too."

"Wait a minute," Beth said, though she couldn't help the warm feeling in her heart as she watched Jenner smile at his boy. "My apartment barely holds the two of us. I don't think it could handle a dog or a horse. Besides, the manager might object."

"I want!"

"I should strangle you right here and now, Jenner McKee," she said, but she couldn't keep the corners of her mouth from twitching into an unwanted smile.

"Like to see you try," Jenner drawled, his gaze suddenly intense enough that she could barely breathe and the large barn seemed to close in. "The results could be interesting, but you might get caught," he warned.

"Caught?"

"Mmm. By the law."

She couldn't stop the pulse at her throat from fluttering. "Justifiable homicide," she said quickly. "Any mother on the jury would agree with me."

His lips curved into a sexy smile.

"Ride outside!" Cody said.

"Not now. It's raining."

"Ride outside!"

"Tell ya what." Jenner's attention was focused on his boy and Beth thought her heart might break as she watched father and son communicate. "You come back here tomorrow, and if the sun's out, I'll see that you ride outside."

"Now!"

"Can't happen now, cowboy," Jenner said. "This here horse's tired, gonna take himself a nap. But when he wakes up tomorrow, he'll be roarin' to go. Then you can ride him."

Cody might have argued his case longer but the door to the barn swung open, and Casey, along with Hillary, hurried in. Wind whipped through the building, scattering loose hay and dust.

"Hey! That's *my* horse," the five-year-old proclaimed, her face knotting into an angry scowl. "Cambridge is mine. My daddy gave him to me."

One of Jenner's eyebrows rose. "And now you're sharin' him for a few minutes."

"I don't wanna share him!"

"Hey, Hillary, is that any way to act?" Casey said with a mock frown. "You're a big girl. You can share."

"Not Cambridge!" she said stubbornly as she crossed her arms over her chest and glared at the usurper astride her horse.

Jenner lifted Cody from the gelding's back. "Haven't I shared my horse with you?"

"Yes, but—"

"We've been riding and I never complained, did I?"

"It's not the same!" Hillary said, her little lips tightening over her teeth, her eyes sparking with fire. "He should have asked."

"That's right and it's my fault. I apologize," Jenner said. "Next time I'll ask."

"Hey, come on, let's not get into a tiff." Casey smiled at Beth and rolled her eyes. "Hillary and I thought that Cody might want to see the new kittens."

"Kitties?" Cody asked.

"Yup. Five of 'em. On the back porch."

"I see!"

"But you have to promise not to touch them, okay?" Casey said gently. "The mama cat, she can be mean when she wants to and she won't want you to disturb them. They're only a few weeks old."

Cody squirmed out of Jenner's arms, much to Hillary's obvious relief. She stopped glaring at her uncle as Cody's feet touched the floor and he raced out of the barn.

"Hey, wait up!" Casey took hold of Hillary's hand and they ran from the barn together. Beth started after them, but Jenner clamped a hand over her arm, forcing her to spin up against him.

"Wha—" she said as his head lowered quickly and his lips captured hers in a kiss that seemed to draw the breath from her lungs. When she lifted her head, her heart was knocking and her bones felt weak. Jenner, as he braced himself against the wall, pulled her closer still, so that her legs fit between his. "But Cody—" she said, motioning toward the door.

"Will be fine. Casey's got a way with kids."

"He doesn't know her very well."

"Won't matter." He looked at her long and hard. Her insides seemed to melt under his direct gaze and she licked her lips. With a groan, he kissed her again, his arms wrapping around her, his mouth branding hers with his own unique taste. The floor seemed to shift beneath her feet and she sagged against him.

Don't do this, Beth. Don't get involved with him again.

But she was already involved. As much as she wanted to deny what she felt for him, it was impossible. His lips were hungry and hard, his hands flat against her back. The outside of her legs rubbed against the inside of his, denim moving against denim, creating friction, creating heat.

Beth closed her eyes as he drew her shirt from the waistband of her jeans, and his fingers crawled up her ribs, searching and exploring. In frustration, he worked at the buttons of her shirt, parting the soft flannel and reaching inside to cup both breasts in his palms, pushing them upward so that they nearly spilled out of her bra. Groaning, he buried his face in the deep cleft he'd created and his breath was hot and wet against her skin, causing a tingle to race through her nerves. Her insides turned to molten wax.

He kissed the top of each mound while his thumbs, through the lacy fabric of her bra, teased her nipples. Inside she was burning, and when he touched a nipple with his tongue, her back bowed, her fingers twined in his hair, and she drew his head closer still, cradling him against her, feeling his tongue and mouth suckling through the lace.

"Beth," he growled, "sweet, sweet Beth." He found the clasp of her bra, unhooked it, and let her breasts swing free. With eager haste, he pulled off her shirt and the flimsy scrap of lace, then began his ministrations again. This time he kissed her, flesh against flesh, wet tongue on anxious nipple, hands splayed over her spine, one between her shoulder blades, the other at the small of her back, his fingertips brushing under the waistband of her jeans.

A sensual, moist heat swirled inside her and she rubbed against him, wanting more, needing to feel all of him. Her fingers worked at the buttons of his shirt and soon she'd discarded it onto the hay-strewn floor with her blouse. His hands burrowed lower, past her waistband, to her buttocks, and she gasped when he reached into her panties, delving to the moist cleft that awaited him.

"Beth..." His finger plunged deep into her and she was on her toes, bracing herself with her hands on his shoulders. "Make love to me."

"Here?" she whispered, vaguely aware that it was dangerous, that anybody could come along and open the door.

"Anywhere." His mouth found hers and cut off further protest as his fingers delved and retreated and delved again, and she moved against him, wanting more, images of their sweaty, naked bodies swimming in her mind. He touched her in that oh so sensitive spot and she bucked, arched against him, rubbed her jeans against the bulge in his. Her fingers dug into his shoulders as her body, like a tightly coiled spring, suddenly found release in a burst of ecstasy that brought beads of perspiration to her face. Her mouth found his and she kissed him hard with a fierce abandon that she couldn't deny.

She reached for his zipper, but he grabbed her wrist. "This...isn't enough," he said, his eyes mirroring her own feelings. "I want more."

"I—"

"I want all of you, Beth." His voice was a raspy whisper that seemed to echo in her soul. "I want to make love to you. All night long. Over and over again until we see the morning together."

She sagged against him and pressed her lips to his neck. "I want it, too." Though she knew she was playing with fire, that she most certainly would be burned, she couldn't resist.

"Soon," he promised, kissing her crown. "Very soon."

"You know, I'm looking for another nurse at the clinic," Skye said, her smile infectious as she stared across the table at Beth. The entire McKee family was seated around the long dining-room table, which was laden with roast pork, potatoes, squash, beans, fruit salad and fresh hot rolls. Max sat between Skye and Hillary, across from Jenner, Cody and Beth. Virginia and Mavis were seated at opposite ends of the table and Casey was wedged between Hillary and Kiki, who, as Beth understood it, was considered part of the family. Reaching for her water glass, Skye continued, "I thought you might be interested in the job."

Conversation and the ever-present sound of flatware scraping against plates seemed to stop. Beth felt Jenner's gaze move toward her. "I don't know how long I'll be in Rimrock," she managed to say. "I've got a place in Oregon City."

Skye lifted a shoulder. "No law says you can't move. I pay the same scale as the city, but the cost of living is cheaper out here." She winked at Beth. "You might want to apply."

From the corner of her eye, Beth saw one of Jenner's eyebrows rise in expectation. "I'll think about it," she said, "but Cody and I are pretty settled."

She couldn't read Jenner's expression, but she felt his hand slide over to grip her thigh.

Virginia seemed to breathe a sigh of relief.

"Rimrock's a good place to raise a family," Mavis interjected. "A nice, quiet little town where everyone knows everyone else by their first name. Not like the city all full of strangers, where you really don't even know your neighbors. And there's so much less crime."

"Unless you want to talk about murder and arson," Virginia countered. Her eyes never warmed as she glanced at

Beth and Cody. "And sometimes small-town gossip can be cruel."

Beth didn't need to be reminded; she'd grown up knowing about the ravages of gossip and she'd promised herself that she would never put Cody through the same agony she'd experienced as a child. Suddenly her appetite waned, and the home-cooked meal, which had smelled so wonderful, seemed to congeal on her plate.

"More 'tatoes!" Cody demanded, and though she was a little embarrassed by his outburst, Beth was grateful for an interruption in the conversation.

"You like them, do you?" Mavis asked the little boy propped on two pillows in his chair.

"Like 'tatoes!"

"Well, come on, Virginia, pass them along, will you?"

Grudgingly Virginia grabbed the bowl of mashed potatoes and handed them to Jenner, who scooped a dollop onto Cody's plate.

"My guess is you'll need this, too," Skye said, picking up the gravy boat as her eyes lingered wistfully on the boy.

Somewhere Beth had heard that Skye, though she adored children, could have none of her own. Beth didn't remember where she'd heard the rumor, and now, as she drizzled gravy over Cody's potaotes, she chalked the information up to small-town gossips with wagging tongues. No, Rimrock wasn't the place for a boy whose rich family wouldn't recognize him, who would be considered a joke, a bastard, Jenner McKee's mistake, for all the years he attended school.

Cody deserved better. As for her relationship with Jenner, she had to face the fact that it would always be just what it was—lust. Even now, with his hand resting on her thigh, she felt it—that slow-burning ember that could ignite into a hot flame with just a look, a movement, a touch.

Somehow she finished the meal, then packed Cody up and said her goodbyes. Jenner walked her onto the porch and she knew by the look in his eye that there was unfinished business between them. There always would be. She'd never been a slave to her passions except where Jenner McKee was involved and whenever he was around, she seemed to lose touch with what was important.

"You don't have to go," he said, his fingers curving possessively over her arm.

She offered him a sad smile. "What's the alternative? I spend the night here?"

"We could go somewhere."

"Where?"

"There're hotels—"

"With Cody."

"Leave him with your mother. She probably wouldn't mind."

"No, Jenner," she said with honest regret. "I don't think that would work. I'm not sure any of this is working."

He dropped a crutch and it clattered to the porch as he wrapped a strong arm around her and kissed her hard on the lips. Her head began to spin and only Cody's laugh brought her up short.

"He kiss you, Mommy!" Cody said, pointing a chubby little finger at Jenner. "He kiss you."

"He sure did," Beth agreed.

"Soon," Jenner said softly into her ear. "Remember."

A thrill whispered down her spine as she turned toward her car, but she caught a glimpse of the window to the den and a figure parting the blinds. Her insides froze when her gaze touched Virginia McKee's just before the blinds snapped back into place.

Dashing across the yard, she heard Jenner's voice with its erotic promise. "Soon...very soon." But she couldn't shake the image of Virginia glaring through the slats, condemning her silently with a gaze as frigid as the bottom of a well.

Chapter Ten

"Tell me exactly what Stone's got." Jenner couldn't hide the irritation in his voice as he leaned against the window and stared out at the dark night. Beth had been gone for hours and he still wanted to chase after her. As if he was obsessed or something. As if he needed a woman complicating his life. No, not just any woman. Only Beth.

He took a long swallow from his glass and felt the whiskey hit the back of his throat, but the liquor didn't drive away his thoughts. Of the kid. Of Beth. Of making love to her. His brain burned with the image of lying with her in an open field, arms and legs entwined, bodies glistening with sweat, mouths anxious.

"Stone's got ideas . . . leads, he thinks. I'm not so sure." Max picked up a poker and began jabbing at the fire.

Virginia and Mavis had retired. Skye had been called to an emergency at the clinic and Casey wasn't back from Dawson City where she'd gone to a movie with an old high school friend. So Max and Jenner were alone, drinking the old man's expensive whiskey. And worrying.

"Stone's got a list of suspects as long as my arm. Some of 'em make sense, others..." He shook his head as the fire, just a few glowing embers, sparked and caused golden shadows to deepen the lines on his face. "Others are too farfetched to count."

"Tell me about the ones that make sense."

"All right." Hanging the poker back on its peg, Max leaned against the stones and folded his arms across his chest. "A couple come to mind right off the bat."

"People Dad swindled," Jenner guessed.

"Right." Max reached for his drink on the mantel and took a swallow.

Though some of the people in Rimrock considered Jonah McKee a god, others thought that he was Satan incarnate. Jenner knew the man was somewhere in between, although, in Jenner's opinion, Jonah definitely favored the devil.

"Most of the people Dad dealt with—"

"You mean cheated," Jenner corrected.

"He didn't cheat them all," Max said, automatically defending Jonah as he had for years. Then, seeing Jenner's disbelieving stare, Max lifted a shoulder. "Okay, so we both know that Dad made more than his share of enemies. Some threatened him, some took a swing or two at him when they were drunk, and others sued him."

"Fred Donner," Jenner surmised.

"Yep. He's on the top of the list. Dad and Fred exchanged money for water rights, then diverted most of the water from Wildcat Creek to the Rocking M. Donner was left with only a trickle."

"Then there was a drought."

"Yep." Max stretched and his back cracked. "Several years of it. The Donner homestead nearly dried up. Things got worse for Fred. His wife nearly divorced him, the bank was on his tail. Dad had to bail him out."

"By buying his place and incorporating it into the Rocking M."

"Fred never forgave him."

"Do you blame him?" Jenner tossed back a swallow of whiskey and felt its warmth work its way down his throat. His fingers clenched hard around the glass as he considered the crook that had been his father. The homestead had been in the Donner family for over a century before Jonah found a way to incorporate the dry acres into part of the ever-growing Rocking M. And why had he wanted the extra land? Why did he need the extra fields? Because of the damned water rights. The way they'd originally been worded, hadn't proved convenient for the McKee spread, so Jonah had made it his mission to strip the Donners of their family land.

"I'm trying to help Fred out—offered him the homestead and the water rights back," Max said, shaking his head. "All he has to do is repay the original note to Dad, which isn't a whole lot, and I'm willing to let him work it off here at the ranch. Hell, I'd probably forgive most of it."

"What'd he say?"

"I think the quote was something like, 'You can keep your goddamned charity and shove it where the sun don't shine.' "

"So he blames you—or us—for what Dad did." Jenner rubbed his chin. "I've never really liked Donner, but I don't think he's a killer. Or an arsonist."

"Maybe he's never been this desperate before."

"Okay, Donner's on the list. Who else?"

"Randy Calhoun. Dad fired Randy less than a month before he died."

"Yeah, I remember," Jenner said. Randy had been a loyal employee of the Rocking M for nearly fifteen years, but, for reasons no one quite understood, Jonah had humiliated Randy and handed him his walking papers. Randy had always had a little trouble with liquor, but Jonah had put up with it in the past because Randy had been so loyal and good with the stock. But suddenly Jonah had ordered the man off the ranch, fired him in front of the rest of the hands. Made him a laughingstock.

It had been early summer, toward evening, and the sun was just beginning to dip below the horizon. Jenner had been part of a tired group that had spent the day setting fence posts on the line bordering the Bateman place, but Randy hadn't been part of that crew. He and a couple of other hands had worked in the paddocks surrounding the barn, sorting and castrating calves.

Jenner remembered being dog tired as he parked his truck by the garage. Some of the ranch hands had clustered near the door to the machine shed. They'd been smoking, talking and getting ready to go home for the day, but had stopped and were watching Jonah give Randy the ax.

Randy was braced against the wall of the barn, smelling of whiskey and looking as scared as a rabbit staring down the barrel of a shotgun.

"That's it, Calhoun, you're out!" Jonah roared, his face flushed with anger, one hand firmly around the barrel of his rifle.

"But Mr. McKee, you can't fire me."

"I can and I will."

"Wait a minute." Jenner vaulted over the fence and strode up to his father. "What's going on?"

"Butt out!"

"Give it a rest, Dad. Randy's one of the best—"

His father had whirled on him, and his face, mottled with rage, was set in furious determination. "Don't you ever tell me how to run my business, boy," he said, his lips curling in disgust.

"I'm just pointing out that Randy—"

"Back off!" Jonah lunged at him. Jenner grabbed the gun and ripped it out of his father's hands.

"What're ya gonna do, Dad? Shoot him?"

Eyes narrowing, Jonah barked, "If I thought it'd do any good." He whirled on Randy again. "Get out now!"

"Jonah," Chester Wilcox, the ranch foreman, said, stepping in, "I think—"

"Well, don't, or you'll be out of job, too! This is still my ranch, last I heard."

Jenner didn't back down. "What happened?" he demanded. But Chester shook his head, obviously not wanting the story to come out in front of the rest of the hands. "Randy's been with us for—"

"I don't give a rat's ass how long he's been here!" Jonah, snatching his rifle away from his son, spun around, his eyes moving from one ranch hand to the next before landing on Chester. "Make sure he packs up all his gear and gets out."

Randy, nearly sixty, straightened to his full five feet six inches. "I want an explanation, Jonah."

"You really want it? Here in front of God and the rest of the men?"

"Yes." Randy's skin turned the color of bones that had been bleached in the son.

"Fine." Jonah's voice shook with rage. "Aside from being a useless drunk who can barely throw a lasso, you've been cheating me, Calhoun. I know about some of the calves we lost last winter. What really happened to them."

Randy's Adam's apple bobbed nervously. "What's that?"

"You culled 'em out. Sold 'em. That's why we never found any carcasses."

"I didn't—"

"Like hell!" Jonah thundered. "You're out, Calhoun, and unless you want me to call Hammond Polk and have the sheriff's deputies poke around, you'd best get in that damned bucket of bolts you call a pickup and leave. You can pick up your check at the office."

Randy's hands shook, but Jonah wasn't finished with him. He pointed his rifle at Randy, then at each of the hands standing on the far side of the fence. "Let this be a lesson to the rest of you. No one. *No one* screws around with Jonah McKee!"

Jenner had nearly quit right then and there. His father had always been a bastard, but he'd never seen him in action before, and though he'd followed Jonah into the den and pleaded Randy's case, Jonah had turned a deaf ear.

"Whatever happened to innocent until proven guilty?" Jenner had demanded.

"Give it up, Jenner. I know that slimy little drunk's been cheating me for years. I turned a blind eye, 'cause he had a way with the stock and the rest of the men seemed to look up to him. But he was stealin' from me and I won't have it."

As Jonah poured three fingers of whiskey into a crystal tumbler, Jenner had glanced around the room. A man's domain with Indian prints on the walls, an old flintlock mounted over the fireplace, a globe in a mahogany stand sitting near the desk. Leather couch, old rocker, crystal glasses and polished floors completed the picture. Casual, yes, but obviously the office of a wealthy man. What did he care about a couple of calves? Randy Calhoun was nearly Jonah's age and had nothing but a broken-down Chevy pickup, a saddle and a room he rented by the week at the Lucky Star Motel.

Randy hadn't been able to get decent work since. His drinking had made him a regular at the Black Anvil. Yep, Randy had motive and opportunity.

"Randy wouldn't do it," Jenner said, remembering how beaten the man had appeared as he'd driven away from the ranch where he'd spent so many years. "Who else?"

"Corey Stills."

Jenner didn't need an explanation for that one. For years, it had been rumored that Jonah had kept Corey's young wife, Grace, as his mistress. The gossip had been floating around like a bad smell, but somehow Virginia McKee had ignored it, explaining to her children that powerful men were always the target for vicious lies involving their moral character. Why, just look at the politicians in Salem and Washington D.C., always being accused of this liaison or that liaison.

Jonah had been linked with a lot of women ranging from Wanda Tully, the blond waitress who worked at the Black Anvil, to Carol Larkin, once his secretary and eventually vice president of J.P. Limited, one of the corporations owned by McKee Enterprises.

"Dad was involved with a lot of women."

"But they didn't all have jealous husbands who adored them."

That much was true, and Jenner just recently had learned about jealousy. The thought of another man making love to Beth brought a bitter taste to his mouth and his fingers tightened over his glass. "Okay, I'll buy it. Corey hated Dad enough to kill him. But once Dad was dead, why the arson?"

"Who knows? Maybe Stills's hatred has been building for years and he wanted to get back at everything and everyone associated with his old enemy."

"But why not do that while Dad was alive—let him see the destruction, let the old man twist in the wind?"

"'Cause Dad was too powerful. Corey would've been found out and God only knows what might've happened if Dad got the sheriff's department and Judge Rayburn and Rex Stone on his side. Think about it."

"I don't know. Anyone else?"

"Mmm. Ned Jansen's near the top of the list. Dad did a number on him with the copper mine. I tried to talk to him about it, work out some kind of deal, but he wasn't interested, said he'd just as soon spit on a McKee as do business with one.''

"Nice attitude."

"Not uncommon around here."

"And Ned did have an old axe to grind with Dad," Jenner thought aloud. "If you can believe the rumors."

Max frowned and rubbed the back of his neck. "You mean because he was supposed to have been involved with Mom years ago?"

"Well, that's just what they say. None of us were around."

"Come on, Jenner. That's old news. Over thirty years ago."

"Okay, so there are other people who have more recent grudges, right?"

"Yep. Even Slim Purcell has a reason to hate us."

Jenner snorted. "Maybe we should move."

"I wouldn't go that far, but..." Max hesitated, then shoved his hands into the back pockets of his jeans. The worry lines over his eyes deepened. "You know I've started taking precautions, not just around here, but at Colleen's place, too."

"You think someone might actually hurt Hillary?"

Max's eyes flared with fury. "I'd kill the bastard who tried," he said, his face suddenly harsh, his jaw thrust in a challenge. "I don't think it'll come to that. Hell, I hope not, but if I were you—"

"You think Cody might be in danger?"

"Or Beth." Jenner's muscles tightened. "Anyone close to you. I've even got someone watching the clinic and apartment house, though Skye doesn't have a clue. If she did, she'd probably kill me herself."

"Okay, you've convinced me," Jenner said, his thoughts already racing ahead. He couldn't let anything happen to Beth or Cody, and if it meant their going into hiding, well, so be it. Slinging his jacket over his back, he limped over to the desk and opened the top drawer. He sorted through key rings until he found the one he wanted.

One corner of Max's mouth lifted in a smile. "This is one helluva time to take a vacation."

Jenner pocketed the keys. "It's *not* a vacation."

"I guess you won't be showing up for work tomorrow."

"I'll call," he said, reaching into another drawer for a cellular phone and batteries.

"Don't bother."

Jenner grabbed his crutches, hitched his way to the door and shouldered it open. Hearing thunder rumble across the hills, he hiked the collar of his jacket up around his neck and considered his next move.

Beth wouldn't like it, but that was just too bad. If, as she so adamantly insisted, he was the father of her kid, then he owed that boy a decent, safe life and he was going to start giving it to him right now.

For the first time in his life, he was worrying about someone other than himself. His own hide was pretty much useless, but Beth and the boy, they were important.

He drove with a purpose, pushing the speed limit, forgetting that some of his leg movements were limited, and being damned if anyone was going to hurt Beth or Cody. The town of Rimrock hadn't changed in the past few hours; it was the same little town Jenner had lived in most of his life. But now he was looking over his shoulder for a sinister presence, jumping at shadows, afraid that some criminal might be planning to do bodily harm to a woman and child he'd met recently but who had already woven themselves so deeply into his heart that he couldn't imagine them ever leaving.

That thought jolted him and he nearly swerved into the oncoming lane. A horn blasted loudly from a station wagon traveling in the opposite direction, but Jenner hardly noticed. He'd spent his life cultivating the art of being a loner, making sure that he put down only the shallowest of roots, and here he was, thinking in terms of the future with a woman he didn't even trust and a boy who might or might not be his.

He turned off the main road and stopped at an all-night market for a few essentials, then drove straight to Beth's mother's house. A soft light shone through the front window and Jenner cut the engine. It seemed he was forever chasing this woman, insisting she be a part of his life, then pushing her away.

Telling himself he was the worst kind of fool, he hitched himself up the steps and knocked softly on the door. She answered quickly, as if she'd been expecting him.

"What are you doing here?" she said. "Everyone's asleep."

"Good." He reached for her arm, pulled her onto the porch and kissed her as long and as hard as he wanted. Her lips were soft and yielding against his, her body as hungry and anxious as his own. Fire swept through his blood. "Come with me."

"Where?"

"I'd rather not say."

Her smile was tentative. "What is this—twenty questions?"

"Please."

She stopped short and he realized he'd never used that word with her before. "Look, Jenner, I just can't leave Cody here—"

"Tonight, Beth. Now. It's important. Bring Cody with you."

"You want him, too?" she asked.

He hesitated for just a heartbeat. "Yeah," he admitted, surprised at his own emotions. "I want him."

Blinking hard against a sudden rush of tears, she swallowed. "Let me just tell Mom that we're leaving."

"And won't be back for a while."

"Wait a minute."

"A few days."

"I don't know—"

He grabbed her arm more tightly. "Pack a bag, Beth. Now!"

"But why—"

"Just do it," he said, and the tenor of his voice must have convinced her.

"I don't usually let bullheaded cowboys push me around," she grumbled as she pulled away from him. "You have some explaining to do."

"I will. Later," he promised, jangling his keys nervously.

She ducked back into the house. Through the open door, he heard conversation as Beth explained the situation to her mother. Harriet's words were muffled through her bedroom door, but their import was perfectly clear. She wasn't happy that her daughter was taking her grandson and leaving in the middle of the night with the no-good McKee rebel who had knocked her up and left her without a backward glance three years ago. Jenner didn't have to hear the words to get the gist of the conversation.

Within minutes, Beth was back on the porch, carrying Cody and a huge bag. She handed him the sleeping baby and Jenner smelled the soap, baby powder and shampoo that he remembered from his niece, Hillary a few years back. Except this was his son. Well, maybe.

Cody was a dead weight, barely moving as Jenner held him and Beth hurried to the truck to stow the bag in the back.

Jenner couldn't move. He didn't dare try to negotiate the steps with his crutches and carry the boy, so he had to wait until Beth, breathless, returned and retrieved her son, blanket and all. Some bodyguard he'd be, trapped on crutches, unable to carry the boy and run if need be, unable to protect them. He cursed under his breath.

Pathetic, that's what he was. But not much longer. He wouldn't just accept the fact that he couldn't take care of people who might rely on him. If he had to go back to the damned doctor, so be it. If he was forced to spend hours in physical therapy, he'd give it a shot. But he wasn't going to be useless any longer.

Damn it, Mavis had been right. This woman and his kid seemed to be all the motivation he needed to try again. And if he failed? If his leg refused to mend? If, after surgery and therapy and acupuncture and voodoo and whatever else it took, he still couldn't walk, then he'd accept the damned wheelchair and make the best of a bad situation. Somehow.

He didn't really have much choice.

Beth told herself she was nuts—certifiably crazy. What was she thinking, taking off in the middle of the night with Jenner McKee? Her mother's protests echoed in her ears.

"You're making a big mistake, Beth. Think about it.

"It's not that I don't like him, but he's got a reputation! The family's got a reputation! They're users, every last one of them. If you aren't thinking about yourself, consider Cody. He's just a baby.

"I hate to say it, Beth, but Jenner could be using you again. He'll break your heart and never look back. Just like before!"

Those final words kept reverberating in her heart, and she silently vowed that it wouldn't happen, that it couldn't; she mustn't lose her heart again.

Jenner didn't say much and the radio played a steady stream of country music, songs of broken hearts, missed opportunities and regrets, but Beth refused to think of them in terms of her relationship with Jenner. She was content to stare out the window at the night-darkened countryside while Cody slept soundly in the seat between them—his father and mother.

"You haven't said where we're going."

"Does it matter?" His voice was a rough whisper.

"I suppose not."

"Didn't think so." They drove through Dawson City and further east until eventually they turned off the main road and wound upward through the mountains, past stands of timber and along steep cliffs.

Though she had no idea where they were, Jenner drove as if he knew where he was going, turning easily at each fork in the road as if by instinct. Finally a gap appeared in the trees and he parked near a three-story lodge that had seen better days, a huge summer home from the looks of it. It was built on the shores of a placid lake, which seemed to shimmer under the stars.

"What is this place?"

"A retreat, I guess. Dad ended up with it in one of his business deals. I think it belonged to some civic group for a while, but it was originally built as a hunting lodge. We used to come up here as kids, whenever Mom couldn't stand another minute of the old man's B.S. Here... use this." He reached across her, the back of his arm brushing her breasts as he opened the glove compartment and extracted a flashlight.

Beth carried Cody inside and Jenner grabbed a couple of sacks from the back of the truck, which he managed to balance while using his crutches.

The steps were covered with dirt and leaves, and rodents had gnawed through some of the boards, but Beth closed her eyes to the state of disrepair and waited while Jenner fitted an old key into the lock. The door creaked open.

The interior smelled musty and dry, as if no one had stepped over the threshold in years. A haunted house, like something out of a horror movie, she thought. The flashlight's beam seemed small against the dark hallways and shadowed corners. A wide staircase with hand-carved railing and posts curved upward, but Jenner walked straight ahead, through a wide arch into a room as large as a ballroom in a Portland hotel.

"Over there," he said, pointing across the room to a huge rock fireplace. She shone the beam on a massive mantel where hurricane lanterns stood under a cloak of dust. "That's it. Hold it right there." He crossed the room, struck a match against the hearth, and lit each of the three lanterns. The room began to come alive as the lantern light was reflected in the mullioned windows and made shadows play upon the old plank floor. Jenner stripped sheets off a couple of pieces of furniture and found bedding smelling of cedar in a back closet. "We'll put him here," he directed as he opened up a sofa bed in the corner, covered it with blankets and waited as Beth laid Cody gently on an old hand-pieced quilt. The little boy snuggled deep in the bedding, sighed and didn't even open his eyes.

"Why did you bring us here?" she asked.

"A couple of reasons. I'll explain it all later. First I want to see if I can turn on the water and build a fire." He snagged a lantern from the mantel. "Wait here."

"I'm tired of waiting," she said as he hitched himself out of the room, but there wasn't much else she could do because she didn't want Cody to wake up frightened in the unfamiliar surroundings. She shone the beam of the flashlight to the ceiling, three stories above the main floor. Two sets of balconies, one above the other, skirted the huge room on three sides while windows filled the fourth wall. Through the dusty glass, the lake was visible, a breeze raising ripples to gleam in the soft light of the stars and a crescent moon.

She pulled off several more sheets and discovered Victorian furniture, antiques, she supposed, that included gateleg tables, brass lamps, club chairs and sofas, even an old player piano. The walls were decorated with heads of animals—bison, deer, antelope, elk, a mountain lion and even a moose. Rifles, spears, snowshoes and a variety of bows and arrows were interspersed between the furry faces with glass eyes that stared down at her.

What kind of man owned a hunting lodge?

The same kind who owned a ranch, a real estate company, racehorse and a copper mine. A man who had thought that the more he owned, the more important he was. A man who ended up getting himself killed.

Goose bumps rose on her arms and she shivered as she thought of Jonah and wondered who could have hated him enough to force his Jeep off the road. She glanced at Cody anxiously, but her baby was sleeping undisturbed, as if everything was right with the world. He didn't understand about his relationship to Jenner, had never even asked why he didn't have a father, and certainly had no clue that his ruthless grandfather had been killed.

Jenner's uneven gait announced his return. He was dragging pieces of firewood stacked on a sheet.

"Oh, for heaven's sake, I would have gotten that," she said, crossing the room quickly.

"I didn't want your help." He was sweating profusely, though it was cold up here in the mountains. "I didn't need it, did I?"

"It would have been simpler if—"

"Would it have?" he said, his voice rising. "Not for me. I'm not going to ask for help for every little thing."

"This wasn't a little thing."

"It's done, all right?" He made his way to the fireplace, opened the flue, laid down kindling, then stacked chunks of oak and fir over handmade andirons shaped to look like wolves baring their teeth. He struck a match and touched it several times to the tinder-dry wood. "That's better," he said, dusting off his hands.

And it was. Flames began to lick at the logs, casting the room in shadows of gold and causing the sweat sheening his forehead to glow. The cavernous room seemed suddenly cozy and warm. Aside from the quiet hiss of the fire and

Cody's soft breathing, the lodge was hushed, and she was suddenly aware of being alone—really alone—with Jenner and his son.

Beth warmed her hands by the fire. "So now you're going to tell me why you brought me here, right?"

His smile was wicked. "I'll give you one reason."

"Just one?" She couldn't help the teasing lilt of her voice.

"The most important," he said slowly as he walked closer to her and ran a long finger down the side of her jaw. "I wanted to be alone with you."

Her heart pumped wildly as his finger slid lower to the pulse point at the base of her throat. It lingered there, drawing lazy, sensual circles.

"We—we didn't have to come this far."

"I didn't want to be interrupted." He let his finger catch on the neckline of her sweater and she hardly dared breathe. He pulled gently, the knitted fabric stretching before she moved her head. He kissed her softly, his lips brushing hers in a chaste, yet sensual movement. "Come on," he whispered. "I'd carry you, but considering the circumstances, I guess you'll have to make it on your own. Bring a lantern." Cocking his head toward a short hallway, he grabbed the flashlight and hobbled ahead, following the uneven beam.

Beth knew that Cody was fast asleep and wouldn't awaken, so she grabbed the light and followed Jenner. Her heart was racing as he led her into a room as large as her apartment. A canopied bed stood on a dais, though the bedding had long since been stripped from it. Another fireplace rose to the beamed ceiling and Jenner drew the curtains to show off a view of the lake.

"Who used this room?" she asked, sweeping her arm around the room.

"The owner's private quarters," he explained. "Complete with bath, kitchen, sitting area and a bed fit for a king."

Logs had been left in the grate and Jenner started another fire. Carpets had been rolled up against the wall and a chandelier covered with cobwebs swung from the ceiling.

Jenner reached into a cedar cupboard, found some quilts and tossed them onto the bed. Beth smiled as she walked up to him. "Why, Mr. McKee, you didn't bring me all the way up here just to seduce me?" she teased.

"That was the general idea," he admitted, watching her close the gap.

"Good." She let her coat fall to the floor and heard his breath rush over his teeth.

He dropped his crutches as she approached and climbed up the short steps of the dais. When she reached him, he grabbed her roughly around the waist. "I've been waiting for this for a long time," he said, and his lips came crashing down on hers in a kiss that was hot and hungry and wet.

Wrapping her arms around his neck, she kissed him back, and when his tongue sought entrance to her mouth, she opened it willingly to him, feeling him plunge and taste, plunder and explore. He cupped her buttocks, drawing her close to the swelling in his jeans, pulling her against him so that she felt his heat.

The fire crackled and popped as they tumbled to the bed. Still kissing her, Jenner reached beneath her sweater boldly, as if he expected no protests. His hands were rough against her flesh as he delved into her bra, his fingers cupping her breasts, and rubbing her nipples anxiously. "Beth, oh, Beth," he groaned, stripping her of her sweater, then shedding his jacket.

He couldn't get enough of her. He kissed the tops of her breasts, his tongue outlining the sculpted lace of her bra, and she arched her back, moving closer, silently begging him to take more. Through the sheer lace, his tongue laved her nipples, moistening the fabric, teasing each little peak until she moaned with desire and pushed her pelvis closer to his.

A warmth swirled deep within her, growing more intense, pulsing with need.

He kissed first one nipple, then the next, and little goose bumps of pleasure rippled along her skin. She was with Jenner, and her heart opened to him, though she'd sworn long ago that she'd never let him touch her, never trust him again. She cradled his head against her, feeling him suckle her breasts, thrilling as his hands slid along her spine, his fingers dipping past her jeans to touch the dimples in her bottom.

"Make love to me," he whispered, and she couldn't deny him.

Slowly she unbuttoned his shirt, touching the stiff hair on his chest, outlining his flat nipples, watching in fascination the play of muscles in his abdomen. He sucked in his breath and she kissed his navel. His fingers dug into her hair and he held her there, feeling her tongue wet and filled with promise as it explored that little dimple of flesh.

He smelled of soap and tasted of salt and he groaned in pleasure as she moved her hand up his torso and let her fingers explore the sinewy muscles of his shoulders and arms while her mouth left moist impressions on his chest. He bucked when she kissed his nipple and cried out as if he could stand the frustration no longer.

His hands moved quickly. Stripping off her jeans, he touched her everywhere, his hands eager, his lips quick to sear a kiss against her bare skin. He kicked off his own Levi's, and if he experienced any pain while undressing, he hid it well. Reaching into a pocket, he found a packet, opened it with his teeth and handed it to her.

As sweat broke out to slick his skin, she fitted the condom on him. He moaned at the feel of her fingers against his shaft. "Oh, Beth," he whispered. Then as the firelight bronzed his skin, he kissed her roughly again, his mouth molding to hers as he pulled her atop him. He didn't wait for her to settle; instead, while gazing hotly up at her, he lifted his buttocks and impaled her.

She gasped as he started to move and she closed her eyes and threw back her head.

"Watch me," he commanded.

"Wha—"

"I don't want either of us to forget this happened. Not ever." His eyes locked with hers, he rocked up and down, his hands kneading her breasts, his breathing ragged. Slowly he rocked, drawing in and out as her blood heated and her body seemed to fuse with his.

A storm built inside her, hot and savage and wild and she began moving of her own accord, to her own rhythm, a furious pace that caused his eyes to darken as he gazed up at her.

"I can't stop...Beth—"

She let out a scream as the world seemed to collide with some unseen heavenly body. He arched up and cried out her name like a litany. "Beth, oh, Beth... Ahhh!" His voice was hoarse and she was jolted again when he grabbed her around the waist and pulled her down to the bed with him where they tangled together, arms and legs entwined, smelling of sweat and lovemaking.

Jenner's fingers tangled in her hair and he breathed hard against her ear. She listened to his heartbeat and cuddled up to him, noticing the scars on different parts of his body and the way his muscles coiled beneath his skin.

For minutes they were silent, their heartbeats slowing.

"Why *did* you bring me here?" she asked again when she could finally talk. She kissed his chest. "Besides the obvious reason, I mean."

He pushed a strand of hair from her eyes so tenderly she thought her heart might break right then and there. "I thought it would be safer up here."

"Safer?" She laughed, then her smile faded when she remembered another conversation they'd had. "You still think there may be a nut out there somewhere, planning to hurt us?''

"I don't know for sure," he admitted. "But I can't take a chance." He kissed the top of her head and told her everything he and Max had discussed.

Beth held him and listened, but she couldn't help the smile that teased her lips. For no matter what else he said, no matter what theories Max or the private investigator or the police could come up with, one thing was certain: Jenner McKee cared. About her and about his son. There was no other reason he would go to such lengths to hide them. Slowly, whether he liked it or not, Jenner was beginning to accept the fact that he was a father.

She didn't know where that realization would lead, but had to believe a major stumbling block was out of the way. So she listened. As Jenner stroked her hair and kissed her crown and explained just how many people in Rimrock had reason to hate his father, Beth smiled and wondered what the morning would bring.

Chapter Eleven

Beth never wanted to leave. Sighing contentedly, she stretched on the rumpled bedding. She and Jenner had made love most of the night and she had no regrets. Though he didn't love her, she knew that he cared, and caring was a start—a large step in the right direction.

She pulled on her clothes and gazed through the dusty panes of the window to the lake where the rays of morning sun glinted on the ripples. Geese flew overhead in wavering V formations and ducks skimmed the surface of the water.

From the corner of her eye, she saw Jenner walking with his crutches near the lake's edge, and with him, dragging a stick, was Cody. Beth's heart nearly melted when she saw Jenner pause and point to a squirrel racing in the branches of an ancient pine tree.

Rather than disturb father and son, she decided to go and explore the old lodge. On the second floor were bedrooms, some single, some double, some with several sets of bunks, which shared communal baths branching off the balcony.

The third was filled with complete and odd-shaped suites tucked under the eaves. The place was dusty and there was evidence of mice in some of the bedding, but she found only one spot where the roof leaked. All the old lodge needed was some solvent, polish and lots of elbow grease.

On the first floor there were meeting rooms, a dining room, a sun porch, kitchen and baths, as well as the main hall and master suite. In the basement, there was a recreation room with an old pool table, the furnace room, laundry, a wine cellar and larders, now empty. Coal and wood chutes were strategically placed near the back of the lodge and a dumbwaiter connected the floors.

The lodge was a mansion out of one of the stories Beth had read as a child. She climbed back up to the first floor and went to the kitchen, where Jenner had a pot of coffee heating on a huge wood stove. Beth rinsed a cup under a groaning faucet, which delivered only cold water, then poured herself some of the strong brew.

With a feeling of contentment she hadn't experienced in years, she carried her cup to the wide back porch and sat in an old cushioned swing. She rocked slowly as she watched Jenner and Cody by the lake. Jenner's voice was muffled, but he spoke to the boy often, and when he did, Cody tipped his face up, his eyes round with wonder.

This was how it was supposed to be—father and son discovering the world together. Tears burned the back of her eyes as she realized how desperately she wanted this for Cody, how much she'd missed by not knowing her own father. Could she ever deny her son the right to know the man who had helped create his life? Even if things didn't work out between Jenner and her, she couldn't break this fragile bond that existed between these two.

As if he'd read her mind, Jenner turned. She felt her heart close in on itself as her gaze locked with his. She was aware of the breeze that tickled her neck and bent the grass near the water's edge, but time seemed to stand still in that one instant. Cody, turning to follow Jenner's gaze, saw her. He threw back his head and laughed, the joyful sound rising into the sky.

"Mommy! Mommy!" he cried in pure delight. "We find squirrels and birds and snakes!" His little legs started churning as he ran along the bank, then found the weed-choked brick path that led to the porch.

"Snakes?" she echoed as she placed her coffee on the floor and reached out to scoop him into her arms.

"Yeah! Rattlesnakes this—" he held his arms out wide "—big!"

"Rattlesnakes!" she gasped, her heart faltering.

But Jenner only laughed as he joined them. "No rattlers."

"They were! I seen 'em."

"If you say so, pardner," Jenner agreed with a wink at Beth, and she relaxed. "Come on now, I'll make you both some breakfast."

Cody scrambled to the ground and tore into the lodge. His little feet pounded loudly on the floors, and Beth, still outside, could hear him running from room to room. "You've got yourself a good kid," Jenner admitted when they were alone.

"So do you."

"Do I?" His eyes held hers and he drew her into the circle of his arms, kissing her lightly on her forehead, her eyelids and her cheeks before his lips settled over hers and she sighed into his open mouth. Everything seemed so right up here—away from the rest of the world, just man, woman and child. No worries, no gossip, nothing but this tiny little family.

She broke the embrace suddenly at that thought. *Family?* They weren't a family. She was a single mother with a two-year-old son, and Jenner was a die-hard bachelor content to be single. How could she ever think of them as a family? How could she delude herself?

Jenner, feeling her tense, held her even more tightly. "It's all right," he said against her ear. "It'll be all right. I promise."

"You do?"

"Mmm." He kissed her crown again and she leaned against him, feeling his strong arms surround her.

It'll be all right.

If only she could believe him.

They had so far spent three days at the lodge. Jenner had driven them into a small town where the post office, general store and hardware store shared one building. Beth called her mother and explained that they were together and getting to know each other. Jenner called Max, asking about the investigation and checking on the rest of his family.

During the day, Beth cleaned and cooked and spent hours with her son and Jenner. They explored the lake and the woods, startled owls and spied a fawn lying still in the undergrowth. A family of raccoons scavenged near the kitchen at night and it was all she could do to keep Cody from chasing after them, intent on catching one of the smaller masked beasts.

Jenner enthralled them both with the history of the lodge, though Beth suspected his stories of colorful past figures spending time here were embellished a little. Each night as they sat near the fire and Cody listened raptly to this stranger who was his father, Jenner seemed to thaw a little more toward his son. The brackets around the corners of his mouth disappeared and a kinder side of him emerged as Cody tagged after him all day long, his short legs keeping up with Jenner's without any trouble since Jenner was slowed by his crutches.

"You may as well know that I promised Max I'd go back to the doctor and physical therapist," Jenner admitted one night as they sat huddled together on a couch near the fire, stockinged feet propped on the broad hearth, Cody snoring softly as he lay in the crook of Jenner's arm.

"What changed your mind?"

Jenner stared at the bright embers and scowled. "You did. You and Cody." He turned to look at her and his eyes were as clear and blue as the lake outside the back door. "You know, I hate like hell to admit it when someone is right and I'm proved wrong, but when Mavis wrote to you, she knew what she was doing." His eyebrows drew together forming one thick line. "I guess I'd given up, decided that if I couldn't ride and rope and brand and all that nonsense that seemed so important—" he waved his hand as if he was brushing aside an inconsequential fly "—that I'd just give up. Then you showed up with this little dynamo and bang! My whole world was turned upside down. Everything I'd ever believed in..."

Her heart nearly stopped beating and she realized there in the shadowy room how much she'd come to love this rugged loner of a man, not with the silly schoolgirl fantasies she'd harbored all those years before, but with a love based on trust and understanding and the knowledge that he could stir her blood as well as her soul. Jenner was a hard man, a distant man at times, but he was honest and strong.

"Anyway." He slapped his thighs and Cody shifted. "I guess I wanted to pour myself into a bottle and drown." He slid her a glance. "Not a very practical plan, but it seemed to keep the demons at bay."

"Did it?" she teased as he slung an arm over her shoulder and his breath whispered across her hair.

"Not very well. I never could seem to get enough booze. Kinda the same way I feel about you." He kissed her hard enough to start her heart pumping with wild abandon. Her arms curved around his neck and she moved closer still, her breasts brushing his ribs through their shirts.

With a groan of frustration, he released her. "You're going to get yourself into big trouble, lady," he warned.

She winked at him. "I'm counting on it."

"Are you?" A devilish light flamed in his eyes and he hauled Cody into his arms and helped the boy into his bed. Once satisfied that Cody wouldn't wake up, he linked his fingers through Beth's and they moved to the bedroom without his crutches, Jenner leaning on her, she supporting him, until they fell on the bed together and he wrested the shirt from her body. Slowly, eyes locked with hers, he made love to her as passionately as they had the night Cody was conceived, as savagely as their first night alone in the lodge together.

The next morning Jenner announced they had to get back. He'd called Max. Things were stable at the ranch and he was needed. Jenner grinned at that. "Yep. Max seems to think I can actually be of some help. One of the men quit last night and the Rocking M's shorthanded. Can you believe it?"

"Yes," she said, her voice catching. Of course he was needed. Didn't she need him? Didn't Cody?

Her heart was heavy as she packed to leave this mountain retreat, but she managed to hide her disappointment. Truth to tell, she, too, had to start thinking about the rest of her life as well as the rest of Cody's. She needed to return to Oregon City and start hunting for another job, but that thought brought a lump to her throat.

Life without Jenner.

Shuttling Cody from the Willamette Valley to Rimrock where, as he grew older, he'd eventually hear the gossip and have to live with the rumors. *Bastard. Unwanted. Mistake.*

But at least he'd have a father's love.

Certainly that was worth the risk and the heartache of facing the taunts leveled at him by other children and the gossips in town. Or was it? Instead of becoming simpler, her life was getting more complicated by the minute. Because of Jenner and the horrid fact that she loved him.

Cody chattered incessantly as they drove back to Rimrock, and with each mile that passed, Beth felt the tension in the cab increase. Her stomach clenched as they turned off the main road and into the lane leading to the Rocking M. The trees lining the drive seemed to bend in the wind and dry leaves scattered as the truck bounced over potholes. Dark clouds clustered in the sky.

"Home sweet home," Jenner said sarcastically as he stopped near the garage.

Max stood in the doorway of the barn talking with Chester Wilcox. Hillary was riding Cambridge in one of the enclosures, her curls catching the late afternoon sunlight as Dani, holding the lead rope, coached her young charge. Cattle milled in nearby pens and the horses grazed in the dry fields.

"Maybe you should take me home first—"

"This'll just take a minute." He slanted her a glance and private little smile. "We McKees don't bite...well, unless it's in the middle of the night when things get a little rough and—"

"Enough. I get the picture," she said, her blood swirling through her veins.

Cody, spying Hillary on her horse, clamored to get out. "Me ride!" he insisted.

"Oh, honey, not now—"

"It's all right," Jenner assured her, glancing at the heavy bellied clouds.

"I don't think Hillary's going to like it."

"He doesn't have to ride Cambridge. We can find him another mount. Come on, pardner." And the two of them were off—father limping on crutches, son scampering through the dust as fast as his short legs would carry him. The dog, Reuben, was sleeping in a patch of weeds near the garage and he let out a quiet woof as Cody raced past.

Beth followed her son and leaned against the rails of the fence. She watched Dani and Hillary while Jenner stopped to talk with his brother and the ranch foreman. Cody was hopping up and down, demanding his attention, and Jenner, after a sharp word to the boy, picked him up and held him as naturally as if he'd done it all his life.

A natural father. She smiled to herself. Wouldn't he die to think of himself, the rugged, lone wolf of a cowboy, now able to read a bedtime story, change a night diaper and kiss scratches and "owies" as naturally as if he'd been born to do it?

So caught up in her fantasy, she didn't hear the sound of footsteps behind her until she felt a breath of chill air against the back of her neck. "So...you decided to come back, did you?" Virginia's voice was cold.

"Pardon me?" Beth turned to face the censure that was Virginia McKee.

"I know what you were doing, don't think I don't. You think you've got your hooks in my boy but you're wrong."

"I don't understand—"

"Sure you do," Virginia insisted in a harsh whisper. "You thought by luring him away with sex and the boy you could make him change his ways, even marry you, but you haven't got a chance. Jenner's only interested in himself—he'll never be tied to a family. And if you think you can pass off your boy as his—"

"Don't even say it," Beth warned, her temper snapping. "Jenner is Cody's father and that's the way it is, even if you've got a problem with it." She stepped closer to the woman who seemed determined to hate her. "I don't know what it is you have against me, and I really don't care. You can think what you want. But when it comes to my son, you'd better be careful, because I won't let anyone—not even you—hurt him."

"Then why did you bring him here?"

"Because I had no choice."

Virginia's mouth twisted into a thin, wicked little smile. Behind her, Casey had come out of the house and was approaching, but Virginia didn't stop. "You may as well know something about me. I'm a lot stronger than I look and I don't back down easily. I was the one who insisted that my husband was murdered when the police were ready to give up and write the whole episode off as a nasty accident. But I proved them wrong.

"I know you came here because of Mavis—that old woman would do anything to convince herself that the McKee name isn't going to die. She and I both know that Skye can't give Max any sons, and Casey, well, that girl doesn't know what she wants, but if and when she does get around to marrying, the children won't carry the McKee name. So Jenner is Mavis's last hope and she pinned that hope on you, as well."

"Because it's the truth." Beth leaned closer to the older woman and held her gaze. "If you have a problem with me—a bone to pick—why don't you just tell me about it?"

"You really want to know?"

"Yes."

"All right," Virginia said, clearing her throat and straightening to her full height. "Isn't it obvious? You bore a child out of wedlock."

"Jenner's child."

"So you say."

"He was involved, too, and I refuse to accept your double standard."

"And now you're back, trying to drag his name—our name—through the mud. The whole town will be buzzing."

"Is that what's bothering you?" Beth asked. "After all the scandal you've endured?" She couldn't believe it. "There's something more, isn't there? Something else that's bothering you."

Beth saw the hint of a shadow in Virginia's eyes—the flicker of a secret—but it quickly disappeared. "I just don't want my son—a McKee—involved with poor white trash,"

Virginia said and turned on her heel, nearly running into Casey.

"How could you?" Casey said as Virginia stopped short.

"This family's name has been dragged through the mud too many times. I won't allow it to happen again."

"Is that it, or are you afraid that we'll all finally come to terms with the kind of man our father really was?" Casey asked.

Virginia's throat worked. "He was a good, decent, hard-working—"

"He was a crook, Mom. He deceived people and cheated them out of their money, then he tried his best to ruin his children's lives. If you face facts, you'll even realize that he tried to ruin yours, as well. It's just that you turned a blind eye to all of his affairs and mistresses."

"I won't hear this . . . this blasphemy!"

"Maybe it's time you faced the truth, Mom, and quit deluding yourself."

"I don't—"

"Of course you do! You always have. Oh, God, I've got to leave this place before I go out of my mind!"

"Don't even talk that way. You tried leaving once before—"

"I was just a kid then, didn't know what I wanted."

"And you still don't!" Virginia said, then stared straight at Beth. "Jenner doesn't believe you, you know. He thinks you're nothing but a fortune hunter, and though you've turned his head for a while, it won't last. Because, deep down, he knows the truth and he'll find a way to prove it." Virginia whirled on her heel and walked swiftly toward the ranch house.

"Don't listen to her," Casey advised. "She's been a basket case since Dad died. Maybe even before."

"She hates me."

"She hates the world." Casey sighed. "Things didn't turn out the way she'd planned. People showed their true colors. Her husband didn't turn out to be Prince Charming and her kids weren't perfect little angels." Casey cast a glance back at her mother, who was making her way into the house. "But none of us should pay her any mind. Especially you. I've seen the way Jenner looks at you, Beth, and he's never, *ever* looked at a woman the way he looks at you. Not even Nora Bateman. As for Mom, she's just going through this thing... what with Dad's death and all. She'll accept you. Eventually."

"I'm not so sure about that," Beth replied, not really certain if she wanted to be condoned by Jenner's mother.

"Give it time. Believe me, anyone who can put up with Jenner is a saint in my book."

"You think he's that bad?"

"Are you kidding?" Casey's eyes twinkled. "He's the worst!"

"I heard that," Jenner said as he came from the barn. He was leading an old gray horse with Cody perched atop.

"Good. Then maybe you'll straighten up."

He darted a quick, sexy glance at Beth. "Never."

"Hopeless," Casey said under her breath. "Hey, Hillary!" Casey waved an arm wildly at her niece. "Looks like you've got yourself some competition."

"I ride, Mommy!" Cody yelled excitedly.

"Big deal." Hillary wasn't impressed.

"It is a big deal," Dani assured her.

"He's just a baby." Hillary tossed her hair and nudged her palomino's sides.

"Am not! Big boy!" Cody replied, then ignored his cousin completely. So wrapped up in riding the gray horse, he didn't catch one of the dozen superior looks cast in his direction.

"Dani's good with kids," Beth said to Casey as the horses slowed. Both children protested loudly and refused to climb off their mounts.

"Yeah. She seems to have a thing about 'em." Casey frowned a little. "She once said something to me about her husband, Jeff, not wanting any. At least not right away, but I think she'd have a dozen of 'em."

"A dozen's a lot," Beth said, but understood Dani's feelings. Wasn't her own biological clock ticking? Wouldn't she love a sibling for Cody—a new baby for her to cuddle? She watched Dani as she helped Hillary from the saddle. Dani had been wild in her youth. There had been stories about her and talk of a child she'd given up for adoption. No one but Dani knew the truth, and Beth hadn't listened too much to the town gossip as she'd experienced her share of it over the years.

"Come on, pardner, you need to meet Gary. He's one of the hands and he'll show you how to brush a horse," Jenner said, leading the old gray toward the barn.

"It's amazing," Casey said. "He's so good with Cody."

"Yes." Beth's heart swelled.

"Who would've guessed?"

Not me. Not in a thousand years.

"The next thing you know he'll want to settle down and have another one."

Beth's heart caught.

With a sigh, Casey slapped the top rail of the fence. "It must be nice, knowing what you want." Raking her fingers through her hair, she gazed across the paddock. "Mom was right about that, though I hate to admit it. I never have been able to figure out what I should be doing with the rest of my life."

Little footsteps sounded in the dust. "You see me ride, Mommy?" Cody asked as he approached.

"I sure did."

"I want a horse."

"Of your own?" She glared up at Jenner, certain the idea had sprouted with him, but he lifted his hands off his crutches to express his perplexity, as if this was news to him.

"Cody's idea," Jenner said.

"We're still debating on a puppy."

"Want a puppy, too. And kitties. You got kitties." He looked eagerly at Casey.

"Hey, slow down," Beth admonished. "One at a time." She checked her watch. "I think we should go. He missed his nap."

"No!" Cody cried.

"Right after a hamburger and French fries!" Jenner promised as he swung the boy off his feet and plopped him onto the top rail of the fence. He held him steady while Cody whooped and squirmed in delight.

"Now who's spoiling him?" Beth said, and Casey chuckled.

"I wish I had a picture. My brother—the father." She winked at Beth. "Take my advice. Run now while you still can. He can't catch you now, but once he gets off those sticks, he'll be hell on wheels again."

"Thanks a lot." Jenner's voice dripped sarcasm, but he flashed his off-center smile at his sister as he covered their bags with a tarp and glanced at the dark sky. "Okay, let's go. Can't keep Grandma waiting."

"See Grandma!" Cody said, running to the truck, and Beth couldn't help thinking of Virginia McKee and her dislike—no, hatred—of her grandson.

As they drove into town, the first raindrops splattered against the windshield, and by the time they'd finished a quick dinner at the Shady Grove Café and Jenner had pulled into the driveway of Harriet's little cottage, the storm was in full force, wind blowing, rain peppering the ground. Cody had fallen asleep in the seat between them, and when Beth reached over to take hold of him, Jenner's hand caught her wrist.

She looked up and found herself staring into blue eyes that were dark with confusion. "What do we do now?" he asked.

Love bloomed in her heart. "I guess we take it one step at a time."

His jaw tightened. "To what end?"

"Whatever we want."

"Then maybe I should make something clear," he said, releasing her and letting out his breath. He held on to the steering wheel in a death grip and stared through the water sheeting on the windshield.

Beth could barely breathe. Something was wrong—horribly wrong. The carefree and loving Jenner she'd known at the lodge was gone and the hard man, the lone cowboy, had returned.

His voice was solemn. "I don't think I'm what you're hoping for," he said, weighing his words carefully. "I'm nothing more than what I look like—a broken-down, washed-up cowboy who owns nothing. I've got a little bit of land, not a whole lot, and probably less than two thousand dollars in the bank. My family is always there to help me out, of course, but I've never taken and will never take their charity. Even though I'm going to work for Max and see a few doctors, there's no guarantee that I'll ever walk again without a wheelchair or crutches or something." His knuckles showed white over the steering wheel. "I've never wanted a wife or a kid or anything that would tie me down. And maybe if things were different..." He scowled. "If I was independent—hell, if I could walk again—I'd feel differently, but right now..."

Her throat clogged, and as he turned his eyes to her, she saw the pain in their blue depths. She couldn't help but reach forward and place her hand against his cheek. He grabbed it and held it against his warm flesh, then turned his head and kissed her palm, leaving a warm impression. "I can't stand the idea of being half a man."

"You're not!"

"And I can't stand the thought of anyone pitying me—especially not the woman I'm involved with."

She couldn't help the edge of anger in her voice. "Do you think I'm sticking around because I *pity* you? Because I *feel sorry* for you?" she asked, astounded. After the past three days together, how could he even begin to believe such nonsense?

"Why *are* you sticking around?"

"Because—" *Because I love you!* "—because of Cody. I—I don't want him to grow up always wondering. Not knowing his father... like me."

"I knew mine. It was no picnic."

"Maybe not, but..." Finally she understood. He was telling her as gently as possible that it was over, that they'd had their fun, that yes, he did care a little, but it was over. For her. For Cody. Oh, God! Her heart squeezed painfully and she swallowed against the lump suddenly forming in her throat. "I—I'd better go...." Condensation had begun to cloud the windows as the rain continued to fall.

"Would you stay here?"

"Pardon?"

"In Rimrock. You could get a job. Skye needs help at the clinic. I could see Cody. We could try—"

"I don't think so," she said quickly when she heard the doubt in his voice. She wouldn't live the life her mother had lived, the subject of small-town gossip. Without another thought, she lifted her son onto her lap. This wasn't the time for goodbyes or making plans. Not after all the emotional ups and downs she'd experienced since returning to Rimrock. She knew that Jenner felt something for her and she didn't doubt that he would come to love his son, but the argument with Virginia and the chip on Jenner's shoulder about the use of his legs were too much to deal with right now. She needed time alone to think. To sort out what she really wanted and what would be best for Cody.

"You don't have to go—"

"I think it would be best. Mom's expecting me and—"

"I mean you don't have to leave Rimrock."

"You want me to stay?"

He didn't answer, just stared at her long and hard, as if he couldn't decide whether to trust her or not. Although he'd seemed to believe in her at the lodge, now that he was back in Rimrock, things had changed. He'd changed. "I want you to do what's best for the boy."

The boy. Not *our son,* just *the boy.* "I—I'll think about it," she whispered as she reached for the door handle. Jenner glanced at the rain and struggled out of his jacket. "Here, you can cover him with this. I'll get your bag."

"It's no trouble. I can manage—"

"I said I'll handle it." Jenner's voice was firm, his eyes narrowed, and she didn't argue with him.

Let him carry the damn bag if it made him feel whole. How could he believe that she cared if he ever walked without the use of crutches? After all they'd shared, why would he think that she pitied him, that he couldn't be a husband or father or— That thought caught her up short. *Husband?* As if they'd ever discussed marriage. Jenner McKee wasn't the marrying kind and she was foolish to think that he would ever change. If she was to stay in Rimrock, she would have to settle for a little part of him, for having an affair, for being one name among many in a little black book. And Cody would know the truth, learn that the man who had sired him didn't care enough about his mother to marry her, that he had other women, maybe even other children. Oh, Lord. She blinked hard, then opened the door. With a firm hold on Cody, she stepped out into the rain. Cody cried out as the rain hit him and the jacket slipped down to the ground.

"Oh, Lord . . ."

"I'll get it," Jenner said, but he slipped a little as his crutch caught the edge of a pothole. Still holding Cody, Beth bent down and retrieved the jacket by the lining. A manila envelope slid out of the inside pocket.

She heard Jenner's sharp intake of breath as she grabbed the dripping packet and the contents fell out onto the wet driveway. "Oh, I'm sorry. I didn't mean—" Her name swam before her eyes, and for a second she didn't realize what it was that she was reading. But as she picked up the soggy pages and recognized copies of her birth certificate, her report cards, credit reports, various other typed documents and Cody's birth certificate, she froze.

"You—you had me investigated?" she stammered, turning to face him as rain ran down the back of her neck and Cody, blinking against the drops in his face, began to cry.

Jenner's face was stony, his eyes without emotion. "I asked Rex Stone to look into your background."

"Why?"

"Because I thought you were a fake."

"Even though your grandmother..." she began, then words failed her. They would never trust each other, she realized, and he would always have trouble believing that Cody was his. Even if all the tests pointed to him, Cody would still be his bastard, his mistake, the reason he had to keep seeing Beth.

"I told Stone to back off," he said.

"But not until you got what you wanted."

Tossing the offensive documents back into the mud, she held her son close to her breast, protecting his head from the rain just as she wished she could protect his innocent heart. "I think you'd better leave."

"I can't."

"Like hell. You didn't want us involved in your life and that's just fine with me. You and all your family can go to hell!" She turned but he caught her arm, spinning her back against him.

"Beth—"

"Don't, okay? Just don't."

He kissed her then. His wet lips captured hers in a kiss that threatened to draw the life from her body. She felt the passion, the raw desire that he inspired, and her heart shattered into a million pieces. With all the strength she could muster, she broke away, and her hand drew back as if to slap him.

"Mommy!" Cody cried and Beth let her hand drop to her side.

Jenner's expression was harsh. "Listen, I don't want you to think, I mean, I'll take care of you and Cody. I—"

"What? You feel *obligated?* You feel *responsible?*"

"Hell, yes!"

"Too late, Jenner. Cody and I, we don't need you!" That was a lie. Both she and her son needed him on the most basic of levels. "Just leave us alone."

"I can't."

"Well, you'll have to."

"No way!" His fingers tightened over her forearm. "That boy's mine, too, and—"

"Oh, so you finally believe me."

"I want to be a part of his life."

"What life?" she demanded, her voice catching. "I won't allow him to be ridiculed by the people of this town, nor will I have your mother treating him like something that should be swept under the rug. He's my son, Jenner. *Mine!*" She hooked her thumb at her chest. "You made your noble gesture, but now you can just bow out." Balancing Cody, she reached into the back of the truck and yanked out her bags, tossing them onto the soggy ground.

"I'm not going anywhere," he insisted, the rain slashing down his face. "You can't take my son away."

"Watch me!" Grabbing one bag she spun around and ran up the steps to the front porch. Water washed down her face and she didn't know if it was raindrops falling from the dark sky or her own tears flowing down her cheeks.

Chapter Twelve

The Black Anvil with its smoky atmosphere and loud patrons didn't lift his spirits. Jenner had downed one beer and was nursing his second. After the fight with Beth, he'd driven back to the Rocking M and, keeping silent about his problems, worked with Max on blueprints for the new stables. Max, sensing something was wrong, but smart enough not to pry, had told him that the investigation into the arson and Jonah's murder was still progressing. The list of suspects was narrowing, even though the leads offered by would-be snitches for their share of the reward had heretofore been busts. Max was still keeping security tight on the ranch, but nothing out of the ordinary had happened.

Jenner hadn't stayed at the Rocking M for dinner and instead had wound up at the saloon with the regulars. Slim Purcell was shooting pool with Fred Donner. Elvin Green occupied his usual stool, and Cyrus Kellogg, Jeff Stewart and a few others clustered at a couple of tables and griped about hunting restrictions.

Jenner wondered where Beth was and if she'd already taken off for the Willamette Valley. The thought depressed him and he tried to think of his life without her—the life he'd found so appealing before she'd shaken up his world. And what about the boy? How could he go on from day to day knowing that there was a kid out there—*his* kid—who needed to be raised properly, with a father? He couldn't help but smile when he thought of the little blond scamp and hoped old Jonah was roasting in hell for trying to screw up his grandson's life.

He saw a movement in the mirror over the bar. Jake was drawing another beer for Jimmy Rickert's glass and Jimmy glanced at Jenner before looking quickly away.

"Think that's about it," Jake said as he slid the mug over to Jimmy. "This is your last."

"You cuttin' me off?" Jimmy's speech was already slurred, but that was a normal state. "Hell, I'm one of your best customers."

"That's why your next drink is coffee. And you might want to settle up your tab."

"Shiii—" He bit off his curse as his eyes met Jenner's in the mirror again. This time he didn't look away. "Well, McKee, surprise, surprise. I thought you gave up hangin' out here."

"I have," Jenner said, startled at his admission. The Black Anvil held no appeal for him anymore and he was sorry he'd shown up. Ignoring the rest of his beer, he left some bills on the bar as Jake fiddled with the knobs on the television mounted near the ceiling.

"Too good for the rest of us since your woman blew back into town?"

Every muscle in Jenner's body tensed.

Jimmy, seeing Jenner's reaction, cackled. "Didn't think we knew, did ya? Hear ya got yourself a son." Another cackle of malicious laughter. "Pr'bly got seven or eight strung out along the ol' rodeo circuit, eh?"

"You're listening to gossip, Jimmy. Never a good idea."

"Yeah, well, I hear a lot. Keep my ears open." His grin was wide. Sly. Teasing. He knew something, all right, and he was enjoying having one over on Jenner. Jimmy reached into his breast pocket for a crumpled pack of cigarettes and lit up. Plucking a piece of tobacco from his tongue, he blew smoke to the ceiling. "Learn more'n I should sometimes, if ya get my drift." Puffing out a smoke ring, he slid Jenner another knowing glance. "Anyone collect on that reward yet?"

"You tell me. You seem to have all the answers," Jenner said, his eyes narrowing thoughtfully on this barfly. If anyone would know what was happening in the Rimrock underground, it would be Jimmy. He knew who hunted without a license, who was sleeping with another man's wife, who'd been in a fight and who was driving with a suspended license. Nickel-and-dime stuff, but the gleam in his eye promised something more.

"I don't know nothin'."

Jenner doubted it. Jimmy had always been a snitch, but the sheriff's department had questioned him repeatedly and Jimmy had come up with an alibi for the night Jonah was killed as well as for the time of the fire. "Twenty-five grand isn't anything to sneeze at," Jenner drawled.

"Petty cash to you McKees."

"Could set a man up, though." Jenner rubbed his chin. "Someone could put a down payment on a ranch or buy a new truck or bet the ponies. . . . Hell, I dunno, a guy could even take a vacation."

Rickert's smile faded and his nose twitched a little—like a rat sniffing cheese. He was hooked. All Jenner had to do was reel him in and the drunk would spill his guts.

"G'night, Jake." Jenner slid a glance at Jimmy. "You, too, Rickert."

He walked outside and smelled the rain that still lingered in the air. The storm had passed, but water filled the potholes in the parking lot. How had Jimmy learned about Beth and Cody? That thought chilled him as much as the wind ripping down from the north, reminding him that winter was just around the corner. Snow had already been predicted for the weekend.

He'd started for his old Dodge when he saw Jimmy stagger out and head toward a battered four-wheel-drive rig that had already tangled with a ditch or two. Both front fenders were crumpled, and where there had once been a headlight, there was now only a black hole.

"Let me drive you, Rickert."

"You?" Jimmy spit his cigarette into one of the puddles. "You're a goddamned cripple. I'll take care of myself."

Jenner's muscles tightened. "You're drunk."

"I hope so . . . the amount of money I spent in there." He swayed a little as he tried to shove his key into the lock. Jenner didn't believe in being holier-than-thou, but he didn't like the idea of Jimmy's truck weaving through the streets of Rimrock, streets where Beth might be driving or into which Cody might inadvertently dash.

"Hard up?"

"I do all right," Jimmy said, still unable to locate the lock. "Son of a—"

"Your truck could use some work. Here, let me help you." Before Jimmy knew what hit him, Jenner had reached forward and snagged Jimmy's key ring.

"Hey, what d'ya think yer doin'?" Jimmy shouted.

"Probably saving your useless neck."

"Don't do me no favors." With that, Jimmy took a swing at Jenner and it was all the incentive he needed. Balancing on his good leg, he slammed Jimmy up against the side of the truck and forced a crutch beneath the sorry little snake of a man's chin.

"Don't even think about it," Jenner snarled as he saw Jimmy's fingers curl into a fist.

"What the hell's goin' on?" Jimmy rasped, his eyes bulging a little.

"You tell me everything you know about the fire and my dad's murder."

"*What?*"

"You heard me. Were you in on it?"

"Hell, no. Are you crazy? I was with Maryellen Inman, I swear."

"Do you swear?" Jenner pushed the crutch a little harder and Rickert began to cough.

"You bastard. Just you wait. You McKees will get yours!" Jimmy's face was turning an ugly shade of red.

"That's more like it, Jimmy. Lay your cards on the table. Maybe you'll get lucky and get twenty-five grand, or maybe you'll end up in jail."

"Damn it, let me up!" the drunk sputtered. "Okay, okay. I know a little, but I wasn't involved. Swear to God."

Jenner pocketed Jimmy's keys and eased up a little, just enough so the snake could breathe but still applying enough pressure to keep Rickert's spine curved over the hood of his truck and his mind on the business at hand.

"Hey, what's going on here?" Jake was peering from the doorway and some of the other patrons were staring through the windows.

"Call Hammond Polk," Jenner growled. "Jimmy here has a story he wants to tell the sheriff."

"So you're leaving? Just like that?" Harriet snapped her fingers, then threw her hands in the air as her daughter stripped clothes from the closet and threw them into suitcases. Her wet bags were drying over a heat vent and Cody, in his playpen, was crying to be let out.

"You knew this wasn't permanent!"

"I know, but I'd hoped." Harriet walked over to the wailing child and picked him up. "What's wrong, darlin'?" she whispered against Cody's curls.

The little boy sniffed. "Want a horse."

"He's been this way ever since Jenner left."

"Well, if you want one, surely you can have one."

"Mom!"

"I'm talking about a stick horse or a stuffed animal or a figurine or—"

"Want a horse! A big horse!"

Give me strength, Beth silently prayed. She should never have come back here; she'd been a fool to think that returning to Rimrock would solve anything and she'd let an old woman's letter get in the way of her common sense. Why? Because, deep down in the darkest recesses of her heart, the place where she'd hidden all her feelings, she'd *wanted* to face Jenner again, she'd *wanted* to show him his son, she'd *wanted* to try to win his heart. Oh, she'd told herself differently, bravely facing him and pretending that she didn't care, but the entire situation had blown up in her face. Now Cody was involved, caring for a man who would never claim him. She zipped up the bag and remembered doing the very same thing—packing her things—at the lodge with Jenner after three blissful days of falling in love with him.

God, she was a fool!

"Stay one more night," her mother said softly.

"Why?"

"Because I need you and I don't want you driving over the mountains at night in this storm. It's raining here and snowing in the mountains. Beth, please." She laid a hand on her daughter's arm. "What will one more night hurt?"

Beth looked at her son, his cheeks red from crying as he clung to his grandmother's neck. She was still too angry to drive safely, and in the morning the mountain passes would be blocked with snow. "All right," she agreed, "but bright and early, first thing, we're out of here."

"Fair enough. We'll eat dinner, then we'll go out to the McKee ranch."

"*What?* That wasn't part of the deal."

"I know, Beth, but I have unfinished business out there and I want you to go along."

"No way. It's over."

Her mother's fingers dug deep into Beth's arm. "Do this for me, Beth. It's important. To me. To you. And to him." She looked at her grandson and Beth felt a quiver of apprehension at the thought of facing Jenner one last time.

Jenner, along with Max and Rex Stone, listened to Rickert's nonconfession to Hammond Polk.

The punk admitted seeing Jonah on the night he died—everyone who'd been at the Black Anvil knew that Jonah had been drinking. But Jimmy, rather than going straight to Maryellen Inman's as he'd first said, had staggered out the back door, slipped near the garbage cans and nearly knocked himself out. He'd seen Jonah arguing with someone, but it was dark, the other man's voice was muffled, and Jonah, after telling the man to go to hell, had gotten into his Jeep and roared away. The other guy had climbed into his rig—a dark blue or black pickup—and hightailed it after Jonah.

But Jimmy was short on details. The suspect had been a man nearly as large as Jonah and he wore a light-colored Stetson and cowboy boots. The description could have fit half the ranchers in the county. Jimmy claimed that he hadn't come forward before because the man had recognized him and had shouted out the window as he'd driven off, "Careful, Rickert. I know where you live. If you squeal, I'll kill you and that woman you're livin' with."

Jimmy had been too drunk to recognize the man, but the words had screamed through his head. Even after the McKees had posted the reward, he'd been too scared to say what he knew. But now he figured that he was owed the money.

As for the arson at the ranch, Jimmy could provide no insight. If the two events were related, he suspected that the same man was behind the fire. Hammond Polk found no reason to hold him and Jimmy was released.

And Jenner was scared to death. Now, it seemed, his mother's crazy theory was dead on and everyone who was involved with the Rocking M was a potential target to some psycho. Including Beth and Cody. And he'd let them get away. Despite the fact that he loved them and couldn't live without that mule-headed woman and her sprite of a son, he'd let them slip through his fingers.

He *loved* them? The thought stopped him cold. For years he'd told himself he didn't love anyone. No member of his family. Not even himself. Yet here he was thinking about a woman and her child and he didn't give a damn whose blood flowed in the kid's veins; he just wanted to be a part of that life. And come hell or high water, he intended to do just that.

"Just tell me what's going on," Beth demanded as she drove past the outskirts of town and headed north toward the McKee ranch. Her mother was in the passenger seat and Cody was buckled in his car seat in the back. A pickup was following them at a distance, headlights bright in the rear-view mirror.

"I guess you could say that I have a score to settle."

"With?"

"Virginia."

"Jenner's mother? Why? What kind of score?"

Harriet frowned. "You'll hear soon enough."

"Look, Mom, I'm not into high drama. Why don't you just tell me—" She noticed the pickup gaining speed, though there was no place to pass as they wound past Elkhorn Lake and into the foothills. "Damn it all."

"What?"

"A truck's been following us. Ever since we left town."

"Whose?"

Beth shrugged and told herself she was imagining things. "You tell me."

Craning her neck, Harriet took a look through the back window, then at her sideview mirror. "Can't see anything but his headlights. It's too dark."

Beth bit her lower lip and told herself to keep cool, that nothing was wrong, that she'd seen too many movies and television shows with car chases and that Jenner's worries about security at the ranch had gotten to her.

"Slow down," Harriet advised. "Maybe he'll pass. I hate it when someone tailgates you on these winding roads."

Beth's heart began to knock. She glanced in the mirror and saw only the glare of headlights. Her fingers were wet with sweat. She eased off the throttle.

"When did you notice him?" Harriet asked.

"In town, at the last light. I didn't think much about it." She slowed a little more, but the truck didn't alter position even though they were on a fairly straight part of the road. "Probably some rancher who lives out this way," Beth said, but she didn't believe it. Her stomach knotted.

"The least he could do is dim his lights."

Clamping her hands firmly over the wheel, Beth stepped on the accelerator. Her little Nova took off, but the truck didn't falter. Within a split second, he was nearly on her bumper.

Keep going. Just keep going! She had no choice and the ranch was only a few miles ahead. Certainly Max with all his security or Jenner would be there to help them. Oh, God, Jenner. Beth's throat closed up and she tried not to let her imagination run wild, but she thought for just a moment that she might never see him again, that he might never hold Cody's little body close to his.

She took a corner too fast and the Nova's front wheel slid off the road and onto the shoulder. Gravel sprayed. The car shimmied and Beth tried not to think about the fact that they were in the mountains, that the road was cut against the cliffs. She braked. The Nova skidded.

"Oh, God!" Harriet screamed.

Cody began to cry. "I scared. Mommy, I scared!"

I'm scared, too! Gritting her teeth, Beth yanked on the wheel and the car careered away from the shoulder and into the oncoming lane.

"For God's sake, watch out!"

The truck bore down on them.

She managed to straighten the Nova into the right lane and stepped on the gas again.

Bang! The truck rammed her car, sending it onto the shoulder again. Harriet screamed. The guardrail caught the fender.

"Oh, God, oh, God, oh, God!"

Metal screamed against metal. Sparks flared. The Nova shuddered. Windows rattled, but the car hung together. Beth wrestled with the wheel.

A second set of headlights appeared in the mirror.

Horns honked and sirens wailed in the distance as the Nova slowed. "Hold on!" Beth cried, bracing herself for the impact of the larger vehicle, but the truck raced past them and Beth stood on the brakes. "Come on, come on," she said, her fingers clenched around the wheel.

The car skidded to a stop as the second truck pulled over.

Beth was shaking as she watched the driver. Jenner! Tears flooded her eyes as she watched him running, limping, throwing himself toward her. He yanked open the car door and dragged her into his arms. "Are you all right?" he whispered hoarsely, his hands tangling in her hair. "Cody...Cody!"

"Out!" Cody cried between broken sobs. "Me scared, Mommy! Want out!"

Jenner reached into the back seat.

"Me, too! I think I twisted my ankle!" Harriet said, her voice shaking badly, and Beth sent up a prayer of thanks that everyone was alive and well enough to complain.

A siren shrieked closer and the lights of a cruiser from the sheriff's department flashed red and blue in the night. Beth hardly knew what was happening. She felt Jenner's arms surround her, felt Cody's little body pressed against her own and knew that her mother was being freed from the car by deputies.

"I followed you out of town, saw what was happening, and used my cellular phone to call the police," Jenner explained. "Oh, God, Beth, I thought—" His throat seized up, and standing in the glare of his headlights, he kissed her and held her as if he never intended to let her go again. "I love you," she thought she heard him say. "I love you and Cody and thank God—"

"I love you, too," she whispered, tears raining from her eyes. He kissed her again until Cody, caught between them, protested.

"It's all right," Jenner assured him as his strong arms folded over his son. "I'm gonna marry your mother."

"You what?"

"I'm gonna marry her. A wedding, you know. That is, if she agrees."

Beth blinked against her tears. Jenner was proposing? Here, on the edge of Stardust Canyon, by her wrecked little car? "Marry a broken-down, useless cowboy like you?" she said, then laughed and sniffed and wiped away her tears. "Get the preacher. I can't wait." She threw her arms around him and kissed him soundly before the quiet cough of a deputy caught her attention.

"I really hate to break this up, but I think someone should tell us what's going on."

"Didn't you hear?" Harriet quipped as she was pulled from what had once been the Nova. "There's gonna be a wedding!"

* * *

It was hours later before they finally reached the ranch
after enduring questioning by Hammond Polk and several
of his deputies. The department was now on the lookout for
a dark-colored, late-model, American-made truck with Or
egon plates and a dented bumper.

The ranch house was ablaze with lights since Jenner had
telephoned Max with the news, and his entire family, in
cluding Skye, was waiting. In the den, Jenner was retelling
the story. "...and so, now that we're all safe, I've asked
Beth to marry me and she's agreed."

"Oh, no," Virginia gasped, but Mavis climbed to her feet
and grinned widely.

"Let me be the first to congratulate you!" the old lady
said.

"Maybe we should make it a double ceremony," Skye
offered, as her wedding to Max was scarcely a month away.

"No." Jenner shook his head. "I want ours just for us."

"But..." Virginia said weakly, then turned her eyes on
Harriet, who was seated in the room.

"The kids are getting married," Harriet said, "and it's
high time they should. Whatever bad blood there is be
tween us has got to stop."

"I don't think this is the place—"

"It's time to clear the air," Harriet said, her lips pursed.
"I know this is hard for you, Virginia, but you may as well
hear the truth. There was a time, years ago, when I worked
for Jonah. He and I—"

"I can't hear this!"

"—were never lovers. I don't know why you believe oth
erwise, but it's not true! Whatever you may think of me, the
simple truth is this. I was never in my life involved with a
married man. Not your husband and no one else's, for that
matter."

Tears began to form in Virginia's eyes.

"Now, listen, I don't believe in sugarcoatin' the truth. He approached me, offered to set me up in my own place, but I turned him down and quit working for him right then and there. I'm not saying he wasn't an attractive man, and if he'd been single, I would have thought long and hard about it, but he wasn't, so I didn't. That's the God's honest truth, and I would hope you're a big enough person not to let some old lie stand between you and your grandson, because if you aren't, you're a bigger fool than I take you for."

Mavis's smile had faded. "She makes sense, Virginia."

"Well, I've said my piece." Harriet stood proudly. "Now, if someone would kindly drive me home—"

"No!" Virginia's lips trembled and she drew in a long, steadying breath. "Stay, Harriet. I, um, I think you're right and if I've misjudged you, I apologize. Whether I like it or not, we have a wedding to plan."

"Another wedding!" Mavis said, winking at Skye and Max. "If only Jonah were alive to see it."

"He's probably rolling over in his grave," Jenner said. "He worked hard to break up Max and Skye and keep me from knowing about Cody."

"He would've changed his mind," Virginia said.

Casey shook her head. "I don't think so. But he'd bit off more than he could chew. Looks to me, at least for you four—" she motioned to Jenner, Beth, Max and Skye "—love really does conquer all."

Jenner linked his fingers through Beth's and led her to the back porch. The sky was dark, the wind chilly, but with Jenner's arms around her, Beth was warm inside. "We could live in Rimrock, rebuild the cabin at the old homestead if you want," he said, "and you could work for Skye, or..."

"Or?"

"We could get the old lodge going again. Hire a skeleton staff and turn it into a kind of hotel and dude ranch."

"Would you be happy with that?" she asked.

His smile, crooked and cocksure, gleamed white in the darkness. "I'm happy with you. Doesn't matter where we are or what we do. As long as we're together. What do you say?"

She sighed and shook her head. "It's about time, cowboy."

"Mommy? Mommy, where are you?"

"Out here. With Daddy."

Cody poked his head out the door. "No, you're not. You're with Jenner."

He hurried over and Jenner lifted him off his feet. "From now on you can call me Dad."

Cody grinned. "Okay, but I can have a horse?"

"A dozen of 'em."

"And a puppy?"

"As many as you want."

"Wait a minute," Beth said, and Jenner's smile faded.

"No way, lady," he said, his eyes turning an erotic shade of blue. "I've waited too long already." With that he kissed her, and Beth leaned happily against the man she loved, knowing that they would be together forever.

Dear Beth,

I've always been a solitary man. Never wanted anyone else around much. Until you and Cody showed up on my doorstep and gave me back a reason to get up in the morning, to walk again, to live, I really didn't give a damn.

You changed all that and made my life complete.

I don't think there are the right words (at least I don't know them if they exist) to tell you how I feel, but each morning when I get up and you're in my arms, I'm glad it's a brand-new day, and each night when I lie down beside you, I'm thankful to be alive.

You and Cody are the reason.

All I can say is that I love you and I'll never stop loving you.

Forever,
Jenner

*   *   *   *   *

A Letter from the Author

Fall 1994

Dear Reader,

I hope you enjoyed Beth and Jenner's story. Jenner is one of my favorite heroes and Beth is just the woman to tame him. I can assure you they, along with their son, Cody, will have a wonderful future together.

The next book in the *Love Letters* series is *C Is for Cowboy,* the story of Casey McKee and Sloan Redwing.

As you know, Casey is the stubborn daughter of Jonah McKee. She's a woman who, upon seeing her brothers find happiness with the women in their lives, is dissatisfied with her own fate. For years she's spent her life as the spoiled daughter of a rich man, but now she wants to strike out on her own and find out who she really is—not as Jonah

McKee's daughter or Max and Jenner's sister, but as an independent woman in her own right.

However, her plans are shattered when she's kidnapped.

When the McKee family receives the ransom note, Jenner won't trust the police or the feds to save her. He contacts an old friend, Sloan Redwing—a rodeo cowboy who's half Nez Percé Native American. Sloan is a strong, silent and proud man whose very presence makes some people nervous. His eyes are dark and menacing and along with his rodeo prowess, he's inherited the hunting skills of his Native American ancestors.

Against his better judgment, Sloan accepts the job and tracks down Casey's abductors to rescue her.

Sloan doesn't want or need the complications of a woman in his life, and he tells himself that Casey McKee is definitely not the kind of woman for him.

Casey wants to be her own woman and doesn't need a man telling her what to do, yet she can't stop her unsettling feelings every time Sloan is near.

In *C Is for Cowboy* the murder of Jonah McKee is finally solved, but the book is really a love story between two very different people trying to discover themselves. I think it's a story that's as explosive as it is endearing. I hope you agree.

If you'd like to write to me, I'd love to hear from you.

Regards,

Lisa Jackson
333 S. State St., Suite 308
Lake Oswego, OR 97034

COMING NEXT MONTH

#925 FOR THE BABY'S SAKE—Christine Rimmer
That Special Woman!

Andrea McCreary had decided to raise her unborn baby on her own.
Clay Barrett had generously offered a proposal of marriage, and soon
realized their arrangement would not be without passion....

#926 C IS FOR COWBOY—Lisa Jackson
Love Letters

Only the promise of a reward convinced Sloan Redhawk to rescue
headstrong, spoiled Casey McKee. He despised women like her—yet
once he rescued her, he was unable to let her go!

#927 ONE STEP AWAY—Sherryl Woods

Only one thing was missing from Ken Hutchinson's life: the woman of
his dreams. Now he'd found Beth Callahan, but convincing her to join
his ready-made family wouldn't be so easy....

#928 ONLY ST. NICK KNEW—Nikki Benjamin

Alison Kent was eager to escape the holiday hustle and bustle. Meeting
Frank Bradford—and his adorable twin sons—suddenly showed her this
could indeed be the most wonderful time of the year!

#929 JAKE RYKER'S BACK IN TOWN—Jennifer Mikels

Hellion Jake Ryker had stormed out of town, leaving behind a broken
heart. Stunned to discover he had returned, Leigh McCall struggled with
stormy memories—and with Jake's renewed passionate presence.

#930 ABIGAIL AND MISTLETOE—Karen Rose Smith

Abigail Fox's generous nature never allowed her to think of herself.
Her heart needed the kind of mending only Brady Crawford could
provide—and their kiss under the mistletoe was just the beginning....

MILLION DOLLAR SWEEPSTAKES (III)

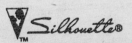

FOR THE BABY'S SAKE

Christine Rimmer (SE #925, December) Self-sufficient
Andrea McCreary decided she was
perfectly capable of raising her unborn child on her
own. Her friend Clay Barrett generously offered a
proposal of marriage, but only for the baby's sake.
Then Andrea and Clay soon realized their
arrangement would not be without passion.... **Don't
miss FOR THE BABY'S SAKE,
by Christine Rimmer, available in
December!** She's friend, wife, mother—she's you!
And beside each Special Woman stands a
wonderfully
special man. It's a celebration of our heroines—
and the men who become part of their lives. Don't
miss **THAT SPECIAL WOMAN!** each month—

TSW12/94

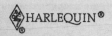 HARLEQUIN®

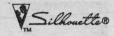 Silhouette®

The movie event of the season can be the reading event of the year!

Lights... The lights go on in October when CBS presents Harlequin/Silhouette Sunday Matinee Movies. These four movies are based on bestselling Harlequin and Silhouette novels.

Camera... As the cameras roll, be the first to read the original novels the movies are based on!

Action... Through this offer, you can have these books sent directly to you! Just fill in the order form below and you could be reading the books...before the movie!

48288-4	Treacherous Beauties by Cheryl Emerson	$3.99 U.S./$4.50 CAN.	☐
83305-9	Fantasy Man by Sharon Green	$3.99 U.S./$4.50 CAN.	☐
48289-2	A Change of Place by Tracy Sinclair	$3.99 U.S./$4.50CAN.	☐
83306-7	Another Woman by Margot Dalton	$3.99 U.S./$4.50 CAN.	☐

TOTAL AMOUNT	$
POSTAGE & HANDLING	$
($1.00 for one book, 50¢ for each additional)	
APPLICABLE TAXES*	$ _____
TOTAL PAYABLE	$ _____
(check or money order—please do not send cash)	

To order, complete this form and send it, along with a check or money order for the total above, payable to Harlequin Books, to: **In the U.S.:** 3010 Walden Avenue, P.O. Box 9047, Buffalo, NY 14269-9047; **In Canada:** P.O. Box 613, Fort Erie, Ontario, L2A 5X3.

Name: _____

Address: _____ City: _____

State/Prov.: _____ Zip/Postal Code: _____

*New York residents remit applicable sales taxes.
  Canadian residents remit applicable GST and provincial taxes.

CBSPR

"HOORAY FOR HOLLYWOOD" SWEEPSTAKES

HERE'S HOW THE SWEEPSTAKES WORKS

OFFICIAL RULES — NO PURCHASE NECESSARY

To enter, complete an Official Entry Form or hand print on a 3" x 5" card the words "HOORAY FOR HOLLYWOOD", your name and address and mail your entry in the pre-addressed envelope (if provided) or to: "Hooray for Hollywood" Sweepstakes, P.O. Box 9076, Buffalo, NY 14269-9076 or "Hooray for Hollywood" Sweepstakes, P.O. Box 637, Fort Erie, Ontario L2A 5X3. Entries must be sent via First Class Mail and be received no later than 12/31/94. No liability is assumed for lost, late or misdirected mail.

Winners will be selected in random drawings to be conducted no later than January 31, 1995 from all eligible entries received.

Grand Prize: A 7-day/6-night trip for 2 to Los Angeles, CA including round trip air transportation from commercial airport nearest winner's residence, accommodations at the Regent Beverly Wilshire Hotel, free rental car, and $1,000 spending money. (Approximate prize value which will vary dependent upon winner's residence: $5,400.00 U.S.); 500 Second Prizes: A pair of "Hollywood Star" sunglasses (prize value: $9.95 U.S. each). Winner selection is under the supervision of D.L. Blair, Inc., an independent judging organization, whose decisions are final. Grand Prize travelers must sign and return a release of liability prior to traveling. Trip must be taken by 2/1/96 and is subject to airline schedules and accommodations availability.

Sweepstakes offer is open to residents of the U.S. (except Puerto Rico) and Canada who are 18 years of age or older, except employees and immediate family members of Harlequin Enterprises, Ltd., its affiliates, subsidiaries, and all agencies, entitles or persons connected with the use, marketing or conduct of this sweepstakes. All federal, state, provincial, municipal and local laws apply. Offer void wherever prohibited by law. Taxes and/or duties are the sole responsibility of the winners. Any litigation within the province of Quebec respecting the conduct and awarding of prizes may be submitted to the Regie des loteries et courses du Quebec. All prizes will be awarded; winners will be notified by mail. No substitution of prizes are permitted. Odds of winning are dependent upon the number of eligible entries received.

Potential grand prize winner must sign and return an Affidavit of Eligibility within 30 days of notification. In the event of non-compliance within this time period, prize may be awarded to an alternate winner. Prize notification returned as undeliverable may result in the awarding of prize to an alternate winner. By acceptance of their prize, winners consent to use of their names, photographs, or likenesses for purpose of advertising, trade and promotion on behalf of Harlequin Enterprises, Ltd., without further compensation unless prohibited by law. A Canadian winner must correctly answer an arithmetical skill-testing question in order to be awarded the prize.

For a list of winners (available after 2/28/95), send a separate stamped, self-addressed envelope to: Hooray for Hollywood Sweepstakes 3252 Winners, P.O. Box 4200, Blair, NE 68009.

CBSRLS

OFFICIAL ENTRY COUPON

"Hooray for Hollywood"
SWEEPSTAKES!

Yes, I'd love to win the Grand Prize — a vacation in Hollywood — or one of 500 pairs of "sunglasses of the stars"! Please enter me in the sweepstakes!

This entry must be received by December 31, 1994.
Winners will be notified by January 31, 1995.

Name _____

Address _____ Apt. _____

City _____

State/Prov. _____ Zip/Postal Code _____

Daytime phone number _____
(area code)

Mail all entries to: Hooray for Hollywood Sweepstakes,
P.O. Box 9076, Buffalo, NY 14269-9076.
In Canada, mail to: Hooray for Hollywood Sweepstakes,
P.O. Box 637, Fort Erie, ON L2A 5X3.

KCH

OFFICIAL ENTRY COUPON

"Hooray for Hollywood"
SWEEPSTAKES!

Yes, I'd love to win the Grand Prize — a vacation in Hollywood — or one of 500 pairs of "sunglasses of the stars"! Please enter me in the sweepstakes!

This entry must be received by December 31, 1994.
Winners will be notified by January 31, 1995.

Name _____

Address _____ Apt. _____

City _____

State/Prov. _____ Zip/Postal Code _____

Daytime phone number _____
(area code)

Mail all entries to: Hooray for Hollywood Sweepstakes,
P.O. Box 9076, Buffalo, NY 14269-9076.
In Canada, mail to: Hooray for Hollywood Sweepstakes,
P.O. Box 637, Fort Erie, ON L2A 5X3.

KCH